DEATH AND TAXES

Tales of a Badass IRS Agent

Mark Zaslove

APERIENT PRESS

First Printing: 2018

ISBN 978-0-9712374-6-9

APERIENT PRESS
2118 Wilshire Blvd. #997
Santa Monica CA 90403-5784

Cover design by John Geralis

APERIENT PRESS

For my son Cole, for making me a better man every day, just by being around.

A dog's head on a stick. A collie, I think—the cloud of iridescent blowflies made it difficult to tell. Fido was impaled in the front yard like a decomposing totem pole, right next to the burnt-out shell of a Cadillac-green 1978 Camaro GTO, about five yards upwind of the rusted kissing gate.

At least it wasn't a six-foot, seven-inch albino Texan singing the aria from Mozart's *Don Giovanni* and accompanying himself on a Peruvian goat's-hoof rattle. That was last week. This week, a dog's head on a stick.

My name's Mark Douglas, and I work for the IRS. Welcome to my world.

"Move in. Move fast. And try not to do anything too stupid," I told my IRS boys.

We stop-and-go'd through the gate single file, then fanned out into the front yard, taking up positions according to job description and proficiency.

Miguel, an overly excited newbie, had a company-issued bullhorn with him. He fired up that puppy and barked out directives right next to my ear.

"Minton, Paul! Or Paul Minton, if you prefer! This is the IRS, or the Internal Revenue Service, as we prefer!"

Rooks, what could you do with 'em? Can't live with 'em, can't Taser 'em in self-defense. I cuffed Miguel upside the head, trying to move him along.

"Just stick to the script, Miguel, would ya?"

He gave me a hangdog look and flicked on the megaphone again.

"We've come to take possession of your worldly belongings equivalent to the amount of six thousand seven hundred and forty-two dollars and twelve cents!"

Old-timer Harry Salt, a thirty-year vet who'd cut his teeth during the glory days of post-Reaganomics and all that entailed, spit disdainfully on the ground, because he couldn't spit disdainfully on Miguel. I could relate.

Our backup, Wooly Bob, was off in the moving truck. That was the team, the crew, the IRS bang-squad, or so we called ourselves outside of company earshot.

Harry positioned himself to the far side of the Camaro. You didn't go into your third decade doing this without a finely-honed sense of self-preservation. I took point and waved Miguel back because he had no sense of self-preservation.

"Mr. Minton!" I called into the house without need of the megaphone. "Why don't you come on out, and we can talk about this? You and I can figure out what to seize and be out of your hair in less time than it takes to have a cup of drive-through coffee!"

"Here!" came a harsh, drunken voice from inside.

A toilet, fuzzy carpet-seat cover and all, came flying through the front window, landing with a ceramic crash right where I had just been standing.

I dove across the porch, coming to a tumble next to the front door.

"Does that settle my account?"

I waved Harry around back. He knew what to do. I waited a minute, then I unclipped some teargas cartridges and loaded them into my riot gun—totally non-government issue, but it beat taking a shot of porcelain to the head if he had another toilet in there.

"I'm giving you to the count of three, Mr. Minton! One, two..."

I fired two rounds through the busted window. I hate playing fair. If they don't, why should I?

A heartfelt "cocksucker!" roared from inside, followed by coughing, spitting, and finally the spasms of committed retching.

I heard scrabbling at the door as desperate hands turned multiple locks. Finally, the door swung open and Mr. Paul Minton, tax evader and tear-gassee, stumbled out, dressed in nothing but his skid-marked BVDs, one hand clutching his eyes and the other in a death grip around a can of Colt 45.

Miguel raced up with handcuffs in one hand and the megaphone in the other, and received a kick to the groin, sending him to his knees, where he threw up on Minton's crusty bare feet.

Live and learn. I never bothered with handcuffs. Minton wouldn't be able to breathe, let alone see sufficiently to bother us, for the next hour, so I hollered for Harry and radioed Wooly Bob to back the truck up.

Miguel writhed on the ground holding his nuts, and when Harry came around from the back, he couldn't help laughing.

"That's gotta hurt somethin' fierce, Miguel. If you were ever thinkin' about having children, you might want to reevaluate your options."

Minton stumbled into the dog's head, knocking it and himself to the ground. He lay there making short, quick "ah-ah-ah" sounds, his face a mass of red irritation that radiated out from his eyes. Teargas isn't pretty, but it sure does the job.

Wooly Bob NASCAR'd the official moving truck of the IRS, a Ryder rental, like Dale Earnhardt, Jr., blowing through the fence and whipping the twenty-footer up to the front door. Then he hopped from the cab and gave me an enthusiastic thumbs-up.

Wooly Bob is anything but wooly. He's egg-bald on top and shaves his eyebrows for effect. He's like a plastic man, all smooth and otherworldly. He says he does it for the "chicks," who he claims "like 'em shaved." I think he's just weird, but he's one of my boys, so what can I say?

I fished out the old WWII gas mask I'd bought on sale at the Tacky Khaki Army Surplus store not far from my home. I hoped "sale" didn't mean "broken," but there was no better time to find out than right there. I wrestled it over my face and smelled stale air, sweat, and something I hoped wasn't dead German.

I strolled as confidently as I could into the house of Mr. Paul Minton, not realizing I was holding my breath. I exhaled and took a small huff. No gas. So far, so good. The living room was decorated in true 1973 splendor, complete with diarrhea-green-and-yellow fiber carpet stained with cigarette burns and dog piddles, a fold-out seen-better-days brown couch that'd been folded out twice too often, a dead lava lamp on a side table, and a couple of copies of last decade's *Playboy* center-folds on a broken Barcalounger. Hardly six thousand seven hundred and forty-two dollars and twelve cents worth of stuff.

"Hey, Mark-o!" called Harry from outside, ever vigilant but never one to actually commit himself to checking on a situation in person if he could help it. "You okeydokey? If you aren't, I can send Miguel in—once he stops puking."

I yelled I was fine and continued my hunt.

According to the records, Minton had something stashed somewhere, unless he'd spent it all on malt liquor. I opened a cupboard and an avalanche of Colt 45 empties poured out.

"Shit!"

Maybe we could recycle them and make a chunk of change that way. It was going to be a long day.

Or was it?

Never fails—people are plain stupid. That last can hit the ground with a less than totally clankity-empty-clank. It was more of a soft thunk. The kind of sound that moollah makes when it doesn't want to be found. I picked the can up. The top had been hacksawed off, then Scotch-taped back together. Amateurish even for an amateur.

I once found a seven-carat, radiant-cut canary-diamond ring—don't ask how much it was worth—that had been welded into a steel pipe, wrapped in asbestos lining, duct-taped, then polyurethaned water-tight and shoved up a cat's pooper-scooper. Swear to frickin' God. Minton's beer can wasn't even a warm-up.

I popped the top and found the can stuffed with a roll of hundred-dollar bills. Fifteen thousand five-hundred dollars' worth. I counted twice. I took sixty-eight bills, left change and a receipt, taped the top back on and, just because I'm a petty son-of-a-bitch, mixed the loaded can in with the others. Let Mr. Paul Minton figure it out for himself.

Back in the semifresh, dead-dog-tainted air, Minton still lay splayed out on the ground gasping for breath and feebly clawing at his eyes.

I nodded to Harry, who nudged a toe into the fetal-tucked Miguel before asking, "We good to go?"

I smiled. "Got what we needed."

Bending down beside Minton, I offered some final words of advice. "The United States Internal Revenue Service thanks you for your cooperation and hopes that in the future you will always remember to pay your taxes on or before April fifteenth, unless you fill out a form two-five-three-oh that allows for an extension. Have a nice day."

I headed for the truck, where Wooly Bob was already redlining the engine in neutral.

As a token of camaraderie, or perhaps simply that he didn't want to have to wait, Harry helped Miguel, his handcuffs, and his megaphone to his feet and helped him tiptoe to the truck, where he tossed him into the front seat—Miguel clutching his nards in pain—and hopped in himself. I got in last, and we peeled out in a cloud of victorious dust as Minton squirmed on the ground, the dog's head beside him, again covered in flies.

All in a day's work for your boys of the IRS.

***

I'm kind of a glorified accountant. Glorified means that after a long week of auditing tax returns earmarked for criminal prosecution and carpel-tunneling my hands-on government-issued keyboards left over from the 1990s, I get to go out into the field with my bang-squad buddies and—without a gun—physically do unto others what they think we're doing unto them already with the income tax. We're the United States government's own repo men.

That evening, papers filed in triplicate—not nearly as bad now that everything is computerized—"I's" dotted and "T's" with whatever "T's" need done to them—my little posse went out to the local watering hole, Del's Bar, for drinks and bullshit.

I washed the faintest hint of teargas away with the first of my allocated three drafts. Two isn't enough and four makes me silly. Usually with women. I've been divorced twice. The last thing I need is to be silly with women again. Three's my limit.

Harry was one ahead, as usual. No matter when we'd start, Harry was always one ahead. I tried to watch closely once, to see if I could spot that change-state moment where we were at none, and suddenly he was one ahead. For the life of me, I missed it, and I was hawkeyeing him mighty close.

I'd once read about something called the Heisenberg Uncertainty Principle: basically, one could not know the position of a subatomic particle and its velocity at the same time. I'm blaming Harry's one-ahead on this Heisenberg guy and quantum mechanics. One could know Harry was drinking, or one could know how many drinks Harry had drunk, but not both at the same time.

Maybe next time I'll spot it.

Miguel nursed his cold one tentatively, a Gladbag of melting ice chips—maternally brought to him by Becky, the hard-ridden but tremendously busty waitress at Del's—placed on his achingly sore nether regions. She had asked if he needed her to help him with it, but he completely fumbled the pass and didn't have a clue. We gave an extra tip to Becky on that one. She may have seen 'em come and go, but she was game.

Wooly Bob didn't drink alcohol, believing solely in organically holistic forms of recreation. I once pointed out that hops, grain, yeast, and water were generally considered organic, and holistic is as holistic does, but he refused. The herb is and always will be his preferred method of relaxation.

And so, the fearsome auditor foursome frittered away another night. That day's topic of discourse: the latest federal tax loophole for those in the upper one-percentile bracket and how it might affect the salary cap limit for the New York Knicks. Swear to God, you get a bunch of red-blooded American accountants in a room together, and they'll find some way to mix sports with numbers.

Harry was of the opinion that basketball players were too stupid to understand the loophole, let alone make use of it. Wooly Bob countered that basketball players had business managers. Which Harry pointed out usually stole from their over-active-pituitary-glanded clients, so using a loophole would be wasted effort. Miguel wanted to know if testicles grew back. We assured him that they didn't, and that his were no doubt so damaged as to have completely stopped generating testosterone, and we began taking bets as to when Miguel would lose his facial hair and begin growing breasts. Harry hoped for some as large as Becky's—"I heard that, you ol' pervert!"—and I hypothesized that Miguel's only hope was to become a lesbian. Miguel ordered another beer and seemed depressed. Go figure.

Your normal night of bullshit.

Until the Human Fire Hydrant marched into our lives.

It wasn't that he was red, or had nozzles. He simply was constructed like a six-foot tall fire hydrant: one solid mass from feet to head. A cylinder of muscle. Even his hair looked muscular. What there was of it, it being clipped closer than a porn star's poontang.

He passed by our table toward the bar, and aside from a brief nodding reflection about the oddity of our fellow homo sapiens, there shouldn't have been any further consideration of him. Unfortunately, it wasn't going to be one of those nights.

It started because of Becky, of course

Now, we think of Becky as a sister. A mammothly mammaried sister, but...well, none of us have ever really had the lack of conscience to go further with her than some slow dancing and the occasional drunken shoulder to cry on. At least no one's admitted to anything more. However, that doesn't mean we aren't territorial. If someone's hitting on Becks, they've gotta pass our standard of approval, a point system with seven categories, each numbering from one to ten, and ranging from financial stability (as IRS agents, we check, *thoroughly*) to knowledge of eighteenth century Italian poets (Wooly Bob can be overly obsessive sometimes). She knows this, and she approves. We got her back, and that glorious front. However, it goes both ways. If she's in trouble, we're there. And that time, she was in trouble.

Spunky the Fire Hydrant transgressed the unwritten code: no hands. You do not lay hands on our Becky unless it's been passed unanimously by the four of us, with Becky getting veto power. Touch the titties, and you Do Not Pass Go, do not collect anything but our undying and ever-burning wrath. And we got wrath in spades; you betchum.

If only we had noticed the Hydrant's friends. All five of them. Each one bigger than the Hydrant. I blame it on the beer. Or that Heisenberg guy. Fortunately, we were the baddest ass accountants on the planet. Just ask Mr. Paul Minton.

Harry ribs Becky all the time, but he took dibs on Hydy. His radar picked it up first, and he was at the bar before the rest of us even registered it as a blip. Giving away about three inches, fifty pounds and a good twenty years, Harry did not flinch. Personally, I think ol' Hare's got a sweet spot for Becky. A serious one. The old bastard.

"'Scuse me, sonny, but we have manners here. You lay another finger on that sweetie—hi, Becky, you okay?—and I'll break it off and shove it so far up your ass, you'll feel it diddling your tonsils."

And he smiled while he said it. Harry Salt's smile makes a shark's grin look downright amicable. Especially when he's one ahead on his beers.

The Hydrant looked at Harry and saw an old guy with a few drinks in him. He missed the smile altogether, so he swung a World's Gym monthly membership I-can-bench-press-three-hundred-pounds punch at Harry's head. He missed that, too.

Did I mention Harry's self-preservation instinct? This hombre's knocked on *Family* doors looking for back taxes and lived to tell the tale. No one gets the drop on Harry. Not only is he fast, he's dirty.

7

"Lesson one, boy-o," Harry instructed. "Never use your fist when there's something harder and handier. Like, say...this bar stool."

Harry swung on the sucker like Barry Bonds lighting up Eric Milton (with or without steroids, I don't give a damn). Good, clean contact right in the sweet spot. It was a thing of beauty. Until the Hydrant's five friends swarmed in, taking Harry down in a dog pile.

Wooly Bob waded in next. He can be a little artsy-fartsy, Marin, California, but he's got balls the size of King Kong's. We know because he's constantly scratching them.

Bob led with his head, ramming the kidneys of the top man on the flesh mountain burying Harry. Without hair, that head is so aerodynamically efficient, it just slices through the air. It had to hurt. I heard the groan, but also heard Bob being snatched up like a six-year-old and thrown across the room, taking out a table of no-longer-called-stewardesses who were slumming it.

"Hey, ladies. Did I mention I'm shaved *all* over?"

He picked himself up and headed back in, only to be tossed on his ass again.

Gotta give Miguel his due. The kid, groined and all, didn't shirk. He knew the code. He took one last slug of beer and marched right over to the fray, and promptly got kicked in the balls again.

Fortunately, Harry rose from the pile at that moment, like Leviathan from the deep, his teeth sunk into the jugular of one adversary, and his hands with a death grip on the Adam's apple of another. He was growling, too. No one keeps Harry down for long. Best I could see, he was standing on the downed body of the Hydrant for good measure.

Wooly Bob, after getting the telephone number of one of the flight attendants—maybe that shaved thing works—went right back to kidney-butting his man and getting tossed across the room.

Which left two for me.

No one ever asks how you become an IRS agent.

Me, I was Marines because my family didn't have any money for college after the divorce. My dad was a university professor who lost his dough through too much love for my Mom, and not enough control of his debit card. He lost Mom because of the loss of dough—she going onto *greener* pastures, if you get my not-too-subtle drift. Dad wanted me to receive a college education but couldn't afford to give it to me; he was busy out on his own trying to keep his ivory tower head above water. So, I enlisted and found I liked the rough stuff. I was good at it. I was also good with numbers, so after I got out, I got an MBA from Washington State, where I did a little football. Just enough to get the girls. I hated the very suggestion of being a CPA after college and thought strongly about the FBI, but the recruiters were a bunch of weenies. Then a headhunter for the IRS got hold of me. Don't know what they looked for, but I musta had the right stuff. The next thing I know, I'd been there for ten years, twice as long as both my marriages put together.

So those two idiots didn't stand a chance. I mean, they wanted to play fair, and the first thing I did was break one guy's knee with a wicked cross-block—long ago outlawed from both college and pros, but that never stopped Coach from teaching us. The sound of one hand clapping is not nearly as satisfying as the sound of one knee ligament tearing. I kipped up and straight-fingered the other poor dumbass's eyes, then scissored him right down to the deck, cutting off his carotids and watching him drift off to dreamland. My sergeant in basic once told us that if you held it too long a person could die. I've always been careful.

At that point, I looked up and saw that Bob's man was wavering. The human body can only take so much kidney trauma. The same should be said of the human body only taking so much ass-across-the-room tossing, but in Bob's case, that just wasn't so. I put the guy out of his misery with a forearm to the face.

I turned and saw Harry was still gnawing on one joe's neck. The other bum was staring in shock as blood began to flow. Discretion and avoidance reaction being the better part of valor, he bounced out of there so fast, he didn't even bother with change, simply throwing a hundred in Becky's general direction and screaming on out through the door. I went over and gently pried Harry's jaws open.

"He's given up, Hare. You did good."

We were Becky's heroes. We had saved her from a pawing worse than death. But for our troubles, what did she do? She went all mushy over Miguel, who didn't even land a glove on anyone.

"Are you okay? You poor thing. Come rest your head on Becky."

And we all know what part of Becky he rested his head on.

"Do you think I can still be a man without my testicles?"

Becky assured him that she did. Some people have all the luck. Well, Miguel was in safe hands, so the three of us left standing went back to our drinks. The Human Hydrant? He lay prone in a pool of his own piddle.

"I had 'em six ways till Monday," said Harry. "Wasn't in trouble for a second." And he winked.

Yeah, I knew he had a holdout on his ankle. I knew he had a permit for it, too. But I also knew it'd get messy if he ever had to use it.

I asked him once, after his thirteenth or fourteenth beer, and he said, "I'd rather be fired and alive, then a working stiff. Get it? Working stiff?"

Then he vomited all over my shoes. Sometimes one-ahead is one too many.

2.

The IRS likes cubicles: they're cheap; they're organized; and they're interchangeable. Like the agents who work for the IRS. All 150,000 of us. It's like a sea of cubicles, floor upon floor, building upon building. There's a touch of color here where someone pinned up a crappy picture their kid drew for them, or Lila got a new beau—which happened every other week—and she put the obligatory red roses on display. But we're basically a gray business with gray people. On the surface. Just like the IRS.

But that's just the tip of the iceberg. Our job is to dig deeper. Down to the financial bone, then crack the bone open and suck out the sweet monetary marrow. We do it with paperwork. We do it with computers. We do it with cunning, intelligence and sheer doggedness. We do it because, aside from the paycheck, there's a numerical beauty to seeing things in balance.

Joe Blow works forty hours a week as a manager of the local Lowes, pulling in sixty G's with fringe benefits, like health insurance for his wife's "feminine troubles" and dental so the kids' teeth don't rot out of their mouths from the constant diet of Coke and Kit-Kats. So JB does his taxes come April, maybe he has a friend, Ronnie, who's an accountant, gives him a break. He takes his deductions, his company has already sent us our take, and at the end of the day, he's in balance. He might even get a couple of bucks back. Life is good, and the hackles on the back of my neck are quiet and orderly.

Now try Duncan Xavier Smithington IV. Dunc does not work in the usual sense. He calls himself a "speculator," which means he takes some of Duncan Xavier Smithington II's manure money (they made their dough bringing pine-scented fertilizer to the world; very big with the tree-huggers and the hoity-toity) and fritters it away on real estate that he rents out to his friends and mistresses, and Arabian horses. Now, Arabian horse people get my hackles up and keep me awake at night. They're worse than drug dealers; swear to God. There is more lying, cheating, and stealing in the horse business than in Hollywood,

11

Wall Street, and the House of Representatives combined. I don't see the attraction to the big smelly things, but the people who do sure go crazy over 'em. And they *never* report their profits. Not once have I come across a tax form that had anything to do with equines that wasn't more than a piece of fiction. And some are certifiable bestsellers.

So here I am, hackles all a-tingling because it's my job to see that the United States government gets its fair share of some part of the horse. And I wanted it to be the good part.

"Mark, did you lay these 7158's on my desk?" asked Lila Everston.

Lila was a helluva looker and even more a helluvan auditor. I'm talking one of those librarian-with-the-glint-in-her-eyes kinda sexy, all gray business suits, with a hint of lace, thick hair pulled back, perfectly polished nails trimmed short, and a man's wristwatch that looked like it cost more than my car. Thousand-watt smile. Short in that fun-at-the-beach, yellow-polka-dot bikini way. And nuclear-physicist smart.

Lila had every tax-code, federal and state, brailed in her brain and could calculate faster freehand than I could on my laptop. I once saw her, called as an expert witness, tear a shyster CEO into itty-bitty corporate pieces, knowing more about the inner workings of his multibillion dollar company than his own accountants. When the poor moron's lawyer tried to lay a little pressure on her, she cited chapter, verse, and line of the lawyer's past six years' income taxes—including his so-called deductibles for his "secretary," the tax shelter he'd sheltered from everyone, his wife included—and promptly booked him for an audit and payback schedule. The judge would have said something but was too smart—everyone refuses to declare this or that, even judges. No, Lila could look like a sex kitten, and she went through men like a chipmunk through pistachios, but deep in her dollar-green soul, she was God's own bookkeeper and the backbone of our department.

"Lila, I did indeed lay those seven-one-five-eights on your already overflowing desk, but, in my defense, I was desperate and completely at sea."

She eyed me, somewhere between quizzical and ferocious, then let loose with the illuminating teeth. "You know, if you had even thought of lying, I would've shoved them so far up your whoopee cushion, you would have been collating them with your tongue."

Then she smiled again. "But, you came clean, so I'll take care of them for you."

"You got that whoopee cushion line from Harry, didn't you?" I asked, knowing full well that only Harry could formulate the sheer iambic pentameter beauty of a phrase like that.

Lila admitted that, indeed, it was a Harry-ism of the first order, helpfully adding, "He has them on a Rolodex on his desk. And, by the way, for the file work, you owe me a drink."

"Sure nuff. I'd make it two, but I'm weak willed and easily compromised, and I'd be afraid for my virtue."

Lila's got this stupid-great laugh that's almost a snort and almost a cartoon, but it kills me. Forget her brain. Forget her body. Her laugh kills me.

"If I wanted your virtue, Mark, sweetie..." She moved closer. "Darling..." And closer. "Honeylamb..." Until she was breasts-to-me, and I couldn't think straight. "I could've had it long ago. Any..." She pressed closer. "Time..." Wrapped her arms around me. "I..." Whispered in my ear, "wanted."

About that moment, my entire body weight was resting in her arms, because my knees had buckled and my socks had melted.

"But it's too late now," she taunted, pushing me away and forcing me to catch my balance. "You're too nice for me. We'd be laughing before we could get my bra unhooked."

"You could *not* wear a bra that night," I offered chivalrously. "Keep things simple. I'd take out my Prince Albert and nipple rings, and it'd be easy-peasy."

And she lost it again with that laugh, going into her upper register: "Your P-prince Albert!" And she laughed until she coughed, then laughed some more

I like Lila. We get along great. She's like the big sister I should have had.

"Look, I'll grab some of your work later this week. I really feel shitty about dumping that stuff, but I was strapped, and you're Wonder Woman."

We went into her cubicle, one giant filing cabinet with an exercycle in one corner and government-unapproved, hopped-up computer, rammed, gigged, and Ghz'd into the stratosphere by some doink or another that Lila had seen for a week or two—it was either one of the bigwigs at Intel or AMD. They all kinda blend together. The thing was a rocket, but he never laid a finger on Lila. Nothing was ever fast enough for her.

"A drink would be more fun, but there is something you could give me a hand on."

Uh-oh. Lila *never* asked for help; that was my "out"—I'd make the offer, she'd turn it down. I went bat-ears in an instant.

"Okay, flack-jacket on, lips sealed, and bullshitometer off. What do you have that you need *my* help for?"

Lila frowned at that but went on explaining. A real bad sign.

"I don't know what I have, Mark. I was going over a Pontus, Illinois, return and there was an odd jiggle, but it didn't mean much. Then I saw the exact same jiggle on a woman's papers from Gallup, New Mexico. And then I remember seeing something just like it seven years ago."

I shook my head. "Seven years ago? Don't shit me."

But Lila wasn't shitting. Her mind worked holographically, and if she saw a jiggle seven years ago, then she damn well saw a jiggle, not a wiggle, not a giggle, and certainly not a fizzle. No, she saw a jiggle. But so what?

"Maybe nothing, but I want to know. So, I could use a little backstopping on some other things while I go deep-sea fishing. You game?"

"For you, I was born game. You give me what you need me to do, and I'm there, any hour, any day. Weekends, too."

She gave me the sweetest peck on the cheek, then smiled. "Don't even start. You know better than thinking that, Mark. You of all people."

I played innocent, though we both knew she'd busted me

"I like rich, shit-ass, messed-up guys who will cater to my every need and treat me like a princess, preferably a goddess. I go through them like cashews and couldn't really give a damn as long as I get off. I don't care if they do, but I've never had a complaint yet."

"I knew that. Remember, I've already had two wives. I only thought, if you were ever on a rebound and wanted to kill a weekend or two."

She cracked up again, and I knew we were square. I was big-boy enough to be aware of toxic when I saw it, but I still wasn't dead, and Lila called to the romantic cut-your-own-throat emotions of youth. Guys never really get rid of those, at least some types of guys. I couldn't completely avoid damsels in distress. I always forgot that those damsels ended up with the prince, because he was the only moron around who could afford them.

"I got 'em, Lila—you just bring them on over and give me a deadline. I'm playing catch-up on some work I missed being out of the office."

We both knew what that meant.

"You boys love playing cowboys and tax evaders. But someone's gonna get hurt one of these days. Why don't we both quit this place, open up a ma-and-pa accounting firm and get rich milking the suckers? Hey, if we can't spot a loophole, no one can."

"But then we'd feel bad."

And Lila and I both knew that. I don't know how it is for *everyone* in the IRS, but she and I, and most of the people I knew, really believed in what we did. Oh, we didn't care all that much about someone hiding a thousand bucks that dear dead grandma left them along with her pewter urn full of granddad. We might give 'em a scare, and they wouldn't do that again. But the bigger fish, the rich ones who have enough, making it tough on the poor ones who don't. It's *unfair*. And I don't know an IRS agent who doesn't feel it like I do. I may not like being taxed, but it's the law, and I made sure that the good guys were rewarded and the bad ones went to jail. Period.

Lila justified, I went back to my office/cubicle/prison/heaven. That was the place it all happened: Mission Control to the moon rocket of federal tax returns that kept my little fevered brainpan occupied 24/7. It was my "glad" place, and I spent way too much time cloistered there, computer burning the midnight silicon, a can of Red Bull at my side, my caffeine-encrusted coffee maker splurting the java. Shame caffeine has no effect on me. I drank it all anyway.

I had an original picture of Republican Congressman Sereno E. Payne of New York, circa 1913, the man who unwittingly got the Sixteenth Amendment passed, and with it, income tax. I say unwittingly because it was supposed to be a dirty trick against the Democrats, never meant to be approved, which it did, almost unanimously, and ended up biting him in the ass, and the rest of us since then. Gotta love a guy like that. I can just imagine his headstone: loving husband and father, founder of income tax. There's something you don't see every day.

I poured myself a cup of now-sludged coffee, tossed in six packets of Splenda, a glug of fat-free, sugar-free, Irish Crème-flavored moo-mix and enjoyed a moment before I dove into the fray.

We IRS slobs usually averaged about forty-three cases a year, not counting assists and bullpen calls like what Lila and I were trading. That comes to about six business days a case—not a whole lot to catch the bad guys and reward the good guys. Nevertheless, we made do by parallel processing and Repetitive Syndrome Insight, or RSI. We use those three letters for *everything*. RSI is simply a fancy way of saying that common mistakes and common cheats occur in repetitive patterns, and once you know the patterns, they're easy to spot. Can you believe it took a bigwig, thrice-PhD'd MIT professor to coin something that every mom and elementary school teacher has known instinctively since the beginning of time? Theoretical mathematicians are almost as useless as morals in a politician.

So, this RSI lets me skim tax forms and get to the good stuff quicker: like little old ladies who still file jointly even though Mr. Little Old Lady died a decade before of an aneurysm brought on by too much brisket and bilinis, or a shoe salesman in Des Moines who's declaring his www.suckulongtyme.com "donations" as business expenses. It's all in the pattern, and once you get the hang of it, it's like those Magic Eye optical illusions they always print in the Sunday papers (back when they had Sunday papers)—they stand out like sore thumbs. Then a quick dip into the data stream of the ol' IRS files, and there you go, case closed, time for a beer.

Except for the occasional glitch. My glitch's name was Rodney T. Gloucester.

Now, the Rodster lived in Phoenix, Arizona, home of the Phoenix Suns, the Arizona Diamondbacks, and the Phoenix Coyotes. Also home of one of the biggest meth labs this side of Panama City, Florida, which is just one big meth lab posing as a hunk of lower Alabama, but that's a whole 'nother tale of crime and punishment. Said meth lab was owned and operated by Rodney's brother Desmond. Desmond H. Gloucester. The Feds had been trying to bust Desmond going on five years, but the yahoo was always a stoplight or two ahead of them: his meth lab was mobile. And not an RV, but a whole house.

When the going got hot, he put the whole thing up on jacks and rolled it at about three miles per hour through the midnight streets of Phoenix to another location, where the Feds had to start all over on getting warrants for the wiretaps, searches, and all that paperwork that makes law enforcement loads of shits and giggles. Rather ingenious, if you ask me. Kinda "Breaking Bad" meets "Trading Spaces."

Where Rodney fit in was, he had a string of cut-rate dry-cleaning plants called Clean As A Whistle that mushroomed the Phoenix landscape and guaranteed your clothes in fifty-nine minutes or you got a free police whistle. Wouldn't you know it, Rodney was using his dry cleaners to—dare I say it?—money launder his brother's ill-gotten booty. Which is where I came in.

See, money laundering is an explicit legal term like extortion, aggravated assault, and jaywalking. It means, and I quote because I have the statue masking-taped to the bottom of my computer monitor, right next to my rookie-year card of Bob Deer, "converting or concealing income from a *specified unlawful act*," or SUA for short. See, the Feds have their own cute little acronyms, too.

Anyway, where yours truly comes in is that the Feds are limited to pursing only the SUA's listed in the federal statutes. The deal with money laundering is this: even if you *can't*, for whatever administrative or political or plain messed-up reasons, prosecute the underlying SUA, you *can* usually *forfeit* the assets that were obtained through the use of the illegal income or were used in the process of its concealment. In other words, if you screwed the pooch, whether you're busted outright for it or not, I can seize your stuff.

All I had to do was show that Rockin' Rodney founded his dry-cleaning kingdom of no starch and same-hour service on some unlawful moola his bro gave him, then seize the moola, the cleaning plants, all the bucks from the cleaning plants that were later invested in Phoenix real estate, the real estate, and, eventually, with a little luck, Rodney. A completely satisfying endeavor. Too bad Desmond was smart enough for both of them.

Desmond was some sort of criminal innovator, a repeat-offending pacesetter, the Nikola Tesla of the shady side. First with the mobile meth house and then with a truly novel money-rerouting scheme based on an ancient South Asian substitute remittance system called *hawala*. Lost you yet? Believe me, I had to late-night a lot of weeks to even figure it that far.

In a nutshell, it's an alternative to traditional banking, and Desmond found a way to utilize it, along with a series of off-off-shore accounts, a phone book full of imaginary identities, and most of the Arizona finance system. The problem was, I couldn't find a weak link before it was invested in brother Rodney's dry cleaners. See, *hawala* makes use of family relationships both here and abroad, and essentially moves money without moving it. Pretty good trick, that, and not being a Gloucester, I was working at a distinct disadvantage.

Ah, I hear you ask, hand raised as in school: "Mr. Douglas? How can a Gloucester be familial with South Asians? Gloucester doesn't sound very South Asian."

My thoughts, too, once I figured the *hawala* angle. And the answer, in true Desmond fashion, was inspired. Seems the big D was not only money laundering, but also wife laundering. He was a bigamist—and not just a bi-coastal one, but a bi-continental one. One wife here in the states named Patricia—a big-bottomed girl who liked 1959 Cadillacs, bouffant hairdos streaked with auburn and platinum, fingernails painted with the state flags, and a need for leather pumps two sizes too small. The other wife, Padma, a New Delhi high-flyer who was burning for a big break in Bollywood and all that entailed—a relentless amount of dance lessons, singing lessons, and acting lessons—and enjoyed shiny things, particularly shiny things that had platinum and diamonds in them, Missoni suits, and imported chocolate truffles. Des didn't pick the frugal ones, that was for sure.

I never would have tumbled on that much if it weren't for a fictitious trail of names on trans-Pacific tickets that led to a single frequent-flyer account. Desmond had thought of everything but that. From there, I tracked the shadow of Padma down, the *hawala* source in all her unbeknownst glory. If only she'd known about Patricia. And I was just the IRS boy to tell her. Provided I could figure a little more out, like how the hell did the money get to Rodney?

And thus, in my stumped state, I sat down at my computer to begin the hunt again. "Once more unto the data, dear friends, once more."

"Hey, Marky Mark!"

Harry slouched his way toward my cubicle, obviously a little worse for wear in wrinkled khakis, "Blow Me, I'm Irish" T-shirt, and his pride-and-joy pair of Georgia Giant Metatarsal steel-toe boots.

"Did you hear 'bout Miguel?"

I had not and said so.

"He's in love. With Becky."

I shrugged. We all were in our own little ways.

"And...here's the goddamned topper—she reciprocates."

I shook my head in serious reality bifurcation.

"You're shittin' me, Harry? Becky's our girl partially because she's like Mount Everest: distant and unclimbable."

Harry began rooting around in his ear with a forefinger, like a wildcatter drilling for oil. "You *do* realize Everest was first ascended on May twenty-ninth, nineteen fifty-three, by Sir Edmund Hillary and his trusty Sherpa guide Tenzing Norgay? And last night Becky was ascended by our very own Miguel not once, but according to the Coke-machine gossip, twice. He's my new hero, the little pissant."

"Some things are better not known by mortal man."

Harry's finger uncorked from his ear, and he gave the nail thorough scrutiny before plunging it back in again.

"Have you seen Miguel to confirm this?" I asked.

At that moment, an off-key whistled rendition of Lynyrd Skynyrd's "Free Bird" came wafting through the office. I didn't have to look up to know...but I did. And there was Miguel looking happier than a government employee had any right to look, and I knew that it was true.

"You're going to have to marry her, you know, Miguel," I pointed out with wolfish matter-of-factness.

The smile dropped from our rookie's face faster than a man with explosive diarrhea pants did when he rushed to the head.

"Harry will be best man, 'cause he is."

Harry gave a sinister, don't-cry-for-me-Argentina smile.

"I will cry her a river, because I'm such a softie."

Miguel began to sweat something fierce.

"And Wooly Bob will be...well, Wooly Bob."

"Did someone take my name in vain?" called Bobby, entering the fray with a bottle of Lemon Snapple in one hand and an overly cream-cheesed bagel in the other. "Hey, y'all. Did you hear Miguel did the horizontal rubbity-rubbity with Becky last night? Twice?"

All three of us stared in unison at the wooly one.

"Huh, guess you did."

"We are planning the wedding as we speak," Harry said.

Wooly Bob's face cracked in glee.

"Can I help? I have a real knack for that sort of thing. My mom has been her Women's League president for the last twenty years, and she taught me everything she knows about social gatherings and their organization, from invitations to cleanup."

Harry got this confused dog kinda look on his face and then sniffed Bob's shiny bald pate.

"Are you sure you're not a liberal communist homosexual? You kinda smell like a liberal communist homosexual."

Bob shook his head, informing Harry, "That's just my mango-avocado shampoo and conditioner."

"You realize you have no hair, Bob." I couldn't help pointing out the extremely obvious. "If a person could have negative hair, that would be you. You are in fact defined by your hairlessness both physically and emotionally and in other, subtler manifestations that I fear to acknowledge. Why, oh, why do you use mango-avocado shampoo and conditioner?"

"Good for the scalp," Bob explained in his straightforward Bobbish way. "Don't want dandruff or itchy noggin. Chicks hate that." Bob ran his hand over his head like a Formula 1 racecar driver over his new car. "You know, Mark, your scalp is looking a bit dry. I can set you up with a pint of the stuff, cheap."

At that moment, I noticed Miguel trying to inch away, slowly slinking behind one of my filing cabinets in readiness to flee. Not a chance.

"I'm thinking an afternoon wedding. How about you, Harry?"

"Afternoon's good by me. More time to drink," he replied, patting his stomach, already thinking about it full of booze.

Miguel had sweated completely through his shirt, the stains under his arms reaching all the way around to his back, uniting in a nervous ocean of perspiration. I bet he was having second, third, and fourth thoughts about bedding our Becky.

"It was only one time. We're not even dating."

Harry went nose-to-nose with Miguel, a frightening sight from Miguel's point-of-view. Especially when Harry went all "I eat shits like you for breakfast."

"You're *not* dating. You're getting married. We will not have you leave our Becky in the lurch. Understand?"

Harry pushed himself even noser-to-noser with Miguel, a move that defied topological mathematics as well as many assault-and-battery laws across the nation.

"But, but I don't even know if she likes me that way," sputtered Miguel. "It was kinda physical. We didn't talk much. I mean, I like her and all."

Harry gave a growl that set even the hackles of *my* hair standing on end. For Miguel, it was pants-wetting time. He was soaked upper and lower with a funky bouquet that was both vile and piquant—not at all appealing. I thought, if only Becky could see him now.

"You 'like her and all?' That's the best you can do? You little dickless wonder—"

"Um, no, Harry," I promptly, enjoyably, and with all seriousness corrected, "'Dickless' he's not, or he wouldn't be having to get married."

Harry churned that one through his synapses and agreed. "Point." He backed away from Miguel but kept the thousand-yard stare. "You little bladder-control-less wonder."

And that's when Miguel's bowels let loose in terror. Which, coincidentally, was the exact moment Lila arrived.

"What's going on? And what's that smell?"

Harry couldn't help himself, and smirked. "Love is in the air."

I lost it. I couldn't breathe for laughing so hard. It was gonna be one hell of a wedding, that was for sure. You betchum.

3.

Rodney T. Gloucester dearly loved a clean collar and a sharp crease in his pants. I knew this because the Fed wonk, Daniel "Tightass" Juarez, had shown me surveillance photos of Rodney from all times of day and night ad nauseam. Clean collar. Creased pants. Period. Even shorts, bathing suits, and from one fuzzy telephoto-lensed pic, underwear.

Tightass's moniker did not come from me. I had no first-hand experience of the sphincter control of any FBI agent and hoped to always remain so ignorant. Nope, Daniel's loveable title derived from the fact that in his deep, sordid past, he ran with some street thugs known as the Slicers, short for Slice & Dice, whose dire rivals called themselves the Ice Nines. Good to know there was at least one semiliterate sci-fi-fan gangbanger out there with a sense of humor. They were like the Bloods and Crypts only more vindictive, if such a thing were possible.

One fine summer's day, Daniel and his Slicer buddies met up with an equally numbered group of Nines for a business transaction— of the pharmaceutical persuasion. A desired amount of illicit white substance and a price had been agreed upon the day before, and everyone was on his best behavior, meaning weapons were limited to semiautomatics and knives. Unfortunately, along with leaving his Saab-built AT-4 antitank weapon behind (imagine that: good cars *and* good weapons), the numero-uno Slicer somehow found himself short twenty bucks. A miscount or something. Could happen to anyone making a drug deal with archenemies, I'm sure.

No one but Daniel had any *dinero* on them, but he refused to fork over the necessary twenty. The man was tight with the dollar. Tensions ran high, no doubt, but Daniel did not succumb to the peer pressure. Suffice it to say, the deal fell through.

That night, after a few shots of Jim Beam and a couple of doobs, Daniel made his way home but did not arrive. Jumped by at least seven assailants, he was beaten to a pulp then dragged to a tattoo parlor where in a wonderfully cursive hand the word "tightass" was inked onto his butt cheek (or so he told me). He never found out if the Nines or the Slicers did it, but neighborhood legend had it that the effort was unified, the first in the gangs' histories.

The next day the newly christened Daniel "Tightass" Juarez took three buses and a train to the nearest FBI office and agreed to infiltrate his own gang and testify in court. And he did. He then worked hard in school and with a letter of recommendation from the presiding judge in the case of the Slicers and some killer SAT scores, he ended up at Williams College for his undergrad work in poly sci and from there he went onto the Feds. Now he was my thin-tied, dark glasses albatross.

Actually, Juarez wasn't a bad guy for a Fed. His time on the street gave him a sense of humor somehow, which is more than I can say for most FBI grunts. That definitely was a plus in my book. He was still tight with a dollar, which I continually ribbed him about, but he was good people to work with.

And he wanted Rodney and Desmond Gloucester real bad. A man after my own black heart.

Here's a little secret: most tax cheats are caught, not because of all your tax-dollar-financed hard work and diligent detecting by us "revenuers," but because somebody squeals. Somebody who is mad at the cheat, normally. Ex-spouses, ex-employees, ex-employers, feuding relatives or neighbors, heirs that are pissed off by a will, such things as that are tax cheats made on. It's just an unpleasant fact; the grass is always greener in the other person's yard, and it's better to give a call to the IRS than to receive one.

My buddy Juarez couldn't nab the Gloucester boys through the *Miranda Rights, get a confession, bring out the hoses in the back room* way, so he came to me with a modicum of hope and an Old Testament desire to see justice done. Just the kind of stuff the IRS likes.

Tightass took the case to me and lit a fire, hoping against hope that yours truly would be wilier than the evildoers. But I'd been stumped along the way, having discovered Patricia and Padma, but nothing else. Desmond covered every little thing in his money-laundering scheme like an anal retentive on Ritalin with a double-espresso chaser. The twice-wife angle earned both my ire and respect. But to Juarez, the bi-spouse goodness was the key.

"Despite some underground porn films to the contrary, a man's only got one dick, so more than one hole is just overkill," was the way he put it. "If you follow the hole, it'll lead to the money."

That was the point I scratched my pointy head in confusion on.

"Are we talking about women or untraceable income?"

Tightass meant both. Then it hit me. I rousted Desmond's latest 1040 and did the IRS eyeball, scanning quickly and letting the subconscious part of my brain look for trivial oddities and abnormalities. Didn't take long; it was right at the top. Filing status: married filing jointly. I scooted down to line 6c and counted six dependents—three from each wife. He was double dipping and declaring two wives and all their kids as exemptions. Well, la-di-da, there was something you don't see every day outside of Utah. There's such a thing as being *too* anal retentive.

Musta been the smile I borrowed from Harry that alerted Juarez, because suddenly he was all Fed-ears.

"You found something?"

I nodded.

"Something good?"

I nodded again. "Two somethings, actually. The bozo—"

"That's <u>Mr</u>. Bozo to you and me," Juarez threw in, as a way of criminal rights respect, or something. Who can figure the FBI brain?

"Well, Mr. Bozo got a little too fancy in the pantsies and declared both his wives on his tax form, reaping more money on his return than he should have. Five thousand six hundred and forty-two dollars more at rough estimate."

Juarez started laughing so hard he got red in the face, little flecks of saliva raining down like bacteria'd mist.

"This guy is pulling in seven digits a year from meth and he cheats on his taxes?"

"It's a time-honored tradition after all," I said.

This was indeed funny as hell, but hardly spittle-sprayingly unheard of. Yeah, yeah, yeah, everyone knows about Al Capone. Best piece of publicity the IRS ever had, even if people still hated us—at least in the year of our Lord 1931, they hated us a little less. But we've done the dirty to criminals large and small since 1927's Sullivan ruling opened the gates to all and sundry, and loved every single squirming second of it. Most people simply don't know, and we like it that way. Heck, Wooly Bob's hung an electronic sign over his desk that keeps track of each criminal busted in real-time. We're still way behind McDonald's, but ahead of the smoking-deaths billboards, which only goes to show there's always something to strive for.

Juarez wanted to know what to do next, but I had to think, which meant hitting happy hour at Del's. Tightass needed to get back to wifey number four—would that be Mrs. Tightass, or did she keep her maiden name?—so it was just me and the boys.

Then I remembered Miguel and Becky.

None of us had ever seen Del in all our knock-back years of going to the bar. Like the mythical yeti, the ever-elusive Del had "sightings" rather than physical encounters. A tab signed and left behind the counter; the crash of someone moving in the storeroom, but then not there; the image of an old crotchety-faced woman in the foam of a beer glass. Nothing tangible.

Being IRS agents, we, of course, checked the records. Nothing there either, except a business filing so squeaky clean, if we didn't like the bar so much, we would have certainly checked into it with tweezers and a magnifying glass. I know Harry once staked the place out three nights running, but he came up with nada.

"Weirdest thing in the world. The lights went out, but no one left. You think she sleeps there, maybe in the back with the bottles?"

It was an enigma wrapped in a conundrum all washed down with too many shots of Herradura tequila. "Live and let live" is my motto, when I don't have anything better to say. Del's corporality simply didn't matter as much as Del's booze.

Harry nodded toward Miguel and Becky, who cooed and cuddled at the bar, she on one side leaning her balcony over, and he blissfully happy on the other. "They're disgustingly cute in an 'I want to rip his pancreas out with my teeth' sorta way."

They oogly-wooglied each other and gave "hummingbird" kisses. As a goad for drinking to excess, it worked wonders. I couldn't funnel the booze fast enough, and Harry was his usual one-ahead. Miguel's happiness depressed us no end.

"I'm thinking a June wedding for our ass-end-of-a-baboon compadre," Harry snarled, looking like the wedding planner from the seventh circle of Hell, fire in his eye and pupils dilated. "The bride would wear white, and the groom would be in black and blue."

Wooly Bob got all teary-eyed; though it might have been a mist of lime zest he twisted into his root beer. "I love weddings. I remember when my sister, seven months pregnant and out to here …," he motioned about a basketball's size out from his belly, "came down the aisle, my dad's fingers death-gripped in her hand, a rictus smile on her face as she braved the nuptial commencement. I wanted to cry, but I'd smoked a spliff of hash-oiled Thai-stick with the husband-to-be earlier and had absolutely no control over any of my involuntary muscles."

"Isn't that why they're called 'involuntary?'" I said.

Bob tapped a manicured fingernail against his hairless chin; I swear he's made of plastic. "Hmm, that's true. All I know is that I'd gone completely catatonic, toes to nose. And, lo-and-behold, so had my sister's fiancé! We had to prop a caterer under him, pry his mouth open with a dessert spoon, and put the cover band's mic up to his lips to hear the 'I do.' Fortunately, good Thai stick has a manic phase about two-thirds in, and hubby came out of it long enough for the wedding dance—Don'tcha just love 'Enter Sandman?' How romantic can you get?—before completely going comatose for the next eight hours. My sister was *not* happy with the kickoff of the honeymoon, for sure. I know better than to mix those kind of organic H-bombs now. We want Miguel in fighting trim for propagating the species."

"Bite your tongue, or I'll bite it for you," Harry said, the bile in his voice as thick as day old pus. "Our Becky is pure as the driven snow and better be on birth control, both oral and condomial. Miguel will breed over my dead and stinking body. Could you imagine a brood of little Miguels let loose in the free world?"

We all sat stunned and motionless.

"Don't you move my stud stallion," Becky mooshy-mooshied at Miguel as she rounded the bar with our next order of drinks. "I'll be right back with a surprise."

Miguel brightened like a five-year-old on Christmas. "I bet I can guess."

In unison, we all chugged our drinks and held our glasses out for more. Becky, a beatific smile on her face, sashayed over with a bottle of Patron Platinum, some Napoleon brandy, and a hard-to-get two-liter bottle of Gale's root beer (we're talkin' the good stuff). Something for the each of us.

"On the house, guys. From Miguel and me. Isn't he the cutest?"

The next sound was simultaneous pourings and drinkings of drinks as fast as humanly possible.

Harry could finally take it no more; like a man whose leg had been amputated in his sleep and *must* pull the sheet back and look, no matter what the bloody consequences, he forced his mouth into the necessary shapes and asked, "What. Do. You. See. In. Him?"

Now, we love Becky with a fire that is both sex-driven and sisterly innocent. A combination that provokes blindness of the severest kind about imperfections. Yet, if push came to shoving back, we know that her makeup is from Target and her shoes from Costco, the lightest of wrinkle lines are beginning to roadmap the corners of her mouth, and zaftig as she is, one day the chains of gravity will destroy all that is holy. We *know* that, but we *love* Becky. What we'd never seen before is the incandescent glow that came over her, transforming Becky the Barkeep and holder of our hearts to Becky's In Love.

"He's not handsome. He's not rich. He's not that smart. And …" she dropped her voice, "he's only so-so in the sack...though very enthusiastic."

Harry had stuffed his forefingers in his ears and was mantra-ing, "I don't hear this. I don't hear this. I don't hear this."

"But, he's my soul mate."

Just like that, metaphysics had won her heart. Who knew that Plato, Aristotle, and Epicurus held more sway than Mammon, Eros, or Athena? I couldn't just let it rest, though. For the good of Harry and belching, swaggering, consumerism-driven manhood everywhere, I had to find out more. So I spoke the fateful words: "How can you tell?"

There is a moment in everyone's life where reason, logic, and just good sense flee the room as fast as their scrawny little legs can carry them. There's no excuse. I never should have asked. It's like asking about the meaning of life, the chicken and the egg, or why, if God is a benevolent God, he let the endoscope be invented. There are no answers, and there are an infinite number of answers. In Becky's case, it was infinite, or near as we could tell.

She started on the warm, tingly feeling she gets behind her knees when Miguel walks into the room with his shirt half-tucked, half-untucked into his two-sizes-too-big corduroys, worked her way through the rosary of his adorable breakfast peccadilloes—the way he slurps his Captain Crunch cereal, butters his toast on *both* sides, the yellow yolk that dries like a canker to his upper lip that he *always* forgets to wipe—took flight into a rosy repetition of Miguel's bathroomarial delights, and began to reach Mach speed as Becky headed stratospherically into the realm of birthmarks, knuckle lines, and the baby-like softness of her "sweet-alope's" cheeks. I, with my last sober ounce of self-preservation, did not ask which cheeks, thank the Lord and pass the ammunition. It was brutal. It was scorched earth. It was, obviously, love. You betchum.

It wasn't until half-past eleven that Becky ran out of steam, and we ran out of whatever high-proof patience we had. How Wooly Bob survived was anyone's guess. My conjecture was he took to snagging hanks of the herb from some secret stash pocket and swallowing them whole in an effort to anesthetize. Harry looked as if he'd just been told Santa Claus not only didn't exist, but in fact, the man whose lap he'd been sitting on for the last ten minutes actually was his sweaty-palmed, child-molester-esque Uncle Oliver who had breath like day-old pepperoni pizza and unsightly oozing sores on his inner thighs and was dressed in his mother's red cocktail dress, the contents of the vacuum stuck to his face with some whitish goo that *wasn't* Elmer's glue.

Ironically, our savior turned out to be the very causer of our pain, Miguel. He missed his "tater-tot" and needed some "huggy-buggies," stat. Becky spread her arms as if she were landing a jumbo jet and rushed over to snuggle. Hideous did not even begin to describe it, but a rescue was a rescue, so we bought Miguel a drink—"Aren't they the sweetest, Miggy?"—and got down to brass tacks, once we pulled them from our bleeding ears.

Harry wanted to kvetch, but I managed steer the conversation around to bigamy, money laundering, and the inalienable rights of man to become so greedy that neither crime nor punishment were an adequate deterrent. Which is why we the faithful believe the IRS was invented in the first place.

So I told them about Rodney T. Gloucester and his brother Desmond H. and the geniuses that they were.

It took the better part of twenty minutes, but when I finished, neither Harry nor Wooly Bob had as much as a toothpick's worth of thought for Becky and Miguel.

"Da-a-a-a-amn," Harry said for the fourth time. "That's some deep shit, Mark-o. That guy's so thorough, I bet he don't crap without wiping twice with bleach to ensure there're no prints."

Wooly Bob likened it to a puzzle of Richard the Third convolutions, "The Gloucester name runs true."

"I know you had a good education, Bob—I read your file, remember, right before I tossed it in the trashcan and hired you despite it," I said. "I've seen your Ivy League credentials, your degrees in things as varied as theoretical ethnocentric biology and ambiguous dipolar statistical engineering. I even read the part stating you had an IQ of one seventy-five- plus. Nevertheless, I still don't hold it against you, except at times like this when instead of giving me answers, you obliquely reference Shakespeare at me. I've read the Bard, too, and you don't see me spouting any 'now is the winter of our discontents' at you, do you?"

Wooly Bob humbled up right then like a newspaper-swatted puppy after making wee-wee on the carpet. "Sorry, man. It's just been a long night."

"I'll drink to that," said Harry, raising and downing a shot of brandy.

"And I got carried away. Shouldn't've done it."

"I'll drink to that, too." Down the hatch went another glug.

Wooly Bob held out a hand for a shake. "Forgive me, sahib. Won't happen again."

I shook his hand, well, 'cause he was one of mine, for good, bad, or worse. We were all a little weirded out by the Becky/Miguel extravaganza. It rankled and pleased us both at the same time.

"Okay, so what do I do? I'm thinking this double exemption in the spouse department might be a shiv into the ribs, but I don't know how to worm it to the heart of the *hawala* thing. Brother Desmond's a clever bastard, that's for sure."

Harry got that Harry look he gets when his little Harry mind was working overtime on something usually involving ritual sacrifice, anemone poisoning, and Internal Revenue Code, Title 26, Subtitle A, Chapter 1, Subchapter B, Part II, section 71, or thereabouts. It was a look I came to know, love, and fear, if only for the certain vindictiveness of it.

"Whatcha got?"

Harry's look went nova in clarity, like seeing the hard white bones beneath the skin, the soft-sloppy brain inside the skull, the sticky-delicious peanut butter at the heart of a Reese's cup.

"We need a squealer, right?"

Bob and I nodded. It always came down to a squealer.

"Suppose you're, for just a drunken second, concentrating too much on ol' Des? And Des' wives, P-1 and P-2. Just...kinda walk with me on this one. Suppose you took a skinny at the Rodney's wife's income."

"But Rodney's not married," I pointed out while grabbing a handful of cashews from the bowl. At least, I thought they were cashews; we'd downed a particularly large amount that night. Coulda been anything from pretzel nuggets to I-don't-want-to-think-about-its. It was getting later and later.

"Yeah, ain't that great? But if he were, I bet he could take a deduction or three, now couldn't he? What we need to do is lure him into matrimonial exempt status and then take that self-same exemption and plumber's helper it so far up his bung-holier-than-thou that when he sings his favorite Bing Crosby song, our audit papers come out his mouth."

Hmm, creative use of audit placement.

"But what makes you think he likes Der Bingle?"

"*Everybody* sings Bing Crosby songs in the shower. 'I'm dreaming of a whi-i-ite Christian, just like my daddy used to know.' "

Wooly Bob scratched his head on that one. "Are you sure that's the way the words go?"

"They do down in Alabama, Slick," Harry said. "And if you think that's a bit strange to your liberal, left-wing, commie-lovin', shell-like ears, you should get a snippet of the southern version of that good-ol'-boy Bachman Turner Overdrive favorite, *Takin' Care of Business*."

There was a pause. And another, longer one. Neither Bob nor I wanted to ask, but it was just so damn tempting, even if Harry was grinning like a lunatic at us. He knew it to be only a matter of time and tainted curiosity.

With quiet inevitability, Bob and I scissor/rock/paper'd it, and I lost. "Rock beats scissors."

I turned to Harry, fearing for my sanity, and put the query to him. "Okay. Tell us."

Harry sang at the top of his lungs to the tune of *Takin' Care of Business*—"Bakin' carrot biscuits, every day! I'm just bakin' carrot biscuits...every way!"

Bob and I groaned, and Harry laughed so hard he spilled his beer down his chin. Then he went into CCR's *Bad Moon Rising* for an encore: "There's a bathroom on the right!"

"Please, no mas! No mas!"

But then Wooly Bob got into it (and to the tune of *Purple Haze*): "'Scuse me, while I kiss this guy! Nahh, naaah-naaah, nahh-nahh-nahh-nahhh-naahh."

"Et tu, Wooly?"

"Oh, you like the blazing guitar stuff, eh?" And then, to add insult to injury, he went into *Stairway to Heaven* in his best, or worst, Robert Plant falsetto. "And there's a wino down the road...I should've stole his Oreos!"

I slapped my palms to my ears, screaming, "Make it stop! Make it stop!"

Then, in agonizing two-part harmony, these sick monsters went into Bruce Springsteen's first album—afterwards covered by Manfred Mann—classic, *Blinded By The Light*: "She was blinded by the light! Wrapped up like a douche, another boner in the night! Blinded by the l-i-i-i-i-ight!"

It hurt as only horrible mondegreens could when sung by sadistic tenors. I screamed again, "Becky! Check!" then reached for my wallet, tossed a fifty across the bar and raced for freedom, the two of them yelling their final assault on my senses as I cleared the door to liberty, a twisted take on my second favorite Simon and Garfunkel song, *I Am a Rock*: "I am a rock, I am in Tha-a-a-i-i-i-land!"

4.

I hadn't seen Lila for a while, but I busy-beavered her files and dropped them off at her cubicle. No sign of her except yet another expensive bouquet of flowers with a note of undying love attached. I know; I read it.

Hey, Lila woulda read it to me if I were there; she always does. Then we'd snigger a little at the sheer purple prose of it, or the misspellings of words like "luv" and "bobo" (they meant "boo-boo"), or simply the fact that someone's favorite lyrics were from The Wind Beneath My Waves.

We were best buds, even if she was the sexiest thing on two legs. Maybe that was part of it. It had been a long time for me between relationships, but I did enjoy the kindness of beautiful women, even if I wasn't doing the flesh fandango with them. Maybe even more that way sometimes. Things were complicated.

I used to like complicated. Used to be my first, last, and middle name. If there were a stadium of full of staid normal people with one psycho-bitch-gave-head-like-an-angel-but-rip-your-heart-out-with-a-rusty-spoon woman, I'd hook up with her. *Every* time. No shit. Swear to God. It's a gift.

Anyway, since my second ex—She Who Will Not Be Obeyed—I've sabbaticalled it from the wide, wide world of relationships. It hurt too much. And for what? Something I could do with my hand and a little Jergins? It all came back to molecular biology—that sneaky little punk testosterone. Why else does a person voluntarily put themselves in penal-system closeness with a complete emotional stranger they'd met at a bar at some point (as if bars were a culling method that led to statistical meaningful representations of rationality), forging legal chains and constant complaints for nothing more than an evolutionary spasm? I wasn't down on relationships; I just never wanted one ever, ever again. But I did miss beautiful women, so Lila helped me there.

She quota'd my beautiful-women needs and threw in wit, charm, and intelligence to boot. And boots, too. Killer, thigh-high leather ones that, coupled with the shortest mini-skirt that could be determined legal in forty of the fifty states, always made me feel like a teenager, a pervert, and a New York metrosexual, all at the same time.

Files closed and stashed back at her desk, I made pointed notes on her flower card, triple-underling the "thee's" and "thou's" in the faux Ye Olde English style of courtship. This guy better be stinkin' rich and not just rich. I then put a smiley face on it and went back to my cubicle grotto to think more about Rodney Gloucester.

Harry, in his own malicious way, was onto something. I pulled out the Rodster's tax returns for the last ten years and started eyeballing his marriage status boxes. Single. Single. Single. Single. Single. Single. Single. Single. Married filing jointly. Hoo-ya! When did the under-brother get hitched? I was going to have to send him a gift. I wondered where he was registered. Crystal was always nice. Everyone liked crystal. Or a lien against his earnings. They're *never* out of fashion.

The IRS was a tricky customer. The closest biological metaphor I could think of was a starfish and a mussel. A starfish kinda gloops along until it hits that muscular mussel. Then it takes its little teeny-tiny starfish feets and slowly works one of them between the bivalve's valve. Then another. Then yet another. Finally, it applies pressure, slow and steady. Quicker than you can say clam chowder, the mussel's splayed out like a big-tata'd hooker at a bachelor party—something else that Rodney didn't have.

We only required the smallest of gaps, and we were into mussel. I looked at the wifey's name: Donna Gloucester. I wondered who ol' Donna was. A friend of the family? An ex-girlfriend? No real-time girlfriend would ever acquiesce to being a pseudo-wife; they wanted the genuine article: ring, house, and good divorce lawyer. Maybe it was the name of Rodney's dog. Wouldn't that be disgusting? Brought a completely new meaning to the word "furball."

I needed more info, and I needed it from the definitive source of info. The "burning bush" of data. The yin, yang, chicken and hardboiled egg of personal facts. That meant a phone call to my histrionically friendly DMV registrar, Bennie "I'm Not A Large Black Woman" Jones.

See, Benz worked with quite a few large black women at the DMV and liked to make it completely clear that he was not to be mistaken for one. Once he even had a T-shirt printed up with that very phrase upon it, but the LBW's corralled him in one of the stalls in the men's room, forcibly removed his shirt from his back, and stuck an "I Obey Oprah" pin on his shrunken, tofu-white chest. At five feet and change, I doubted the women broke a sweat doing it. To this day, Bennie swore it was consensual, but what the hell that meant was anyone's guess. Suffice it to say, he was dating one of the women who accosted him.

"Mang! You outta see the sex we got! It's totally fucked up!"

Bennie's data-fishing talents were so often used by me, he was on speed-dial, right up there near Happy Jack's Bail Bonds (another good source of dirty laundry) and Thai Surprise (a take-out place that served Mexican food—which, I guess, was the surprise). One ringy-dingy, two ringy-dingy.

"Department of Motor Vehicles, mang. May I help you?"

Nobody but Bennie answered the phone so lyrically.

"Bennie," I cooed, knowing that he knew that I knew that if I were calling, there was a bonus somewhere in there for him. "My favorite DMV employee. You still fudging your deductibles?"

"Mark mang! You know I am as honest as the dick is long. You no worry about me or my deductibles. Right?"

"I'd have to ask Clarisse about how honest you are, but no worries from me, long or short form." I fiddled with Rodney's tax returns. "So, you have time for me on something?"

Bennie knew those magic words well. He immediately began puffing up with self-serving importance.

"You know, I am kinda busy here. Lotta people getting their registrations renewed today."

I couldn't help but grin at Bennie's transparency.

"I bet they're lined up clear around the block. Nevertheless, I have a generous proposition for you...provided you can fit me into your busy registrational schedule."

Bennie and I danced like this every time, more for practice than purpose.

"For you, mang, I got the time. Whatcha wan' me to look up?"

"Phoenix, Arizona—Donna Gloucester...if she exists and has a driver's license."

"Spell that, okay?"

So I did. I also gave references to Rodney, and some addresses Donna might happen from. Shots in the dark, but sometimes those were the best kind. Then I laid out the carrot for Bennie: "Two tickets to the Knicks Friday night."

"No shit! Really? Like, they're my favorite team ever! I grew up with a Patrick Ewing poster in my room, right next to the one with REO Speedwagon and Che Guevara. I wanted to *be* Patrick Ewing. I kinda look like him."

"If the 'Beast of the East' were really short, Hispanic, and had no hops, you'd be the spittin' image. Swear to Christ, Bennie."

"Don't take Hey-sus's name in vain, let alone Mr. Ewing's, or I will get Clarisse to mess you up. And don't think she can't do it to you. She's a big girl with a lot of anger that I suspect had something to do with her early upbringing."

My pal Bennie the psychiatrist.

"Hey, I was only commenting on the facts, Jack. You have to admit, the similarity is stretching it a bit." I heard Bennie grumble on the other end, but life was like that. "So, the tix okay for you?"

"Sure, mang, didn't mean to complain. They good seats?"

"Got 'em at a repo for a shit-don't-stink neurosurgeon who owed three-fifty-K in back taxes—ten rows back behind the bench."

"She-e-e-e-e-et! No fuck! You are my best friend! What's mine is yours. I will name my firstborn after you."

"Bennie, your firstborn is named Bennie Jr. I met him, remember?"

"Oh, yeah. I forgot on account of because he's livin' with my first squeeze, Ramada, that complete bitch and a half. Okay, I will *rename* my firstborn after you. How's that? I will call him Mark Mang, in your honor."

I concluded my Bennie moment with salutations and the knowledge that if there were a Donna Gloucester, my b-ball lovin' buddy'd find her and weasel back to me in no time flat.

"Adios, amigo."

And so came lunchtime.

Now, lunch at the IRS was a unique time of day. We were a governmental agency, after all, so it split fifty-fifty between those who went out for a meal and those who brown-bagged it. And then there were those of us who ate at the cafeteria.

I liked the cafeteria. My mom never let me eat at the one when I went to school, so that was my revenge. Comfort food as far as the eye could see. Mac and cheese. Mashed potatoes. Salisbury steak that was actually day-old meatloaf. Or at least that's what I thought it was. Green Jell-O cubes! Heaven on the cheap. Oh, and little chocolate milks that you poked a straw into. Gluttony, thy name is cafeteria.

My friends thought I was weird.

Harry relied on the power of Quarter Pounders to make it through the day. Supersize fries. And a chocolate shake. Miguel was a dyed-in-the-wool, fish-filet fanatic. He chowed three at a sitting, with eight of those little tartar-sauce packets on each one. Wooly Bob? He didn't eat lunch but liked to get Happy Meals for the toys—"They're collectibles."—and sit on the lap of the life-size Ronald McDonald statue out front and tell it what he wanted for Christmas: "... and a pony. And a Nintendo. And some guava scalp exfoliator..."

I was just a stick-in-the-mud. I had to have my cafeteria food. On a tray. Trays were very important to my inner elementary school child. The one that unscrewed his Oreos counterclockwise, then scraped off the white junk with his lower teeth.

"Hey, Slick." Lila sashay-shimmied next to me. "Wanted to thank you for the homework you did for me by buying you lunch, but I see your tastes are wa-a-a-a-y out of my league."

I carefully placed my chocolate milk in the upper-right corner of my tray, my chips on the upper-left corner, my tuna sandwich still unopened in its triangular cocoon of plastic to the lower left, my napkin and plastic settings carefully to the right of my plate, which was heaped with some brown stew, or it could have been meatloaf and gravy. The Oreos rested comfortably on the lower right, waiting expectantly for dessert.

"This some sort of religious ritual, Mark?"

Lila tilted her head to the side like an impish siren in Ferragamo and Cavalli.

"It's every lunch I never had as a kid growing up."

She snatched a chip, replying through the loud crunch, "You're weird."

See, told you my friends thought I was weird.

"I owed you on the paperwork, kiddo, so we're more than even," she said.

"What're you doing slummin' down here? Thought for sure you'd be gallivanting about with a billionaire or three."

"I gallivant less than you might think." She reached for an Oreo but I glared her down. "A bit territorial on the Oreos aren't we?"

"You can have as many as you want, *after* you finish your lunch."

Yeah, yeah. I know I sounded like a psycho from Pacoima, all "Jesus told me to climb up on the top of that water tower with the fifty-caliber rifle and sniper the passing yellow VW Bugs with license plates from New Jersey," but I was just playing around. I enjoyed Lila's company no end.

"So what's up with your super-secret, deep-sea fishing trip? Catch anything?" I asked.

I removed the plastic from my sandwich like a bridegroom his virgin wife's clothes on their wedding night. Had ever a sandwich been so well treated?

Lila gave me a strange-o glance, kind of a cross between confused, perturbed, and don't-fuck-with-me-or-I'll-make-party-favors-out-of-your-intestines sorta look. I'd never seen that one before. Was it for the way I treated my sandwich, or my question? Couldn't be the question, could it?

Lila nuzzled herself up to me, dropping her head down so her hair swept across my cheek, a brief touch. "You know ..." she huskied her voice something divine and terrible. "Something came up."

"Like the African elephant raging in my pants? Down, Simba! Down! No peanuts for you!"

She cracked up in that exceptionally Lila way. "No...*peanuts*! I think you have more than enough peanuts!"

I offered Lila an Oreo. "Wanna cookie, little girl?"

"Why, Mr. Douglas...are you trying to bribe an agent of the Internal Revenue Service?"

"Will it help me any?"

She took the cookie and—just to screw with my little male noggin—split it halfway and ran her tongue up and down the white filling.

"You are so going to hell in a hand basket for that," I said.

Then she popped the whole thing in her mouth and chomped. "Tricks of the trade, Mark. You know that."

She proceeded to eat the rest of my Oreos, licking each one slower than the one preceding it, while I gave a few karmic thoughts to coming back in my next life as a cookie.

By the time I realized she hadn't answered my question, I'd already gone back to my cubby, burrowed into a stack of past-tense papers like a mole to ground, running my fingers lightly along my computer keypad, crunching and re-crunching numbers in an economic frenzy worthy of the late-great Dr. Milton Friedman. Between the two thousand seven hundred and forty-three dollar deduction for argyle socks and the six hundred eighty-nine dollar deduction claimed for the Q-Tips (you got me—some people will claim *anything*) that nagging tickle at the base of my monkey brain started screeching in true primate fashion.

Odd she avoided answering. Lila glorified candor. "I only say things behind people's backs I say to their faces—repeatedly," she'd oft time quoted to me, chapter, verse, and episodic anecdote. We both called 'em as we saw 'em, one of the reasons bonding us like epoxy. Which made her reaction doubly strange. I scratched my ear and thought for a moment, then let it pass. I'd catch up with her and really grill her about it.

That was the last I ever saw of Lila, though.

Bobbsie "Zimmerman" Dylan may have said it best during his weirdly iconoclastic journey through Christianity: "You're gonna have to serve somebody." In me and mine's cases—us bang-squad buddies—that somebody was so far away from Jesus Christ as to beg a description in detail.

Aroon Kumaar Vijah Smith (the gatekeepers at Ellis Island thought Singeteem was too long a name, so they shortened it, moved a few letters around, and then released it back into the wild) stood six feet eight inches in his stocking feet and looked like a cross between Manute Bol and Mahatma Gandhi. With a penchant for extremely ugly but loud ties—usually of some lime green persuasion—suits dating back to the early Sixties, and the musical tastes of a thirteen-year-old girl, Aroon was a trial to the laws of the universe and a misunderstanding waiting to happen. With an accent thicker than panang sauce, most of the time he was completely incomprehensible, and that's the way we liked it. Can't follow an order if you didn't understand it.

What he wasn't, though, was stupid.

I'd once eyeballed the diplomas on his walls, nailed up there next to the faux-casual shots of his wife and family—all eight kids ranging in age from two to ten. Mr. Aroon matriculated for only five years at various universities, from Dartmouth to Chino, but there were six degrees up there: economics (MA), applied mathematics (PhD), business administration (MBA), doctor of jurisprudence (JPA), engineering (another PhD) and a final one from the Fashion Institute: apparel design. Go figure.

Anyway, this incongruity in motion led, and we followed, when we could figure out what the hell he was saying. Or writing. Our boss's memos were legendary. His spelling made Mandarin look like a cinch to decipher. Who spells "cat" with a "k," a "u," *and* a "b?" He didn't care; he just sent another memo with a completely new set of spellings. You betchum.

Ding! E-mail hit my machine. Then another and another and another. Sounded like xylophones in my head. Mr. Aroon was communicating. I started clicking them open as fast as they bulleted in, but somehow he wrote them quicker than I could read them.

Something that looked like "eels eet hey but the eagle laffs at midnight" popped up. Odd. It actually made sense, but was of no help to me. The next one seemed to read: "Xberta, lagoosha san mithwa heck." Getting somewhere...or not. It went on from there until I figured out that Mr. Aroon wanted my week's summation a day early for some reason.

I tallied up my cases, cut-and-pasted from my Excel sheets, and printed the whole thing out. Then I printed them out again; my boss sticklered everything and wanted me to be looking at what he looked at when we were looking over whatever it was we were supposed to be looking at.

The Big Office took two elevator stops to get to. Shoulder to shoulder with brown-suited revenue grunts who took pride in their brown suited-ness, I attached my special clip-on identity badge—the one marked with my name, my smiling face, my thumbprint, and retinal scan (no, not *rectal*, but I'm sure they're trying to find a way to add that to the list)—and braved the journey to the executive floor. There I grabbed my special hall pass that waited for me at the front desk, handed out by a Sherman Tank of a woman, Claudia Faberge Constantine—I shit you not.

I gave my most gallant smile, the knight-in-shining-armor one that said: *You can trust me, swear to mutherfrickin' God*, then gave it my best shot. "So, what's Mr. Aroon want me for, Claudia?"

The Cerberus of secretaries didn't even glance up from her two-hundred-words-a- minute transcription of court records she collated and shunted into the system for a hobby.

"His name is Mr. *Smith*. And I am Miss Constantine."

"Right, Claudia. Of course you are. We've met before. Many times."

It was fingernails on the cliff edge, and I'd only been there thirty seconds. How can it be possible for one human to do this to another? Then she looked up at me. Maybe she wasn't human.

Basilisks could supposedly turn men to stone. Medusas, too. Svengali could hypnotize with but a glance, and demons could pull a man's soul out through his eyes. Claudia Faberge Constantine had them all beat in spades. She could make a man's testicles retract so far back into his body, they lodged in his throat. Puberty was not an option around her.

"Yes, Miss Constantine. It won't happen again, Miss Constantine."

I sat down demurely on the regulation lumpy couch of off-gray leatherette and waited like a penitent on Good Friday. She had a gift. A terrible, horrible gift, and if there were a God, He/She/It would have to pay dearly for creating a Miss Constantine.

Mr. Aroon finally claimed my attendance in his office after only a twenty-minute wait. Not bad, overall; though twenty minutes with Miss Constantine felt like an eternity in the Eighth Level of Hell. The moment I entered the Big Office, I felt again the whole wonder and majesty of the Internal Revenue Service. It was a shrine to the tax code. Every inch of wall space—except for his many diplomas—bricked three-deep with every book ever written about taxes. I mean *every*. And, as far as I knew, Mr. Aroon had read them all back to front.

"Mr. Douglas. Thank you for coming up so quickly."

There was an arachnid-ness about Mr. Aroon's six feet eight inches as he bent and folded it into the federally issued office chair that he made his home. It was a combination of knees, elbows, and the spider look he had. I shuffled my files, making time, trying to figure what it was about.

Then I noticed the two impeccably dressed gray-suits sitting in the corner, unmoving, sunglasses glued to their faces. Uh-oh. I smelled trouble with a capital "T" and that rhymed with "P" and that stood for...uh-oh.

"I gather you are friendly with the Federal Bureau of Investigation."

Not a question, a statement: was there something with the Gloucester files I'd done wrong? No one said I couldn't play in the park with Agent Juarez. I'd done it before, and if not standard operating procedures, it wasn't banned. Something smelled fishier than a day-old Subway foot-long tuna sandwich, and I recognized what: feebs.

"I need the copies of the files you worked on for Lila Everston," Mr. Aroon said, his voice soft but if-you-don't-you're-dead demanding.

Lila's files?

"You know they're just scut-work I did as a favor she did for me."

Mr. Aroon held his hand out.

"Nothing in them but noise. A few holdouts and odd deductions, but nothing revelatory. Mostly paper pushing, which is why I'm doing it for her while she moves on important stuff. Lila stuff. You know."

Hand still held out. I sorted through the files, glad I'd brought them, and handed them over.

"What's up, boss?"

Mr. Aroon looked at the files, fanning them open and snapping a memory of them before holding them out for the Feds, one who silently opened up a briefcase and put them inside, closing it with the click of a lock.

After that, no one moved.

No one talked.

No one did anything.

Sometimes overstaying a welcome gleaned tidbits of knowledge, kernels of information. Unfortunately, sometimes those bits and bytes weren't anything you wanted to know.

Finally, Mr. Aroon unfolded from his chair, standing up and up and up until he looked down on me.

"Ms. Lila Everston has been killed."

The next thing I knew, I was downing five tequila shots, one right after the other, and asking for another five. After that, I didn't remember anything.

5.

"Juju Klondike? What the hell kind of a name is Juju Klondike?"

"He's a killer eunuch," Juarez explained, tight-lipped and nervy.

I squeegeed my ear with a forefinger. "Come again?"

"No cash and prizes. Without the family jewels. Joey and the twins are missing. The wedding tackle has gone the way of the buffalo. He's crotchless in the crotch; nuthin' from nuthin' leaves nuthin'."

Juarez looked unstoppable at that moment, rolling freely with the verbal dice.

"Really?"

"Captain Winkey and his two first mates have gone AWOL."

I held my hands up. "Okay, okay—enough with the euphemisms. I get the picture."

Imagine that. I'd always heard that Hitler only had one ball...no doubt part of the reason he was such a friggin' psycho. Well, this guy had no balls and no bat. We were talkin' cut off at the root by his own twisted grandfather in order to make him *tougher*. Now Klondike took it out on the whole world, for a fee. Nature? Nurture? Incredibly nasty.

Juarez shook his head as if he could hear a rattle inside, then went on, "It sent two of our best profilers to the psych wards trying to figure out a theoretical mindset for this nutso tofutti. Wasn't going to happen. We don't even try anymore. He's unpredictable as he is thorough—and he's never been tapped yet. We only know his name, rank, and serial number. And he scares the crap out of me."

"So, why are you telling me about this nut, er...nutless whack job?"

"Lila Everston. She twinked something that no one else could have possibly twinked."

My eyebrows shot up so high they nearly wrapped to the back of my head. "Lila was extraterrestrial when it came to that."

Juarez was anything but happy, his voice dropping low as he replied, "Somehow she figured the who, what, and where of some people who are the type of people who hire people like Juju Klondike. And we think he killed her for it. With pleasure. And he took his time..."

I don't get angry. I haven't gotten angry since...well, since I came back from basic training, head shaved, muscles screaming, and found my stepdad hurting my mom. For twelve years I had little-kidded the fact that he slapped her. Twisted her arm until she cried. Left bruises sometimes where I wasn't supposed to see. Smiled while he talked to her like a blue urinal cake in a public bathroom.

Oh, he was an upstanding guy: all big business and rotary club glad-handing. It took the wind out of his sails when I went military: "Who the hell goes into the military voluntarily, you scrotum-sack lug nut? Street trash and idiots volunteer. I thought you had brains Mr. Valedictorian Football Star."

I shuffled my feet and mumbled nothings, ashamed as only my stepdad could make me feel. My dad dad couldn't pay for me to go to college, and stepdad wouldn't waste his money, for all his words and high-falutin' innuendos. He humiliated my mom and treated me like skin rash. But after my thirteen weeks in jarhead hell, I realized I wasn't angry at my drill sergeant, at the Marine Corps, or at my fellow street trash and idiots, who I kinda liked. I was angry at my stepdad.

And he was into his second gin and tonic when I slung my duffle bag through the front door of my old home, dressed in my Bravo uniform, my hair just growing past peach fuzz.

"Well if it ain't the conquering hero. Whatcha doin' back here, Marine? Wash out, come to cry to your mama?

He laughed and splashed more gin in his glass.

I don't think it was what he said, but I never could get it straight with my shrink years later. I don't think it was that I knew he hit my mom with all the gusto of a born bully, reveling in his own invulnerability, though I'm sure that, at the core, the hitting was key. It was the look on his face that insulted me, opened my blind eye to the helpless cycle inflicted for the last twelve years.

Of course, hurting my mom yet again triggered it.

Oh, he tried to be playful, but I could see him staring at me as she walked out, proud as punch to see her boy a man. And it was that smile she had for me, and never for him, that really set him off.

"Honey! Look at you! Why didn't you call me, tell me you were coming home? I would have made you a special dinner. I have rib eye in the fridge. I still can. I know how much you like your rib eye. And mashed potatoes. I'll fix up a pot of them for you."

She hugged me like only a mom can, and he eyeballed my mom, microscoping for weakness, frailty, or just plain chinks in the personal armor we all carry like fingerprints.

"How come you don't make a special dinner for me?" Stepdad said. "I bring home the bacon every goddamn day. He's just an idiot without initiative, working for a bunch of other idiots who like to play with guns."

Mom knew that voice. She knew the implications, the ramifications, and the intent. I'd like to think that Mom put up with it for twelve years because she had me around, helpless. Maybe that wasn't the best way to handle abuse, but it was a way. Dad failed her monetarily. Stepdad failed her psychologically. Maybe she knew I wouldn't fail her physically.

So Mom ignored him, which only wound him up more.

"You think a few months marching around like a tin soldier gives you some special dispensation? I have grunts like you working my warehouse for below minimum wage."

I turned to my stepdad. He wasn't small. He was a beefy, ex-athlete gone to seed, six feet four of water polo back-in-the-day. I never liked water polo players; they always acted like five-year-olds with tans. All of them. Stepdad was no exception. Maybe too much chlorine seeped into their nasal passages when they were young. Or they took too many dunkings, the air cut off from their brains too often. Whatever it was, they thought they were golden gods, even when they were just fat-asses. Besides, I was a Marine, and you don't screw with the Marines: Semper Fi, motherfucker.

I smiled at Stepdad. "You know, I hear it's illegal to pay them so little. Better watch out someone doesn't report you."

For one instant, just a micro-second, I could see his pupils dilate, like he recognized the steel behind the words; that he acknowledged that things had changed, and he'd better step back and reconsider his stance on life, the universe, and his own overrated hide. I saw the gears whir, the neurons fire, the conclusions reached. That moment could have changed everything, even my anger. Then I watched his jaw set, and his small-penis insecurities rise up to overcome reason.

"Who's gonna drop the dime, you?" He laughed, shambling over, his gin-and-tonic courage sloshing. "I know everyone in town who even pretends to be anyone. You make a call, and maybe I'll just have them toss your butt into jail for being a little shit. No bail. How 'bout that, boyo?"

I kept smiling. "I won't be in town long enough. I have my MOS training to go through. Gotta learn to kill good."

"Big words, sonny jim. You wanna drink?"

That took me by surprise. He never offered me a drink.

"Sure."

He poured me a gin and tonic, and I took it, letting the bite of ice and alcohol roll down my throat.

"That'll put hair on your chest." He turned to Mom, demanding, "So where's that special dinner? I want mine charred through and through. Same for the Marine."

"Mark likes his medium rare," Mom said in my defense and that of the rib eye.

Charred? What kind of an asshole ruins perfectly good rib eye?

"That's not the way I like it, honey, and this is still my house, as far as I know."

Drink or no drink, this was just a power play. They taught us all about that in basic training: when to avoid them and when to go head-to-head.

"I got thirteen weeks of pay burning a hole in my pocket. Why don't I take both of you out? You don't need to cook, Mom."

Stepdad didn't like that in the least. It made him look weak and bitch-slapped, which was what I wanted, I guess. Hard to tell at this late date.

"Mr. Marine's got some cash? Imagine that. Twelve years of sponging, and now he's gonna take me out to dinner. Gonna pay me back-rent, too?"

My mom surely knew what came next, and over the years I wondered if this was what Dad saw in her when the bank accounts dwindled to nothing, and she threw him out. I sometimes dream about the look on her face at that instant. The force of it. The sheer clarity of righteousness and manipulation that went into pulling the mask of victory into her features like a red cape to a bull. Mom knew what she was doing with all the forethought and consideration of murder one. She executed her plan, and I do believe it *was* a plan, with absolute precision. And neither my stepdad nor I could do a thing to stop it. Not that we wanted to.

"John, don't talk to Mark that way. He's a man now."

The implications of that were so insulting, my stepdad could only laugh. "He's a snot-nosed little shit, still and always will be. Now go make some rib eye."

He grabbed her arm, as she knew he would. Too hard.

"John, you're hurting me."

Those were the words I needed to hear for the anger to vomit forth. Twelve years of helplessness at the hands of this man, and those words unlocked the shackles of my temper. Forget that my mom stayed with him to be hurt. Forget she inflamed his own inadequacies for him to hurt her. No one deserved to be hurt, especially Mom. Even if that hurt meant freedom for her.

"Let her go. *Now*."

My stepdad didn't see the punch coming. I didn't give him a warning. I'm insanely fast. I'm very, very strong. And at that moment, I had thirteen weeks of boot camp torture welling up behind that hit, twelve years of anger and a partridge in a pear tree.

I drove his jaw sideways, tearing it loose from its ligaments. Then I caught his kneecap with the heel of my foot and drove it straight down, ripping it like cardboard. I wanted to drive my fingers into his throat, but something stopped me. I'd like to think it was decency, but I'm not sure I had any at that moment.

He still hung onto my Mom's arm, his body shocked into immobility. The pain hadn't reached his brain yet, but the understanding that it shortly would, had. He stood there, unmoving.

Mom looked at him calmly. "John?"

Then Stepdad crumpled to the ground in complete silence. His knee gone, his jaw shattered, he should have been screaming, but it was as if some shred of courage crawled into his soul like a sneak thief and inspired him to propriety. He never made a sound during the 911 call. When the paramedics arrived, he kept quiet as they drove him off.

Afterwards he hollered bloody murder through his lawyer, but that day, I shut him up.

He tried to get me arrested, but the Marine Corps sticks by its own. I had friends in the high places my stepdad liked to say he did. Seemed the assistant DA was USMC. So was the judge. And no one seemed to like my stepdad. So charges simply vanished, still-birthed and aborted. I went back to Camp Pendleton with a smile on my lips, a song in my heart, and some good rib eye in my stomach. Mom never divorced him.

It's not like I hold a grudge, but I never let my stepdad's villainy go for some reason—call it divorce guilt, Oedipal leanings, or just straight-up dislike. But the first person I ever audited when I got confirmed in my new IRS job was good ol' stepdad. Got a gold star from my boss for thoroughness, too. Steppie got fine-tooth anal-probed like an HMO patient being examined for prostate cancer. He never knew what hit him, and, just like with the Marines, I had the full force of the United States government to back me. Little fuckin' son-of-a-bitch.

But I didn't get angry anymore.

Until then.

The world was not a pretty place. It was singularly screwed up most of the time, without conscience or reason, but Lila made it better. Her up-and-at-'em confidence, that neon-glow intelligence, the sexy smirk she got knowing that if she had to, she knew where the bodies were buried, each and every one of them. But the world had buried her, all because she believed the good guys should win and the bad guys should be punished. And it took a long, long time to enforce the lesson, in the most painful, humiliating way possible. *That* made me angry. I didn't know how, or when, but I was going to have this bastard's balls on a plate, even if he didn't have any. That was a promise I solemnly swore before God and the FBI. Juarez knew that's what I'd do. He planned on it, though it didn't matter one bit to me. Sometimes being predictable was its own reward.

6.

The funeral looked like a *Forbes* Who's Who of billionaires. Lila never slummed when she could go first class. Acres and acres of black Armani, Missoni, and Zenga dotted the immaculately kept lawn like a Milan fashion show for the dead. The kind of limos that weren't rented following the hearse in Blue Angel formation perfection. Dialects from around the world all murmuring to each other in ritual and sadness. Lila shining-starred even in death.

I used my Internal Revenue hindbrain and calculated that thirty-percent of the global wealth was tied up at that shindig. If someone dropped an A-bomb out at Forrest Lawn, the world's economies would've hit the crapper and driven civilization back to the Stone Age. But an army of highly professional bodyguards in tailored pinstripe Kevlar body armor, Glock 33-armed, stood ranked to stop the attempt with their lives, and no doubt everyone else's lives around them as well. Man, would I have liked to audit all of them just once...

Despite the mourners that overflowed the mortuary, I felt empty and alone. What the hell had happened? Why kill Lila? And why saddle me with the conscience to do something about it? I ain't nobody's hero. But I knew I needed to do something, if only so I could go into a men's room with mirrors above the urinal and be able to look at my reflection while taking a piss. But I didn't know where to begin, except for the paperwork. Somewhere, Lila found something with that laser-razor brain of hers, and I had to do the same...without being butchered in the process.

And as I looked around at all those golden-parachute, CE-asshole, collagen-injecting, monkey-pineal-gland eating, picture-in-the-backroom moneyfuckers, I realized that if I ever needed a favor, I knew where to go. Someone underestimated the friends Lila had. And he'd pay for it in dollars and cents and blood.

Del's had a Sunday football crowd of Miller yahoos and Bud loudmouths, all innocent, but noisy on a noiseless day. Harry sucked on a beer, not even one ahead, as Wooly Bob played darts in a corner, taking overly careful aim because he had to. Miguel Becky'd while Becky Miguel'd, but it didn't amount to much. They knew Lila, but she was *my* friend, and their respect mostly focused on me.

Harry waited for me to ask, but I needed more scotch. A lot more scotch.

"It was a blip," I finally began. "A hiccup."

Harry nodded, trying for drunken sagacity.

"They always are. I remember when Wilcox, back in Ninety-one, caught a whiff of cartel money. He wanted to set his dominoes up in a line and didn't tell anyone until they found his head in a dumpster behind the Yack In The Box on Main and Seventh—you know, the one with the really crispy onion rings? And then they found his hands in the mailbox outside the new post office on Lexington and Russell, stamped Special Delivery. His feet popped up at that Bubble Busters carwash over near the Olsen off-ramp seven-one-one on one of the rotating brushes, kicking the shit out of someone's Hyundai, while his torso made a guest appearance at the Midtown Gigante Market between the fresh chorizos and the week-old menudo. No one saw anything. No one ever does."

I took another gulp of scotch. There was a color scotch gets, when it's good scotch, that reminded me of a moment of my life when everything added up on the plus side. It was in college, and my girlfriend and I, sharing the top floor of a duplex with two other students, were sitting in the kitchen, which was redwood paneled then stained green—don't ask—and I was cooking breakfast. Omelets, I think. I looked over and saw her hair touched for a moment by the sun, and I rushed headlong in my mind to the end of my life, and it was a good life, and I wasn't afraid to die. That's what good scotch tasted like: a good life, not afraid to die.

"You know we'll help."

I knew they would. They were my bang-squad boys.

"I'm not even sure what to do yet," I said. And I wasn't.

Harry gave a Harry smile and blessed the proceedings, "Find 'em, assess 'em, fuck 'em up real bad. The usual."

"We're out of our league, though, Harry. We're accountants. No matter what we play on weekends."

"Speak for yourself, Marksalot. That's just my hobby. What I really want to do is direct." Harry put his glass down and looked at me hard with the Harry look before giving me the rundown. "We're the I-R-fuckin'-S. We can do this because no one else will. Just watch, the feebs'll flake and everyone else will look the other way like baboons at a baseball game. You, me, Wooly, and maybe that pencil-pud Miguel will do this together, along with a hundred of the "little people" we've audited over the years who owe us, or *will* owe us come next April fifteenth. You need someone, I got the tax returns to get 'em to help, yes indeedie."

All the plumbers and stockbrokers, dentists and environmental lobbyists. Who wouldn't want to do a "favor" for their dearly beloved Internal Revenue Service? I had access to disciplines that all the police departments put together couldn't touch. I took another sip, the scotch rolling along my tongue like high-proof molasses. An army of tax evaders, conmen, frauds, and accountant-ly challenged idiots who put their faith in their CPAs. Minions of well-meaning cheaters all at my disposal, each compliantly putting their particular expertise at my fingertips, in service of finding the killer. Lila would've liked it that way.

"First thing to do is find what Lila found. You know anything about locks?" I asked Harry, knowing full well what the answer would be:

"Nope. But I know a guy who does."

The guys Harry knows run the gamut from Caltech field-space physicists to one-legged Dublin chimney sweeps—"Makes it easier to get up and down the flue." There was even a semi-articulate gorilla in there—"I knew Chummy's owner for years—an anthropological linguist who met a nasty end trying to talk to some irritated bonobos."

The weekend came with no bang-squad jobs, so I ratted around my place in paint-splattered sweats and a ripped camo T-shirt from a Marine reunion: "We Came. We Saw. We Killed Everyone." My sentiments exactly.

About noon, after I scrounged up a two-day-old Subway twelve-inch tuna from the fridge and tipped back a couple of Boddingtons (that's a British beer to the unbeerish), then decided that facing the day required too much effort, so I wandered back into my bedroom, closed the drapes, punched up a pillow and lay down for a nap.

No sooner had my head hit soft pillow, then some jackass began slamming my door with what sounded like either a sledgehammer, or the jack handle from a 1952 Desoto.

"Go the hell away!" I yelled, with a tuna and beer burp at the end.

The banging continued, accompanied by counter percussion from something smaller and brick-like. Possibly even a brick. I left the cozy comfort of my blankets, reached under the bed for my trusty Hank Aaron baseball bat, signed by Barry Bonds, and headed for a meeting with destiny. Or at least someone's head.

Out in the hallway, it was cacophonic cubed, and I began to question the future integrity of my front door. I hefted my bat, stood back from the door, waited for the "one" beat, and whipped it open just as they hit.

Three bodies tumbled through my entrance like the Keystone Cops on speed. The back of the head I was aiming to "park" with my bat looked distinctly like Harry's, so I checked my swing and rolled him over with a jerk. Yup, Harry.

"What the hell you trying to do to my door, Harry?"

Rising to his feet like some aging mammoth, he pulled up his two companions as he stood. One, an extremely cute brunette with a silly, apologetic smile, dressed in a silver-spangled short skirt that barely came down far enough down to keep her warm, a black leotard with a revealing scoop in front, and a black matador's jacket. The other, dressed in white tie and tails, complete with top hat. Christ, the circus had come to town.

Harry eyeballed me in his Harry way, then broke into what he affectionately referred to as a grin, but could also be found in the dictionary listed under words like scowl, glower, and fanged grimace.

"Ta-da! The cavalry has arrived!"

Harry motioned to his two companions, who struck a stage-worthy pose, she in a presentory position, and he in an aloof but knowing way.

"Marky Mark, may I present, straight from a six-night engagement at the Starlight Lounge and Truck Stop in Boise, Idaho, the Great Zibaldo and his lovely assistant, Devon."

The Great Zibaldo promptly waved his hands in a magically delicious kind of way and, quicker than you can say Doug Henning, began to pull half-dollars from the air, behind his head, from between his assistant's scrumptious cleavage, much to her blushing chagrin, and almost from my nose, but my hand reflexively shot out and grabbed his wrist in a break-hold and brought him to his knees.

"Any money up my nose is deductible and mine, so leave it there, or I'll do the appearing cast trick on your wrist." A reply that made the assistant crack up.

And that's how I met Devon Pontac. She was born-and-bred Boise, with the Great Zibaldo being her ticket out of the desolation that was Idaho. The name came from a mother with a yearning for fine butter and no other vision in life than to have her daughter grow up and be...*special*. But in a good way. Devon was...in a good way. But that came later; at the moment, I held the wrist of a magician in one hand and wasn't completely sure of what to do.

"Harry?"

"Let go of Waldo's wrist, Mark," ordered Harry. "He needs it to help you."

I let go of the wrist, and the Great Zibaldo rubbed it to get the feeling back. "Robust grip, there. Ever thought of going into showbiz? I could use a strong-but-silent type. The pay's not good, but you get to see the world."

I looked at the magician in disbelief: there's chutzpah and then there's a dissociative break from reality that should be looked at by a competent psychotherapist. I began to suspect old Waldo Zibaldo here had the latter.

"Before you dismiss Waldo here summarily, I believe you asked for the aid of a person who could pick locks, yes? The Great Zibaldo has no peer this side of Cincinnati. And what's more, he owes me a favor."

The list of favor-owing people in Harry's life could defy the calculations of the latest supercomputers all working in tandem.

"Mr. Salt does not exaggerate. I studied under Albert Boscini of St. Louis, who studied under the great Guatemalan escapologist Manfred Hombre, who knew a magician who had actually *seen* Houdini!"

Waldo hit a pose, punctuating the sheer amazement of that statement.

"Are you sure about this guy, Harry?"

Harry raised an eyebrow in a smug way and bowed to the Great Zibaldo, presenting him my front door.

"Mr. Zibaldo, if you please."

Waldo flexed his fingers and pulled up his sleeves—"Nothing up my sleeves but wrists"—and proceeded to lock and unlock my front door without key or even locksmithing tools. I have to say, it was impressive.

"Waldo used to be a second-story man before I fudged him on a tax return and extracted a promise to go straight and narrow," Harry said.

The Great Zibaldo looked both chagrined and huffy, trying to excuse is misdeeds, responding, "I was young and fell in with the wrong crowd. Still, I was able to perfect my craft while staying behind bars at the expense of the taxpayers of this good state."

Devon looked hard at Waldo, not happy, as she reminded the magician, "You never told me you were an ex-con, Waldo. You know how I feel about criminals."

"My apologies, Miss Pontac, but it didn't seem pertinent to our business relationship."

Devon turned to me in half confession. "My father went away when I was six; turns out he liked to rob banks but wasn't very good at it. I still get postcards at Christmas and my birthdays."

"Of course," I said kindly, still not sure why I seemed to be tolerating the invasion of my territory. "So if Zibaldo is so great, how come you were banging on my door?"

"I respect the individual's personal privacy too much to enter without asking. You know, the Constitution and all that," Harry explained. "So, can we come in?"

After a round of my patented, warm artichoke dip with Ritz crackers—"This is really yummy," Devon gushed between bites—mixed nuts and a few beers, Harry got down to business.

"Waldo here is willing to give Lila's file cabinets and home safe a shot, if we tag along to help out," he began.

"There is no lock that has been invented that the Great Zibaldo cannot—"

"Yeah, yeah, Waldo, you got the gig already," Harry said and turned back to me. "I figure Lila had the formal stuff at IRS central, but probably, if it were touchy, squirreled away the real dirt somewhere else. She was a careful one."

I flinched at that.

"Not careful enough, I guess."

Devon did an odd thing then. She put her hand on my shoulder, softly, but with enough intent that I felt it. "Your friend told us about what happened. I'm sorry."

For some reason I let her keep her hand there without shrugging. I'm not really a touchy-feely kinda guy, but...

"We'd have to go to the office at night. I think Phil's on shift tomorrow, which would be best. I don't want to have to try to explain to Mr. Aroon what a magician was doing rifling through our unmentionables. As far as Lila's stash boxes, I know she kept a safe at her apartment and a safety deposit box at her bank. She used to cache her high-frequency gifts there. You know, baubles over four carats and such."

Harry looked thoughtful for enough time that Devon and I finished off the dip, both scrapping the bowl for the last scraps, then said: "I think I know an on-duty-cop friend who might get us access to Lila's, but the safety deposit box has me stumped."

Devon chirped in, mouth stuffed, but cute, "That's an easy one. Just get another safety deposit box at the same place and go from there." We all turned to her, and she reddened, embarrassed. "I saw it in a movie."

Harry and I shrugged at each other.

"Works for me," I said.

An agreeing nod from all set it in motion.

The first place to go was the office; Lila's formal files would give us the who-done-its for everything else. So that Sunday, pass cards in hand and a couple of non-regulation guests in tow, Waldo in his full magician's black tails attire, Devon in a tight-fitting pair of black sweats, high-top black Keds, and a black turtleneck that sure caught my eye, Harry and I went to work.

Now, normally, we probably wouldn't get past the front door without being stopped and given the fourth degree, but Phil had the night, and Phil was well...Phil.

Picture a short, white Rastafarian with a penchant for Dub and spliffs the size of a rolled-up Sunday New York Times, enough Pop-

Tart crumbs in his beard to feed Biafra, a gold front tooth from a brief sojourn running with a Hispanic gang called the Asesinos, and a Southern accent so strong you'd think you were listening to outtakes from "Gone With The Wind," and you'd have a work-in-progress idea of Phil. No one quite knew how he got a job as a night-duty guard at the IRS office, or how he managed to keep it, but some things were best left unknown, perhaps. Obviously, someone like Phil was a consequent discovery of someone like Harry, and by the transitive property of somewhat equality, a discovery of mine.

"Hey, Phil," I called out, interrupting the guard's vacant stare. "How's it hangin'?"

Phil gave two slow-motion blinks as his dilated irises focused on us. He blinked again and processed the information. "Mark! How y'all doin', mon?"

I went through some strange handshaking gyrations of Phil's invention. Harry followed suit.

"Want you to meet a couple of friends of mine..." Harry began.

"Da-a-a-ang! That's the biggest penguin I've ever seen! Totally doob, mon. Where'd you get him?"

We all looked at each other perplexed until Phil bound to his feet and circled the Great Zibaldo. Earth to Phil! Come in, Phil.

"Can I pet him? Can I? Can I?"

The look on Waldo's face said it all, so who was I to burst Phil's bubble?

"Sure, Phil. Knock yourself out."

Waldo took it like a good sport, I had to say that. Maybe it was all the kids' birthday parties he'd done, but he stood passively as Phil checked him out. Devon kept a quiet giggle going the whole time, and even Harry's mood improved from sardonic to Cheshire Cat grin. A good time was had by all.

Finally, as all good things must come to an end, Phil grew bored of penguin handling and goofy-smiled back into his chair.

"You guys workin' late?"

"Just stopped by for a few files."

"Okeydokey-pokey, bra."

And thus your personal secrets were kept safe by the U.S. government employees, *E pluribus unum*.

Lila's cubicle had a cordon tape across the front, which we gingerly moved out of the way. Nothing had been touched, and knowing bureaucracy, nothing would be for years to come. Knickknacks and curios dotted the desk, and a brief wave of Lila swept over me, potent and pure. I missed her a lot.

Then Devon was there again, close to me, a hand on my arm, a tender look for me in her eyes. Neither of us said anything, but it did help, and she must have known that. Deep down, I appreciated it.

The Great Zibaldo threw his head back in preparation for his "show," flexed his fingers, did some really nauseating finger-cracking (kind of a cross between a close-mic'd bowl of Rice Crispies and a pneumatic drill hammering cement) and approached the huge file cabinet that took up half the workspace. He made some mystical passes, had us all say "abracadabra" three times, and popped the lock in nothing flat. I watched closely, too, and still didn't see the trick. He was good.

"Ta-da!"

Waldo waited, waited some more, then Devon motioned to us, and we realized the magician was waiting for applause. Which we then heartily gave him. He bowed and said it was all "nothing." Such humility.

I slid open the first cabinet drawer, Harry back-seating over my shoulder. "A" through "G"—I knew there'd be something here, but didn't know what form it would take, or where. Only choice: look through everything. I began passing files to Harry.

"It'd be something recent. And if I knew anything about Lila, cross-referenced to something else. Look for the lavender post-its—she liked her links eye-catching, and to her, lavender was both feminine and a statement color."

Devon nodded. "Your friend knows her stuff. Lavender is a psycho-luminescent."

I looked over at this magician's assistant with the five-dollar words, questioning. "Psycho-luminescent?"

"Studies have shown that the brain is hard-wired to certain frequencies of light, probably from evolutionary tendencies. Psycho-luminescents are certain windows of light that cause neurological responses in humans who have predispositions towards mental ambiguity."

We all looked dumfounded.

Devon gave a shy smile. "Basically, certain colors make us feel certain things."

Harry laughed. "So, there's some substance to the fact I'm a Winter?"

"Oh, absolutely," Devon assured him. "There's direct causality."

We returned to looking for clues as if nothing had happened.

We found it in the "T's" a reference to a Fred Tumurbaatar and nothing else.

Damn, why'd it have to be the Mongolians?

7.

Mongolians. We had a memo about them titled: "Organized Crime In Mongolian Immigrant Populations Entering United States Territories Both Illegally And Legally." Basically, we were talking Mongolian Mob. And if the Russian Mob was tough, the Mongolian wise guys made the Ruskies look like Nancy Boy kindergarteners playing tea party in their Sunday best. The Mongolians were meaner, tougher, and with a vastly more difficult language. Populated by guys with names like Gansukh (steel-axe), Batsaikhan (strong-nice), or our boy Tumurbaatar (iron-hero), they were tongue-crackers to pronounce and knuckle-crackers to take on.

But the really scary part about the Mong Mob were not the soldiers but the bosses. Women ran the whole organization since time immemorial in a sort of matriarchal eat-your-young kinda way. That's what made them so dangerous. Don't let the names fool you— Altantsetseg (golden-flower), Narantuya (sun-beam), Oranchimeg (artistic-decoration), Sarangerel (moon-light). They were all stone-cold black widows who took pride in being tougher, stronger, and more sadistic than any man.

Of course, the Mongolians were at the root of it. Who else would hire someone like Juju Klondike? It suddenly made perfect sense. Somehow, Lila had stumbled on something in a tax audit that fingered the Mongs. Damn...

Next stop: Lila's apartment.

Harry's love affair with police departments all over the country began with his great-grandfather being a beat cop in Chicago during the Twenties and his father being a NYPD undercover narcotics agent during the Serpico years. Harry bled blue as surely as Tommy Lasorda. But at no time in his life did he ever want to put on the badge.

"Too many rules to follow," he explained once.

"And the IRS is so Wild Wild West and lacking in forms and regulations?" I'd pointed out.

"Trust me on this one, DeMarkation: there's no bureaucracy like PD bureaucracy. They *live* for triplicate, and their idea of an up-to-date computer is a Commodore Sixty-four circa nineteen eighty-two."

Nevertheless, the extended family that was police departments took in Harry as a double legacy and opened their arms to him as one of their own, if a bit of a black sheep. A week didn't go by without someone sending a letter or postcard to him telling a story about Big Bob Salt (great-grandfather), or Slick Sandy Salt (father). Harry had enough info to write an encyclopedia of anecdotes.

So when Harry needed a "favor," there was always someone willing to give it to him "on the house, and say 'hi' to your dad for me." Ridiculous.

For Lila's apartment, Sergeant Wallace did the trick. He gave Harry carte blanche to nose around as long as he didn't mess anything up—which was an almost infinite amount of latitude when you thought about it, which we didn't—and made sure to lock the door after he left. No sweat. We trooped right over after we'd file-cabinetted Lila's cubicle.

Yellow police tape crisscrossed Lila's door, X marking the spot. I'd been to her place more than a few times, usually for cocktails with whomever'd been moth-to-a-flame'd to her that particular week. Lots of small talk about Dubai, the current trend in the Dow Jones, and if a certain professional sports team should be bought and/or unloaded, choose one. Always good booze and better appetizers, and I was usually odd man out, so any available cuties always came my way. I suddenly didn't want to go inside.

Waldo was already working on the locks—Lila had four—when Harry caught my eye with a questioning glance. I shrugged manfully, but my stomach felt like a ball of barbed wire.

That's when the shooting started.

I know the sound of automatic weaponry from my Marine days. It's not pretty. Every muscle in my body contracted as I torpedo'd to the ground. On the way, I grabbed Devon and got her beneath me in the dive. A note about the male Sympathetic Nervous System: even in a moment of unbelievable danger, I perceived how soft and curvy Devon was. Go figure. I guess that's evolution for you.

Harry beat me to the ground and had somehow shimmied himself behind a potted palm for good measure. That was twenty-five-years-plus of self-preservation for you. I couldn't see anything but the tips of his work boots. And the Great Zibaldo? Swear to God he vanished in a puff of smoke. We're talkin' David Copperfield good, and that's *including* when he was dating Claudia Schiffer. Quite the magic trick in itself. Maybe I'd jumped the gun on ol' Waldo.

Speaking of guns, a steady stream of fire raked the front door, wood chippering it to splinters. I did a quick ear-count and came up with two guns blasting simultaneously. Any hero in me knew that the better part of valor on this one was to stay as flat as a pancake. Having Devon sandwiched under me didn't hurt either. She squirmed real nice.

It seemed like minutes, but couldn't have been more than twenty seconds, when the shooting stopped, and we heard a vehicle peel out and head down the street. Harry stayed hidden, but I leapt up to see what I could see, which was mostly tan van with Canadian license plate. Canadian? Obviously only two-thirds as good as an American van. Couldn't catch the number, but I doubted it mattered. Since when were Mongolians using Canadian vans? How the hell would I know what kind of vans Mongolians would use anyhow?

A flash of light, a puff of smoke, and Waldo was back among us.

"Neat trick, Waldo. You're gonna have to teach that to me someday," Harry said as he got to his feet. "Could come in handy sometime."

The Great Zibaldo bowed. "I'm sorry, but a magician never reveals his tricks."

Harry sneered, and Waldo moved away.

I helped Devon to her feet. "Sorry about that. I didn't have time to think."

Devon rewarded me with a shy but lovely smile. "If you hadn't have done that, I'd still be standing there. Besides, it was fun."

"Lady, you've got a weird sense of fun," I replied.

She grinned back at me. "You don't know the half of it."

Hmm, food for thought. But right at that moment, I could hear sirens. I wanted to hightail it out of there, but Harry wouldn't hear of it.

"We didn't do anything wrong," he explained, while checking his pockets for something.

"We were sorta breaking into a police investigation, I believe."

"Nonsense. We're concerned citizens who heard shots and, much like the bear that went over the mountain, came to see what we could see."

Three black-and-whites roared up and slammed on their brakes, spotlights stabbing at us. Then came the megaphones: "This is the police. Put your hands up and step towards us." Wow, just like on television.

Harry, who had been rooting around in his pocket, was first to put up his mitts, but in one of them was an old, tarnished badge. A spotlight caught it "just so" and it glimmered like a star in the firmament.

"What's that in your hand?" went the megaphone. "Is that an NYPD badge?"

"I'm Harry Salt."

"Harry?" The spotlights flicked off and the police officers hurried up, holstering their guns. "You son-of-a-gun. What're you doing here?"

The lead cop was a monster of a man, a good six feet six with his old-style afro'd hair adding another five inches. He gave Harry a hug and lifted him off his feet—no easy achievement—and swung him around like a dad giving a kid a *Superman*.

"How the hell are ya?"

After Harry returned to terra firma, he introduced the colossal cop to the rest of us. "Kids, this is detective Levon Amadeus DeCarlo, and if you're wondering, his mom was a piano teacher and his dad was a steel worker. I've known Lee since he was under six feet, which is saying a lot."

Lee nodded to us. "A pleasure, I'm sure. Any friend of Harry's..." Lee smiled. "Has got to be trouble."

I stepped forward and shook Lee's massive hand, "Ah, you *do* know Harry well, then."

Introductions went all around, including the other five police who'd come with the detective, each and every one a certifiable good egg. Of course, after the pleasantries, the bullets came next.

"Nope, don't know a thing. One second, the night was quiet, the next, the roar of gunfire. Chinese QBZ-95 assault rifles with caseless ammunition, but...that's just an uneducated guess on my part."

Lee eyeballed Harry closely, but only got a "What, me?" look out of it. The cops went to work on the forensics, and we faded into the shadows, Harry nodded toward the back.

"I figure we got about twenty minutes before they hit the inside of Lila's place. Let us do a little reconnoitering of our own first."

We tiptoed to the back entrance, and with a finger-cracking dexterity, Waldo opened the rear door.

A note of time-out. We should have been freaking. We should have been screaming at the top of our lungs and running as fast as our little frightened feet could carry us *away* from that place. Hell, we'd just been shot at. By automatic weapons. With lots and lots and lots and lots and lots of bullets. At the very least, we should have been cowering in the back of a police car, blabbing our brains out and begging for protective custody. I know that's what I would have done, if I weren't an IRS bang-squad veteran. And if Harry weren't an IRS bang-squad veteran. We'd been shot at many a time, and although we never liked it, it didn't faze us anymore. But the Great Zibaldo and Devon—they weren't acting right.

"You two don't have to come with us, you know. Guns kinda queer any deal Harry might have had with you."

Waldo raised himself up to his full, regal, illusionist height— which wasn't very much—looking as if I'd just called his momma something his momma shouldn't ever be called.

"I'll have you know, before I was a master magician, before I was a so-so burglar, before I was wearing long pants, I, Waldo Zibaldo, lived in Compton. Need I say more?"

I gave Waldo the once-over twice: Compton could be pretty rough gang territory. He didn't look like a banger, especially being all pasty white, but there was a certain to-hell-with-everything steel in his eyes. Maybe he did know a Crypt or two back in the day. But Devon...

"And don't worry about me," she said, putting on a face she'd obviously learned from an old movie. "I have six older brothers. Not a lot scares me."

"Did your six older brothers come armed with rapid-fire urban assault rifles?" I asked, remembering that she *was* from Idaho.

Devon gave a crooked grin. "Worse. I can handle myself. Besides, it's exciting."

Exciting. Now there was a word you didn't hear applied to attempted murder every day. I'd like to meet those older brothers...On second thought, maybe not. Either way, we went 'round back and got inside.

I'm glad we needed to move fast; otherwise, the echo of Lila inside would have overpowered me. As it was, the place strongly perfumed of her spirit. From the delicate antique furniture to the sparse-but-high-tech kitchen, it was Lila through and through. No photos, but she was everywhere.

I knew her safe was hidden in the floor under her couch, so we struggled to move the huge leather thing without tipping off the cops outside. All that in near-darkness, only illuminated by a carefully aimed flashlight and some of Zibaldo's "fairy dust"—which made a cloud of firefly-like lights that circled his head. It looked pretty darn fairy dusty to me.

Safes proved to be a little harder for Waldo than front doors. Almost too hard. He cracked his fingers, cracked his toes, he even cracked his neck, but couldn't crack the safe.

"Sorry, I'm a little rusty on picking combo locks from the outside. I'm usually stuffed inside of these things."

I glanced over at Harry, who understood: maybe we should jam Waldo inside a safe next time. And drop the safe in nice river somewhere. That led to the sea. Right near the Marianas Trench.

Fortunately, I knew Lila's mind. It was as beautiful as she was, and twice as fast. The question was what numbers would she use for her super-secret safe combination? Birthday (not that she'd ever admit to having one), social security, lotto picks would never do for her. Perhaps an arcane stock tip leaked by a disrobed CEO, or the last digits of a Malaysian Prince's Swiss bank account. Naw, too mundane. It had to be something totally Lila.

And then I had it. The only number that would mean a thing to Lila. "Try thirteen, forty-three, forty."

It worked. Six pairs of eyes stared at me, and I shrugged. "Pluto's MPL number."

More stares.

"See, when Pluto got demoted to an asteroid, the Minor Planet Center gave it a number. Lila was so offended, she called a very influential Parisian 'friend' of hers, screaming into the phone that number and nothing else, and the next day, the International Astronomical Union started the dwarf planet list, with Pluto being number one. That wasn't good enough for Lila, and she broke off relations with her friend. I'll always remember that number because it pissed her off so much."

No one said a thing for a moment. No one knew *what* to say. I had to agree with them; that was Lila in a nutshell. Pluto being a planet meant more to her than all the money in the world. Go figure.

The inside of her safe, big enough to stuff a body into, would have made Mr. Tiffany jealous. There lay the acquisitions of the life of a very beautiful and inconstant woman: diamond baubles that shone like stars, gold and silver, platinum and pearls, rings, necklaces, watches, and even a tiara. I'd never seen Lila wear a one. I think she kept them as counters, like poker chips in a friendly game, but that was it. She knew she was ahead, and that was enough for her.

Harry gave a low whistle, and I had to waggle a finger at Waldo, who I just *knew* wanted to practice the "Disappearing Jewelry" trick. Devon? She laughed.

"Now there was a woman who knew the importance of saying 'no.' "

And that was it. No big eyes, no awed "oo's," nothing but a laugh. I think Devon and Lila would have gotten along.

"Lookie, lookie." Harry pulled up a vanilla file stuffed with papers. Then another one. Then a third. We didn't know what we had, but we knew it was what we needed. I nodded, and we headed back out.

I was behind, and before I left, I turned and took one final look, one final breath. That single thought that would be the very last moment of Lila, except my memories.

"Mark?" Devon called quietly to me.

I turned my back on Lila and went out into the night.

8.

I had Tightass in my cubicle the next day. He waited there as I walked in and didn't say a word, snugged down in the chair behind my desk looking like a priest in a confessional. Only his eyes moved, following me as I entered.

I ignored him, went over to my trusty Mr. Coffee and began the morning ritual of caffeinezation. I didn't really like coffee, but I tried, constantly. It was a social thing, and a ritual thing, but I didn't really go for the taste by itself and have never been buzzed for a second from it. Still, I had two strong cups every day, with lots of Splenda and evaporated milk, and pretended I was one of those lucky people who gets a jolt out of the sludge.

"I'll take a cup," said Juarez. "No sugar, no cream."

I fixed him his right after mine, and we both sat sipping.

"We found the van."

"What van?"

"The van carrying the fun-loving people who shot at you last night," Juarez said as he finished his coffee, then waved the cup for more.

I obliged. "Figured they were just some high-strung, trigger-happy, on-vacation Canucks down to catch the summer breezes,"

"Thought you didn't know of any van..."

"I don't work for you Juarez. I work for your boss, the United States government. You got anything to tell me, spit it out; otherwise, I ain't got shit to say."

Tightass worked his coffee like a mountain climber does Half Dome: piton by piton, rock by rock. Finally, he offered, "Neighbor across the way heard the shooting, saw the van. Local boys found it outside Genghis Khan's, that Mongolian all-you-can-eat barbecue down on Federal."

"No way."

"Way. Smelled of overheated rifles and cheap caseless. Not a damn print anywhere, though. Someone was Mr. Clean about it."

I eyeballed Juarez closely to see if he were sandbagging me. Didn't look like it, but you never knew with a feeb. Still, I had to be sure. "You do a data dance and find who owns the restaurant?"

Juarez nodded and handed me a sheet of fax paper.

"Some guy named Paul Antioch, forty-five, no priors, no credit problems, couple of speeding tickets. His family's from Arizona, and he's been here for ten years or so. Nothing to hang your hat on."

I'd already flipped my monitor around and was banging on the keyboard. "He married?"

Juarez picked up the fax from the desk and scanned it. "Yeah, he's married."

I kept typing.

"It say who to?"

Juarez looked closer, but came up blank, shaking his head.

"That's okay. I got it right here. Paul Antioch is married to one Erdenetungalag Antioch."

"Excuse me?"

"Erdenetungalag Antioch. Your boy Paul has a taste for more than Mongolian *barbecue*."

Juarez hopped over to my side of the desk, and I do-si-do'd back to my own chair. He looked at the monitor and smiled.

"You're not supposed to be able to do this sort of thing."

I smiled back. "*Really*? I can do anything I can get away with. And if you don't think so, I'll audit you until you do. So, gonna take a closer look at that restaurant boy?"

"Why? 'Cause he has a wife with a funny name? Probably her idea to do the restaurant in the first place, and he's gotta foot the bill. Bet she was a mail-order bride, and this is her revenge: fire ass forever."

FBI agents were not necessarily known for their imaginations. That was okay, though—I already had plans. "Don't sweat it. So, other than the van, what did you want to ask me? I know it wasn't my coffee that brought you here this early."

I continued to type.

"Just figured you might want to give a little insight about the shooting. Not often you get twelve hundred rounds of caseless aimed at two such loveable characters as you and Harry Salt."

"You forgot about the magician and his charming assistant. Perhaps someone wanted to find out how they sawed a lady in half really, really badly. Or maybe he didn't restore someone's card to their satisfaction. Maybe he missed a piece or something. I bet you've seen stranger things over at the Federal Building, huh?"

"Truth is stranger than friction. But I know that was Lila's place, Mark. I don't give a diddly you were there. I just want to know if you found anything I need to know about. We went over that place, but you were her friend."

Juarez looked at me hard.

"You know about the safe, I bet."

He nodded.

"But you don't know what the files mean."

He shook his head.

"And you were hoping I would happen by and take a look at them."

He smiled.

"Which, I graciously did. How polite of me."

"So? Can you enlighten me?"

I flipped the monitor around again and played show-and-tell, having called up all three of Lila-files tax returns and cross-collated them as far as deductibles. One was a welder from Pontus, Illinois. Another, an airline pilot who keyed out of Miami, and the third was a daycare proprietor in Gallup, New Mexico. Ba-bingo, just like Lila said. A most unlikely trio for interest, but there they were, and Lila was never wrong.

"Yup, those are the files. We fine-tooth-combed them but came up nada. No ties that we could see, and...well..." Juarez looked embarrassed. "We'd need to get a consultant anyways to decipher the tax data, and since you're with the I-R-S, and we'd come to you anyway..."

I left Tightass hanging like his sentence. I know FBI guys walked around with permanent hard-ons against the world because somewhere in time someone thought that's what FBI agents should do and put it right in the manual, first page, but just about then I didn't give two farts and a weak bladder for that kinda attitude. He could have just called and bought me a drink like he normally did. Something wasn't right.

"What the hell's going on? You're acting like a grunt, and you never act like a grunt to me. A tight-sphinctered, enlarge-prostated tightass, but never a grunt. Before I play connect the dots with these files, you gotta come clean with me, or sip coffee till your testicles shrivel."

There was a thing that Daniel "Tightass" Juarez did which made him a formidable adversary. It had nothing to do with smarts. Or toughness. Or training. What he did was that in the middle of a situation, win, lose, or draw, he could actually listen, and having listened, he could act upon it. And that's what he did.

"Look, we know through the vine about Klondike but haven't a clue who hired him. Zippo lighter on why, but since Ms. Everston was I-R-S, it couldn't be an accident. Klondike doesn't make mistakes, and his fees are not quite...trivial. Or easy to get."

"There's more?"

Juarez finally tipped it.

"It's not just money he asks for. This is all hush-hush and without complete verification, but he likes...children, boys. He likes to..."

And Tightass, in all his FBI-ness, couldn't go on. But I could guess, and it pissed me off even more.

"He likes to cut 'em like he was cut. You guys follow a trail of castrated kids, and that's how you tell if this sick shit's done the hit. You ought to be ashamed of yourselves."

Juarez looked me in the eye, nodding, "We are. But it's how we knew who'd done your friend so quickly. The kids are usually left bound and bleeding somewhere nearby. This one was lucky. He didn't make it."

And that epitaph seemed right. A fate worse than death, they called it. I couldn't tell who deserved worse: the killer, or the person who hired him. Both at least deserved death, and then some. I was a step ahead of the feebs, but to stay that way, I needed to be quicker. And to stay alive? I needed a lot of things for that.

When Juarez left, I called Harry, but got his voice mail. He was probably nose deep in ferreting out an audit. He never answered when he was in the middle of what he called "bustin' chops."

Then I remembered Devon; she was off to the bank to get a safety-deposit box. Now why did that bother me? I stuffed my tremor aside and took stock: eunuch killer with a sadistic bent, Mongolian Mob run by strong women with a sadistic bent. I was beginning to see a pattern. And since I didn't have a sadistic bent (well, not really), I understood what was worrying me. Devon was a civilian.

And she was awfully cute.

The Gloucester brothers then reared their money-laundering heads. I'd put out a feeler toward some Phoenix friends—Harry ain't the only one with friends—and I got three e-mails back from them. Each told me a little more in the Gloucester saga and reinforced my feeling that Rodney was not only the weak link, but the key to snapping the whole chain.

Unfortunately, I didn't really give a damn at that moment. Still, Lila wouldn't want me to be a complete slough-off, even over her own death. I could just hear her: "What, you can't do two things at once? No wonder I never had sex with you." And then we'd both crack up.

My phone buzzed. It was El Diablo herself—Claudia Faberge Constantine—inviting me to come up to see the boss, said the spider to the fly. Jesus, what's the matter now?

I elevatored up and for once, the 'vator was empty. Another bad sign. The rats always knew when the ship was going to hit an iceberg, or something like that. I steeled myself for bad, bad news. I'd normally be worried, but by then, I didn't really give a tinker's damn.

When the doors opened, Mr. Aroon Kumaar Vijah Smith's She-Wolf-of-the-SS secretary was smiling. At me. I didn't even know she was capable of that. It looked weird and unnatural, sorta like a pig in a micro-bikini, or birthday cakes in the shape of a squid. Both unappetizing and thoroughly scary.

"Um, good morning?" I ventured.

"Isn't it just," gushed the Big Bad Wolf. Weirder and weirder. Next thing you knew she'd be asking me how I was doing. "And how are you this fine day?"

I had cancer. Terminal cancer. Everyone knew it but me, and this was how they were breaking the news. I was the walking dead, and they were taking pity before jettisoning me into the cold blackness of space. That was the only thing I could imagine, other than the Earth's magnet poles reversing to account for Constantine being nice. And smiling! Eu-u-u-u, gave me the whoopin' willies.

"Care for some coffee, Mr. Douglas?"

Okay, enough was enough. It was a dream. A nightmare. The world had gone mad. All of the above. None of the above. I began to flop sweat under my pits.

"No, thank you, Miss Constantine."

"Oh, well...you're missing some very good java. I have a Kona blend that's to die for."

Java? Kona blend? Pleasantries? It was worse than I thought. *Way* worse. Fortunately, Miss Constantine said that Mr. Smith was ready for me. In less than two minutes! I couldn't wait to go inside, while some part of me, probably my spleen, knew better and wanted to run very fast, very far.

It just got weirder.

Mr. Aroon stood waiting for me, a set piece at the ready. "Lila was a good Internal Revenue employee. She shall be missed."

I hemmed, hawed, and agreed, beginning to add some observations of my own, but he cut me off. He wasn't finished yet.

"But she's gone, and I've a need to replace her. I want you to take her section title and step into her shoes, as it were. You have the seniority and the experience, and I believe you have the respect of the rest of the department."

Suddenly, it all dominoed into place. I was getting a promotion, which was the last thing in the world I was expecting. My face must've looked scrambled and over-easy at the same time because I was *that* confused.

"Why not Harry? He's got seniority on everyone but God, and he's a good man in the clutch."

I didn't know which to fear more, the job offer or Harry's vengeance if I fobbed it off on him.

Mr. Aroon did something with his jaw that seemed disturbingly like a cross between a yawn and a boa constrictor eating a mouse. "Erm...ah.... Mr. Salt is a respected and valuable employee, but there's a certain transience about his approach that relegates him to a nonexecutive role."

"Transience?" I quipped. "He's been here *thirty* years!"

"Yes. But he's never taken it seriously."

Mr. Aroon had a point: Harry and serious never mixed. *Thorough, vengeful,* and *mischievous* might be words to describe Harry's approach to revenue-ing, but *serious* probably wasn't. It embarrassed me that I thought that; it meant I might be the right guy for the job.

Mr. Aroon mistook my hesitancy. "It comes with an increase in pay and a new cubicle."

"I kinda like my old cubicle. Can't I keep it?"

I hated moves: the packing, the unpacking, the lugging of the boxes. I believed the lowly sea sponge had the right idea: swim around until you found a place and never move again until you die.

"No, a new position requires new surroundings, otherwise the rest of the staff will not be able to visualize your increased responsibility and tend to treat you as you *were*, rather than as you *are*."

That sure sounded like some page from a biz-ed book to me: compelling on paper, but oh-so-untrue in the harsh halogen lights of life. Then it hit me. He wanted me to move into *Lila's* cubicle.

"Look, I'm sure there's someone better suited for this—"

He waved his long, crooked fingers. "You are suited because I say so. If you sit in her cubicle, no one will object or balk. You were her...*friend*."

For a moment, a blink, the stutter of a neuron unsure which pathway to take, which direction to fire, I contemplated aiming a fist at Mr. Aroon's bureaucratically smug face, maybe wiping his smile and nose across it. Instead, I asked, "Did you pick me because of my qualifications, or I fit the chair?"

My boss steepled his fingers, a spider doing spider pushups.

"A little of both. Don't minimize the weight of context. Ms. Everston cast quite a shadow; filling her high heels will not be easy."

And that was a joke. Mr. Aroon never joked, which made it both more surreal and threatening. Inhuman is as inhuman does, and I recognized a *fait accompli* when it bit me on the ass. I took the job, the raise, and the cubicle, and I took my pride and stuffed it deep inside, jack-booted it down and covered it up with a graveful of dirt and regrets.

When I left, Miss Constantine handed me all the necessary paperwork, in triplicate, already finished and ready for my signature. I signed twenty-seven separate times, initialed ten, and collected a new pass card, set of keys, and a completely new persona, at least in the eyes of the IRS. I was another Mark Douglas, and I felt it. Then I thought of Devon. Harry and I needed to meet her and the Great Zibaldo at noon.

My first official act in my new executive position was to take a long lunch. Perfect. They wanted me; they got me, warts and all.

I had a theory that men of a certain age and financial bracket got the car they fantasized about when they were fourteen. Mustang, 'Cuda, or Ferrari, once the monetary wherewithal came in, they must have what they'd always longed for. It might be updated, it might be the very one that used to sit next door. But at some point, guys did that.

Harry must have lived next door to a construction site all his life, with a chop shop down the street, and a serious Hispanic radio station blaring. First, stepping "up" to get in the passenger's seat was never a good sign. Then into Corinthian leather bucket seats each with its own cup holder and 360-degree Swivel-Master controls that could go from upright to reclining in two seconds and one spinal spasm flat.

With a souped-up 500-horsepower under the huge diesel-powered hood, flame-painted with devil girls and red bulls, a custom short rig housing God-knows-what in the back, Harry was the extremely proud owner of a deluxe, one-off , AC-460 Mac truck, complete with large-titty silhouetted girls on the splash guards and a special horn that blared the opening notes of *Guantanamera* when yanked. Couple that with a fridge full of cold ones beneath the driver's seat, a proverbial Easy Rider rifle rack on the roof, and a set of fuzzy dice hanging from the rear-view, the Saltmobile always turned heads wherever it went. And despite the decibel-breaking, pain-threshold-passing roar as it went by beyond the speed limit, there wasn't a cop within a hundred-mile radius of Sacramento that dared pull Harry over. Sometimes the police got it right.

At the moment, Devon eyed it suspiciously. Waldo had obviously seen it before, because he shrugged it off and began jabbering to Harry. I sidled up to the magician's assistant and caught a draft of her: lemons and myrrh. She wore a charcoal business suit that looked dry-cleaned instead of recently bought, with sensible leather shoes and her hair pulled back with a clip. I'd give her a loan in a second; just fill out the form and the money was yours.

She caught me looking and smiled. "Not my normal M-O, but not a stretch, either. I legal secretaried for an ambulance chaser back in Idaho for almost a year until...well, stuff."

"His wife find out he was filing torts with you during lunchtime?"

Devon wasn't tall, but in that moment, she towered over me with metamorphosic ease.

"Give me a little common sense. You musta been chewed up and spit out pretty hard."

"De nada."

"No, he caught me with his wife." She smiled Buddha-like and serene. On her, it looked good. "Hey, she was hot. Smokin'. And I was in my experimental years. I'd sneak out and catch up with her whenever her hubby was in court. One day a client settled for less and the lawyer came home to find more, catching us mid-delicto."

You betchum.

And I almost fell for it. Fortunately, she couldn't hold the straight face long enough and started laughing. A really great laugh, by the way; part melodious and part peanut butter.

She giggled, going all Little Miss Innocent on me. "I could see the thought balloon big as life, right over your head. You have a very dirty mind."

"Me? I'm not the one serving up a main course of titillation with a side-order of hot lezi action. What's a boy supposed to think? I'm only human, or at least most of me is."

She kept cracking up. "*Most*...of you?"

"Well, I have a baboon heart, a pig spleen, and you don't want to know what part of the horse I got."

And there I was thinking I was being clever.

"The ass?"

She couldn't breathe from laughing, and I knew I'd lost that round, shot with my own words. I laughed, too.

"Hey, cut me some slack. I'm tryin'."

Harry did the cutting at that moment. "You two having fun? Waldo wants to do this fast. He has an afternoon birthday party to do, and he hasn't set up yet."

"Doves to pack and scarves to stuff up my sleeves, you know." Devon mock-whispered to me. "Guess where he puts the rabbit."

We lost it again, and the Great Zibaldo shot us a dirty look, part false superiority, part butt-of-the-joke frustration.

Harry waited, finger drumming on the Big Wheel, before trying to be all adult. "We finished?"

"Nope. I want to know where the—" I began, then Devon punched me in the shoulder. "Ow!"

She turned to Harry, her hand snaking toward him. "We're ready. Here's the key to the safety-deposit box. I put some envelopes and jewelry cases in, both empty, to look like something."

"Good thinking," Harry said, hefting the key as if judging it for balance.

"She learned misdirection from the Great Zibaldo! Of course it's good thinking."

Waldo held his hand out for the key, and Harry plunked it down. The magician examined it, holding it up to his eye like a jeweler a diamond ring.

"Not even a challenge. How close is our box to the other?"

"Across the room, about twelve feet. But there's a glass wall on one side. You can see in from the manager's office."

Waldo thought for a moment, then nodded, as if coming to a conclusion neither good nor bad, simply necessary.

"Right. Then we need to make sure the manager sees what we want him to see. We'll switch lock boxes, take our time, then switch 'em back."

"Just like that?" Harry asked.

Waldo looked hurt. "I *am* a professional. I'm thinking the Inner Eye Illusion might work."

I smiled, knowing bullshit when I heard it. Harry frowned, also knowing bullshit when he heard it.

Devon whispered to me, "You'll like this one, I bet."

"Does he pull a rabbit out of some orifice or another?"

Devon grinned. "No, that's the Inner *Bunny* Illusion. This is more about misdirection. But I'll need to prepare." She volumed up to Waldo. "I have to run back to my apartment to get ready, Waldo."

"Right. Show time in..." he glanced at his wrist, no watch, did something shazammy and, voila, a watch. "One hour."

***

An hour later, I had become a full-fledged member of the Great Zibaldo's Traveling Magic Show and Illusionarium©. Harry waited in the getaway car, as he termed the Saltmobile, while Zibaldo, dressed in top hat and tails, readied to enter the bank.

"Isn't that a little obvious?" I asked.

"Part of the illusion," he assured me, shooting his cuffs and placing his hat *just so*.

Devon had on a stylish overcoat, which seemed an odd apparel on such a sunny day, but I didn't ask.

Waldo entered the bank first, flourishing his topper and speaking in his "stage" voice, which meant shouting five-syllable adjectives and demanding to be heard, which he couldn't help being.

Devon counted off sixty, then took my arm tightly, and we herded in next.

What greeted our eyes made *theatre in the round* look downright monocular. The Great Zibaldo had started his show without us, pulling coins from the air, people's noses, the guard's bullet holder, and clanking them into his top hat. We're talking *hundreds* of coins. The whole bank looked on, captivated. With a final wave of his hand, a waterfall of silver dollars gushed from the bank manager, Mr. Don "Curly" Isakson's mouth. "Curly" must have been a previous incarnation's nickname, as the present noggin was a hairless wasteland of the epidermal soul.

After the applause, Waldo espoused his need for a secure bank in which to do a "supremely amazing feat" on live television "a week from today." Mr. Isakson imagined all the publicity inherent with that and demanded to know what he could do to help.

"I was thinking," Waldo said, "of doing an escape from a security-deposit vault. The key to my shackles would be locked in one unknown box; I, blindfolded, straight jacketed in the room, with only five minutes to get out or alarms would sound, and I'd be carted off to the pokey."

Curly clapped his hands together in glee and assured the Great Zibaldo of the bank's help. He then asked his assistant, Mira Slopowski, to see that Mr. Zibaldo got a look at the safety-deposit boxes, which was our cue to lead the way before them.

Waldo was in rare form, like a theatrical impresario, pointing up high to this and squatting down low to peer at that. Slopowski went out and back to whatever business Slopowski's did, leaving the three of us alone to the safety-deposit room. With a smiling Curly waving at us through the glass.

It was at that point that I found out about the Inner Eye Illusion. Devon took off her overcoat.

Da-a-a-a-amn.

It was like discovering an unknown da Vinci by rubbing away at a picture of dogs playing poker, or realizing Sasquatch was living next door in the foreclosed, one-story ranch house, drinking your beers and borrowing your lawn mower. Devon had on a black, spaghetti-strapped dinner dress that revealed a body that made the phrase "architecturally sound" sexy. I expected a heavenly choir and cherubs with their hosannas. My socks melted, and my eyes popped out.

She grinned. "Told you you'd like it."

Curly's eyes were also riveted, which is when Waldo made the first switch, and I looked into Lila's safety-deposit box, and my eyes popped out even more.

9.

If you know how to read a tax form, it can be more informative than 411. We at the IRS could Braille a person's life from which lines they skipped and how they dotted their decimal points. It was more damning in court than all the eyewitnesses any five-hundred-dollar-an-hour attorney would muster. No muss, no fuss, just the facts in black and white with our red ink all over it.

Lila's safety-deposit box had three tax returns in it. Nothing more. No jewels. No stacks of hundreds. No insider-traded stocks, bearer bonds, or account numbers from the Caribbean. Three tax returns that smoking gunned her. She knew, or she'd never'd socked them away there. Somewhere in the pages a bit of radioactive accounting Geiger-countered Lila's eye, and she put them away for safety's sake. And for mine. In the end, she understood I'd follow. No matter what. I was too stupid not to, and she smilingly counted on that. It was Lila's "I love you" in the only way that mattered.

"Damn it."

I don't know how, out of the hundreds of millions of tax returns filed by businesses and individuals over the last few years Lila could find these three. That's why Lila was Lila, I guess. But she did, and that meant something fundamental, like Planck's Constant and the number of woodchucks that could chuck wood. I caught the names—nothing. Then I caught their declared occupations: truck driver, veterinarian, and restaurateur. What the hell did that add up to?

Then I saw the Form 1040X. They'd all taken the nontaxable death gratuity based on the Military Family Tax Relief Act of 2003. Odd, but hardly unique; they'd lost someone overseas. I riffled through to the backing documentation: copies of death certificates, etc.

Ulan Bator. Mongolia's capital. The deceased had all been assigned to the U.S. embassy there when they died. One private, one lieutenant, and a full-bird colonel serving as defense attaché, security-assistance officer, and liaison for PACOM, the military's Pacific Command. Shi-i-i-i-i-i-i-i-it. Mongs and military Siamese-twining it.

78

That was the connection Lila laughingly wanted me to follow. But to where?

Then the room flashed Valentine's Day red and filled with smoke like a thermite detonation with a hint of Altoids. The Great Zibaldo abracadabra'd a grand finale, and we shilled frantically. I felt the safety-deposit box snatched from my hands, then another jammed back into place. A frenzied Isakson began banging on the vault glass. I could hear Mira Slopowski enter, then leave just as fast, coughing violently.

"Nothing to fear!" shouted Waldo, everything orchestratedly under control. "Can I have a volunteer from the audience?"

That cued Devon to take my arm and whisk me from the bank, no one giving us a flicker. The clutch of her hand on my arm made me lock-step her stride. It felt good. When we hit the sunlight, I started stringing a succession of sneezes that climbed into the teens before stopping.

Devon still held my arm, as we waited for the light at the street corner to change. "You have a deviated septum, don't you? My Uncle Bernard sneezes like that. His record is eighteen in a row. I counted."

"You counted? Do you do ceiling tiles and cracks in the sidewalk, too?"

"O-o-o-u-u, someone's sensitive about their nasal expulsions, aren't they?" Devon had recoated herself on leaving the bank, but the afterimage of her still lingered in my mind. I'd forgive that impression anything. "I was seven, and Uncle Bernard took pride in his accomplishment. He also could waggle his ears and play Beethoven's Ninth Symphony with a blade of grass."

"Ah, *Uomo Universale*, a man of varied accomplishments. I like that. I've been known to write haiku in the batter of a pancake before cooking, as well as make matchstick guns from clothespins."

Devon cracked up. "Poetry pancakes? I have to have some of those. What do you punctuate with?"

Straight-faced: "Walnuts."

Devon tossed her head back in laughter, catching a strand of hair across the bridge of my nose. She was all teeth and gasping breath. "I...I have *got* to have some of those. With lots of syrup."

"Is there any other way to eat pancakes?"

The light changed, and we trotted across the street to the car. Harry waited with practiced ease, a carton of grape juice and a microwaveable 7-Eleven burrito half finished, a smudge of bean on his cheek. He gnawed a bite for a moment, then popped the locks on the doors of the Saltmobile, and Devon and I hiked in.

"So, Marky Barky, show go okay? No one get hurt, weaseled, or arrested?"

Devon looked at me in confusion. "Weaseled?"

"You don't want to know," I said, but that only kicked her imagination into overdrive. "Does it hurt?"

Harry turned around, that smudge of bean looming igneous rock-like. "You have no idea, if it's done right."

"Now you *gotta* tell me."

Harry smiled his Harry smile and turned back around. "So where's Waldo?"

"Still 'wowing' the people. Last I saw, which wasn't much because of the flashy/smoky stuff, he'd begun pulling doves from handkerchiefs, and the doves weren't too happy about it."

"Doves are mean and anxious birds," Devon said. "And, given half a chance, they're cannibals. They are the Donner Party of the avian world."

"No way. Those nice cooey fluffballs are vicious?" I could not believe it.

"Oh, yeah. Maybe not in the wild, but cooped up three or more to a cage, shoved in S&M-tight holders and kept under someone's smelly armpit for an hour? They go carnivore in an instant. And once they get the flavor of blood..." She clacked her teeth together. "Sometimes it really does taste like chicken."

"I call bullshit," Harry said from up front. "You're gonna have to Discovery Channel that for me, or I'm not buying it. Show me where the little birdie bodies are buried, and I'm good to go, otherwise, you're lyin' out your pretty little ass."

Devon held it for another five seconds, then cracked a smile bigger than Idaho. "I'm never playing poker with you."

"Was it something I said?"

I'd been distracted. It was a long day. The sun was in my eyes. Maybe it was that smile. "Okay, I'm gullible. Says so on my birth certificate. What do I know from birds?"

At that moment, the Great Zibaldo arrived, knocking on the window of the truck. Harry buzzed his pane down and looked down. "We ordered lunch an hour ago. What took you so long?"

Devon and I gave a round of applause.

Waldo didn't blink, he simply took a bow. "Was I not perfection in motion? The great Thurston couldn't have done it better."

"Was he the guy on Gilligan's Island?" Harry asked. "The one with the overbite accent and the withered piece of wife named Lovey? No self-respecting billionaire would ever have a shriveled up pootie like that. He'd a traded her in for three eighteen-year-olds and a Vietnamese b-girl a long time before. TV—absolutely no sense of realism."

Devon looked at me. "He *loved* her."

I could only go with Harry's assessment: "I mean, the guy *was* a billionaire. He could have bought the genetic plasma to a whole series of nubile family trees and bred for tits and ass. Billionaires never love anyone but themselves, and what their money can buy."

"Amen to that, brother. The bigger the wallet, the younger the cunny...if you'll excuse my French. I bet Bill Gates is secretly doin' zygotes. Wouldn't surprise me in the least."

Devon shook her head in feminine disgust. "You're all ate up with the dumbass, aren't you? The level of jaded cynicism in here is enough to drown a kitten. But I shall rise above the blatant testosterone foolishness and simply say, 'screw you!' "

Waldo hadn't even registered the commotion; he was still basking in the performance glow as he came around the cab and climbed in.

"Howard Thurston was the preeminent magician at the beginning of the nineteen hundreds, and we all owe him a debt for his brilliance: Blackstone, Houdini, even myself. He was *not* on Gilligan's Island."

Harry revved the Saltmobile up and took off with a redlined roar.

"So, what did we get, Markintosh?"

I pulled the trio of tax returns out. "Got a Mong connection through the military, but I don't know what or why yet."

"Shit, I hate Mongs," Harry said as he took a rolling right through the red, giving an emotive middle finger to a hard-honking

SUV. "They never play fair. Give me the Goombas any day. You knew where you stood with the Idees. Some kneecapping, a little neighborhood graft—no big thing. But the Mongs—it's like dealing with a deep-water fish—no commonality. They're Area Fifty-one aliens in my book."

"They killed Lila. They pay. Don't care what they're like. Doesn't matter."

It was simple arithmetic, and I carried the two from long experience.

"Roger that, kimosabe. Mongs just make my butt itch, that's all."

And with that, we dropped the Great Zibaldo and Devon off to ready for their afternoon birthday extravaganza.

"Gotta change, or I'll scare the kids," she said.

"Hey, you can scare me anytime you want," I teased, but she hit me with a full-beam halogen headlight stare, and I backed off, quick. "Just saying, ah—you looked very...*magical* in that outfit."

Devon let me off with a warning and a promise. "I expect a sincere apology in the near future. Preferably somewhere nice, with ambiance and a fairly representative menu."

She gave me a quick peck on the cheek, then vanished in the way women do when they aren't aided by the Great Zibaldo.

Harry and I rolled on back to the office, and I noticed a paint crew whitewashing Lila's parking spot, starting in with a stencil on my name. The paint dripped like tears, or a runny nose. White drips of paint slowly covering up her name. I headed inside with a retributive authority, three stolen tax returns, a new job title, and white dots of paint dripping down the inside of my mind.

Miguel huddled in my new cubicle like a whipped puppy with big, shy eyes. In one nail-bitten, overly masturbated hand he clutched a gift-wrapped box, bedraggled blue bow and computer-printed card. It was about the size of a coffee mug.

"Hey, Mark...er...boss," he stammered in that Miguel-is-an-idiot way he has. "Me and Becky wanted you to have this."

He held out the gift as if it were a biopsy. I looked at him, the box, the bow, at him again. I liked to make Miguel uncomfortable. It was just plain fun, like kicking the next-door-neighbor's trashcans over after they'd kept you up all night with a loud party, or answering the phone and pretending you couldn't hear the person on the other end of the line: "Hello? I can't hear you...hello?" Maybe I had some issues. Maybe not. I took the gift and opened it. A blue coffee mug. Stenciled on the side was "#1 Boss."

"Wow...a mug. Kudos to you and Becky. Very thoughtful."

Miguel got that silly Miguel grin on his face, half dope, half idiot, half brain-dead, all Miguel.

"Becky picked it out herself when I told her you got the bump. She seriously wants to know if you'll come over for dinner one of these nights. She cooks the best green-bean casserole. She puts little bits of bacon in it, and cottage cheese on top like a scoop of ice-cream, and—"

"You moved in together?"

I hadn't been aware, but then, lately I'd been preoccupied. Poor Becky.

"Becky's idea. We spend more time together that way. And I like spending time together. Did you know that she likes to read biographies of military people? You know, like that Robert E. Lee, and General Patton and that Closet guy."

"Closet guy?"

"Wrote about how to fight wars and stuff. I think he was a German."

"Clausewitz. Carl Philipp Gottfried von. Prussian. Military theorist. Wrote *Vom Kriege*."

Miguel nodded. "That's the guy. Becky thinks he's the greatest. She quotes him all the time."

Here was a side of our barmaid I'd not contemplated. "She *quotes* him?"

"All the time. Like the other day, after we were doin' it, she quoted him."

"Interesting. In the original German, or translated?"

Miguel thought for a moment, all gears whirring. "In American. But with a German accent."

Now there was an image: a rosy-skinned Becky, gloriously naked and after-glowing from a bout of sweaty Miguel, quoting Clausewitz with a German accent. If ever I'd been titillated by Aryan uber-alles, that was the vision to do it.

"One of these days, I promise I'll drop by for eats," I said, no matter how unlikely that was. No sense throwing sand in the gas tank of camaraderie, or whatever. Miguel still stood there. "What?"

"About...you know...the Lila stuff. I want to help. I know Harry's doin' stuff, and...I want to, too."

There's a sincerity that truly clueless people have that is usually mistaken for other things. Courage on the battlefield. Loyalty in the face of adversity. Gas instead of a ruptured spleen. It's a sincerity that had tramped down the ages: misguided, misunderstood, misappropriated. It was the sincerity of the dumbfounded, the genuineness of stupefaction, the unaffected idiocy that derived from absolutely not knowing what was going on and having so little self-preservation instinct it wouldn't matter anyway. Miguel had it in spades.

If I were an evil man—and some say I am, but they obviously don't know me very well—I would have taken advantage of Miguel's offer to help. An extra set of eyes, even ones as bovine and lacking intelligence as Miguel's, always comes in handy. But I knew that, despite the fact he bang-squaded for me, he didn't have the final steel to go up against Mongs. Mongs snot Miguels in the morning and scratched their asses with them at night. He'd last long enough to give a goofy get-kicked-in-the-nuts smile, then be slaughtered, and I'd feel guilty about it in the bowels of my bowels. I was tender that way.

"Thanks, Miguel. You'll be the first I call if I need something novice. Honest injuns."

Miguel, no doubt unaware of the true Webster's definition of "novice," took this benediction as if I'd been the Pope.

"You can count on me, Boss."

"I always do, Miguel. Now go left flank some returns—we have a government to finance around here."

And off he went, the eternal imbecile, but *our* imbecile. If only I were as ignorant.

Something nagged at the itchy spot on my temporal lobe, like the beginnings of a second-hand cigar cough when you stepped into a room of Cohibas. *Why a vet's daughter?* I picked up the phone and speed dialed Juarez. I needed a little slime-ball snooping, and no one does that better than the feebs. They live for that shit. Makes 'em feel all-important and superior. Besides, it'd give me a chance to knock on some doors. And I could avoid all my other work piling up and somehow delay my actual first managerial pronouncement. If I didn't say it, it didn't happen.

10.

The FBI had a thing for greasy spoons. It was as if the juxtaposition of squeaky clean and dripping intestinal blockage with little burnt bits somehow gave all-American righteousness a good name. Not that I had anything against a lightly cauterized corned beef hash just gooing with egg yolk, coffee that ate spoons, and a piece o' pie (I like blueberry. hold the mode), but the feebs made a monotheistic religion out of it. Maybe 'cause they were cheap bastards.

Winky's Snack'n'Dine smelled like the 1950s on a crew-cut summer day, complete with Studebaker leather interiors, liquid-blue barbershop combs, and tighty-whitey, nut-hugger Fruit-of-the-Looms. Juarez sat at the booth like a bear shitting in the woods, sucking a malted through a straw with the vigor of a middle-aged hooker at a Shriners after-convention party. There was a banana royale in mid-consume and an order of steak fries submerged in Heinz strategically resting on the table. He motioned to me with a spoon, still doing the bottom-of-the-glass on the malted.

"In Bakersfield, we call that empty," I informed him.

He ice-cream-eyed me, then finished off with a loud frazoo. "We aren't in Bakersfield," he repartee'd back in Joe Friday obvious. "Besides, this is on your nickel."

Even when they were comped, the feds couldn't resist a good greasy spoon.

"So, find anything out that's worth all this gluttonous wallowing?"

Juarez did a face-lunge into the fries while handing me a manila folder. He sounded like a broken radiator with the trots.

"Dad's a veterinarian at a small clinic in Tucson. Mom's a social studies teacher at Polk Memorial High. Dead girl's a lieutenant in the army. See the world and all that."

"I bet you were navy, weren't you?"

"You bet your battleship. Proud of it, too. Got me through college." He ketchup'd his face into a bleeding wound Bozo the Clown would have been proud of.

"And look at you now..."

"Fat, broke, and intelligent—F. B. I."

"Cute. Does that work at parties?" I snatched a fry. Not bad, actually.

"Just flash 'em the badge. That always works."

"So why did the Mongs kill a lieutenant in America's armed forces, the daughter of a dog fixer, and child matriculator?" That was the question, wasn't it?

A grizzled veteran of the restaurant wars ambled up, steel-haired and steel-eyed, "Dorothy" on her name tag as if a blessing of intent.

"You want anything?" she said in a tone that implied world-weary vengeance if I didn't. "The Special's really special today."

"And what is the Special?"

"Chili dog with chips. With real chili—not that vego-spummy stuff they call chili. We have real rat snouts in ours."

The smile said joke, the eyes said "maybe." But who was I to pass up rat snouts?

"Gimme a bowl with lots of crackers. And if you have any Tabasco, that'd be great."

"Right. Tough talk from a guy who's sitting with an FBI wiener." Tightass popped the ketchup bottle for the dregs without a care in the world. "He tips like he's gotta pull the pennies from his own sphincter."

"Hey, the bureau has us on a tight budget. Your tax dollars at work, et cetera, et cetera." He held up the empty bottle, and Dorothy stared at it but did not take it. She left.

"So what does it mean?"

Juarez may be many things, but dumb was not one. "Haven't a clue, but I got a bead on a connection. They all invested in Kobe Beef after they left rotation and returned stateside."

"You mean like *steak* Kobe Beef? Costs a month's pay and melts in your mouth?"

"Japanese specialty. Treat their cows better than their women."

My chili arrived at that moment. Not a speck of cow in it, no doubt. I splattered on the Tabasco to the concurring nod of Dorothy, who had also brought another Heinz bottle for Juarez.

"Why'd you ding the beef and not me?"

I took a spoonful of chili, made a quick prayer, and popped it into my mouth. It chewed like jerky with an aftertaste of motor oil. Definitely the real McCoy.

"Gotta have customs papers a mile long to bring livestock into the country. Easy to track, and they weren't hiding. Don't know why, but there it is."

"Kobe Beef. *Cows*. They invested in cows."

"So their bank accounts say. Came in through San Pedro docks all fine and dandy."

"Cows."

"You're repeating yourself. And not in a good way."

Juarez flooded his fries again, forming a lake of red.

"You don't kill people over cows. Lila didn't die because of a bunch of fuckin' cows."

I pushed the chili bowl away without another bite. Juarez, seeing a freebie, dumped it in with the fries and kept chowing.

Mouth full of eats, he tried to chew and talk at the same time. "Didn't say the Mongolians did it. Just said cows were a connection. Couldn't find anything else but their stationing in Ulan Bator together. They didn't even socialize, from what I gather. Colonels and privates don't mix. There're just the cows."

***

Cows. What the hell did cows have to do with all of this?

I got back from work just after six-thirty, about normal on a very abnormal day. Mooing filled my head, and I knew even heavy drinking wasn't going to get rid of it. I figured a couple of phone calls might. To the right people.

Lila always knew the right people. Movers, shakers, economic bastions of largess: power brokers and billionaires. "Tiny" Jim Walker was anything but tiny. An ex-Texas Tech right tackle who threatened the NFL before completing a business degree and taking the beef business by storm, muscling the competition like so many defensive linemen, and reinventing the slaughterhouse system into a twenty-first century robotic charnel. Along the way, he began to accumulate Fortune 500 rankings, moving higher and higher up the list and collecting more and more ranch land until Tiny Beef Enterprises became the leader in all things bovine. He had an encyclopedic knowledge of animal husbandry, dirty business tactics, and women's lingerie, for more reasons than met the eye, according to Lila, who ran with him for a meteoric seven weeks before she moved on to her next financier, leaving poor Tiny severely calloused and forever trying to measure up. What could I say? Lila had a way with men.

I'd met him twice during his stay of execution, both times at Lila's, both times at dinner parties that would have made five-star Michelin restaurants green with spite. Lila was always effortless and overly ostentatious, but no one really cared. I remember Tiny as being a massive verbal vacuum that seemed to suck words from the air; anyone who talked to him vanished in his engulfing void. He wasn't overbearing, obnoxious, or ex-athletically egotistical. He simply ate words without giving any back. When he talked, it was as if he hadn't. Perhaps he was a throwback to a pre-oral hominid past, a tribal link to an ancient evolution. Yet his present-day successes seemed to belie the need for speech. Maybe it was overrated. I knew I sure talked too much sometimes.

But not then. I needed to talk to Tiny and get something cowish from him. Kobe Beef cowish, with a moo-moo here and a moo-moo there. In black-and-white, honest-to- God-fearin' words. And I knew he would. For Lila. No NFL draft pick could refuse; Lila had known the commissioner.

See, I had the full roster of Lila's exes on my laptop—just in case—and went through the file like a spelunker in a cave: roped, lit, and carefully. I could retire on those telephone numbers and addresses alone, not to mention the "extra" notes in the margins. This major CEO guy liked to be called "Papa Smurf" while being snapped with a wet towel, while that liked amaretto-flavored whipped cream and nipple twisting; another simply wanted Lila to lie very, very still and try to "keep her temperature down." Weird. Disturbing. And so predictable. I finally scrolled to Tiny's direct, super-secret, have-to-kill-you-if-I-tell-you number, lingerie annotation included.

Before I could pick up the phone, a knock at my door ignited my paranoia like an arsonist's wet dream—not too difficult to do in the most benign of circumstances. I hefted my faithful Louisville Slugger, and open the door (never mind that was dressed only in my boxer shorts) and—

—there was Devon standing on my stoop dressed in something mundanely sexy that emphasized her finer points like sunrise on the Grand Tetons.

"You don't get out much, do you?" she drawled, fighting a smile.

"Only to pee and stretch my legs," I replied.

She gave me a toe-to-nose look-over.

"Boxers are okay in my book. I wear them myself."

She walked inside on that remark. Who was I to disagree with underwearial taste? So, she wore boxers...

Once in the apartment, Devon began nosing about with occasional nods and some shakes of the head. She seemed to find my one-tenth-life-size recreation of the Randy's Donuts donut-as-a-coffee-maker whimsical.

"A friend gave that to me."

"You sure it was a friend?" She found my coffee in the freezer next to my frozen, half-eaten Snickers bar and a gallon of Rocky Road ice cream. With a laboratory assistant's accuracy, she filled the brewer and switched it on. "Want some?"

I shook my head. "Caffeine doesn't keep me awake."

She smiled a curiously piquant smile, and I realized I was still standing there in my boxers.

A minute or so later, jeans and a Spunky Monkey T-shirt thrown on, I came out of my bedroom to find Devon fussing with cream, fake-sugar—the yellow packet kind—and filling mugs. She'd chosen the biggest I owned.

"I took you for a cream and sorta-sugar guy. Was I wrong?"

"Naw. I know I should be a big bad drink-it-black dude, but I never caught the habit. My friends laugh at me for it."

Pretty women could make anyone babble like an idiot, and I'd never been the exception that proved the rule. Just call me Ismael.

"Probably not the only thing they laugh at you about, though I think it's endearing: macho with a sweet tooth." She handed me a mug and I sipped. Then sipped again.

"You sure this is *my* coffee?"

She clapped her hands like a Vegas dealer going on break and held them out, palms to me. "Nothing up my sleeves but wrists and hands. It's...*magic*. And a pinch of salt." She took a sip. "You need to clean your donut, too. That'd make it better."

From where I stood, *nothing* could make it better. She noticed my noticing.

"You got something on your mind, Mr. Douglas?"

I still noticed; not one to be intimidated, even by good looks and a saucy smile, or so I swear on a stack of bibles with a cherry on top. "Just curious what prompted this lovely but unexpected appearance by my favorite magician's assistant."

"We have a restaurant to eat at. You haven't made reservations yet. I'm reminding you. In person. Ta-da."

I had plans for the restaurant thing but was somewhat busy, what with Lila's death and all, but who was I to look a gift horse in the mouth?

"I know a great Moroccan place around the corner. You get to eat with your hands."

Devon stepped toward me, and I had both an immediately uplifting reaction as well as one of trepidation, as if a big hungry tiger had decided that I was some sort of two-legged roebuck.

"Good choice. Bad timing. You have to make reservations, *then* call me, *then* come pick me up on the day. You know the drill. Boy/girl stuff."

"I didn't know we were doing the boy/girl stuff."

"Oh, we're doing the boy/girl stuff. I thought you got the memo. *You*. You're it."

"Me? *It*? Why me?" I asked in all ignorance, but with a growing sense of entrapment. Normally, I don't like being in a deterministic universe. Screw Laplace's demon and the Newtonian horse he rode in on. But somehow, at that moment, I wasn't *so* bothered.

"You're clean, not too ugly, keep yourself in shape, you have a good job, you don't spend too much, and when you're excited your pants make me think of the movie Krakatoa, East of Java."

"Kraka—"

"Sexual imprinting at a young age. Sue me. Anyway, I had a friend who only went out with sixty-five-year-old millionaires. I picked you. We'll see who's happier in the end."

She stood toe to toe with me, just the right height. Wrapping my brain around the onslaught took a moment in which her "right height" kept tantalizing me, and how the hell did she know I didn't spend too much? She beat me to the question:

"Come on Mark...look at your place, your clothes. You get your car from work. Unless you're a secret, big-stakes, Capybara high roller, you like money in your account and a little extra for a rainy day."

"I *like* rainy days." I tried to sound offended.

"Me, too."

"Well, at least my FICO scores are bigger than yours," I shot back with a last blundering hope of salvaging some male pride—it wasn't as if I hadn't checked. Hell, I was the IRS!

"Not all of them," Devon said, a bit little girl and defeated.

"No one gives a hoot about TransUnion. It's the cheap, back-alley call girl of FICO scores."

Not a word, then we both started laughing.

"'Cheap, back-alley call girl of FICO scores? Tell me, Mr. Douglas, how do you *really* feel?"

"Best I could come up with on short notice. I'll do better next time."

Devon gave me a quick kiss on the lips, just a speed-of-light flutter, then headed out the door. "I'm relying on you to."

And she was gone as suddenly as she'd come. I didn't have time to even think straight, even more so since I had a call to make. But eventually, *eventually* I was going to sit down and give all this between her and me the once-over twice. Maybe even three times.

***

Take it from me, 'cause I've seen it all in my capacity as IRS over-the-shoulder-peek-a-boo auditor extraordinaire: luxury was a sliding scale thing. To some, three hot meals of Mickey D's quarter pounders with Supersize fries and a ceiling with upstairs neighbors thumping around on at 2:00 a.m. was the Ritz. To others, anything short of a gold-plated Rolls with a custom license plate that read, "SWNKY," simply "will not do, dear." Then there was Jim Walker's private jet. Jesus in a leopard-skin pillbox hat.

First, it was painted, shined and waxed Black Angus black. We were talking stealth black, the black between stars black, the total absence of color black. Lettered—in black—on the side of the plane was the corporate name: *Tiny Beef Enterprises*. Only readable when the light hit it *just right*. And it had horns. Big ol' horns on either side of the cockpit. Ostensibly radar bubbles, but they sure looked like cow horns to me. Don't know how the FAA let him do that, but I guessed money not only talked, it mooed.

Then we came to the inside.

At that moment, I was flying at 40,000 feet, relaxed in—you'd never guess—a Black Angus leather reclining chair. But that ain't all. I was being elegantly served Laysan Duck foie gras and Almas caviar with tiny toasted toasts, champagne (the good stuff; the kind that had limited serial numbers on it), watching the not-yet-released sequel to George Clooney's latest, and being beck-and-called by two equally as expensive twin flight attendants: Dollar and Cents. Swear ta frickin' God, that's what it said on their name tags. The cabin was lined in additional leather—whole generations of bovines gave their all for that décor—and had more electronic gadgets than an eleven-year-old boy's room. My brain whirred overtime trying to calculate the taxes on the sucker. For once, even I needed a calculator, something that, oddly, wasn't available. Go figure.

I'd toyed with the idea of calling Devon just to muckity-muck to her about the "fast lane" I was living in, but realization sank in somewhere after takeoff: this was about Lila, and all this opulence didn't mean shit if it didn't help me find out what happened to her. So I sipped a socially polite amount of champagne, devoured the nibbles and couldn't care less about the movie. I counted down the minutes to landing.

Private airfield, of course, somewhere on the territory lightly referred to as Tiny's ranch. Cows from horizon to horizon. All black. Looked like a rippling ocean of tar with hooves. It was 104 degrees in the shade, and there was no shade; it was Texas. The stink of the locust-number of cows burnt my nose hairs like Drain-O. A Subzero refrigerator in the shape of a black Humvee awaited me, steer horns on the grill. I climbed inside, exhaled hot cow and was greeted by a third attendant, identical to the two on the plane. Her name tag read: Interest. Tiny was obviously a very twisted guy.

Horn blaring to scatter the cows, we eked our way along until we hit a four-lane highway (still on Walker's property) and shot across the landscape in temperature-controlled, sound-proofed leisure. An hour later, the scenery turned into the Swiss Alps, and we wound our way upwards, my ears popping, snow splattering spots higher up. I toyed with the idea that, perhaps, Tiny had built the mountains just to add variety to his holdings, but...no, that would be too much even for him. Wouldn't it?

A log cabin the size of a Bavarian castle hove into view around the last curve. A cross between a monstrous set of Lincoln Logs and the Overlook Hotel from *The Shining*, Walker's abode went beyond Texas-weird. Texas-weird would have been a forty-foot, anatomically correct statue of Roy Rogers with a herd of lawn jockeys around its base. Or kangaroos in waiter outfits greeting guests with trays of Mexican martinis. Maybe the world's largest barbecue pit, a drift of pigs all slowly rotating on the spit like Rockettes in a line with a football team's worth of chefs slathering it all with sauce. It went beyond that. It hop-stepped-and-jumped into weird-weird.

Walker met me as we parked, looking anything but weird-weird. In fact, he looked normal-norma—a guy in jeans, T-shirt and cowboy boots, haircut Army-short, the start of a pot belly, a belt buckle in the shape of an Angus steer. Until you got closer and realized he was six foot eight and moving toward 300 pounds. Like shaking hands with a hydraulic press. And despite the authentic smile, there was that hint of protect-the-quarterback-at-all-costs still in his eyes. No amount of money could buy or sell that look.

"Mornin'," he said after the crippling handshake.

"Jim, I appreciate you seeing me, bringing me down, but we could have done this on the phone. I just need some information about cows."

Tiny gave me that lineman's smile again and shook his head. "This is more than cows, and you know it. Phones don't really get to the root of things sometimes. And besides..." he looked almost shy, if a 300-pound bear with a Black Angus belt buckle could look shy, "... I wanted, kinda, to hear about Lila. Not somethin' for the phone, if you take my meaning."

I nodded. "Sure thing. Lila was never anyone's phone call."

For a moment we both caught ourselves in thoughts, then Walker lowered his eyes, and I did as well. Not much more to be said.

He led me inside, through the solid, sequoia-sized doors that would, mass-wise, look at home on an airplane hangar, and into a complete and perfect all-enclosed reproduction of Dodge City circa 1876—the time of Wyatt Earp and Bat Masterson. Seriously, we were talkin' every saloon, hotel, stable, every mud-filled street, hitching post and stagecoach depot. There were audio-animatronic bartenders, robotic piano players, seemingly real dancing girls, and various and sundry cowboys, Indians, and townsfolk, real or otherwise, I didn't have a clue. Walker gave a much-practiced running monologue of the historical accuracy, rule-bending liberties, and just plain frivolity involved (like the Lieutenant Colonel George Armstrong Custer who greeted us as we entered G. M. Hoover's whisky bar).

"Yeah, Custer never quite got up here, but I always had a soft spot for the stupid son-of-a-bitch. If there's a heaven, it can't be worse than this."

I looked on in wonder. "This" was way beyond Texas-weird. Seemed Tiny had taken a *whim* to the Old West, and it was born like Athena from Zeus's bank account.

"I never tire of it. Makes me feel like I'm part of something bigger than myself."

I looked around: helluva lot bigger.

Shot glasses and a bottle slid down the bar, something I'd only seen in the movies, but appreciated in real life. It was prime, single-malt scotch. Another historical inaccuracy, though I didn't mind a bit. We sipped our *uisge beatha*, neither of us wanting to say the first word that would open up the dictionary of Lila. But I went there for a reason, and it wasn't a whim.

"Wasn't pretty, Jim."

Walker tried to stand tall as I told him what I knew—or at least some of it; no names or contacts—but with each word, that monster of a man shrunk, getting smaller and smaller, like a crumple of paper in a fire, until he was nothing but ash and ready to blow away.

I didn't pull many punches, though I didn't linger on the details I knew; that would have been below-the-belt. Walker's Lila wasn't my Lila, but they were sisters, and we both loved them in our own way. I skipped over the funeral, knowing that Walker hadn't been there because he was on the other side of the world. It broke his heart, but he knew Lila wouldn't've minded. Hearing about one's successors and competitors didn't seem proper.

Then I hit the meat of my visit, the things only Walker could know, and I saw the anger and determination leak back into his face. He wanted to help me and, barring that, kill Juju Klondike. Which, from everything Juarez had told me, would only get Tiny Walker killed deader than his ghost-town Dodge City. No, I was the lucky SOB who was going to get a shot at Klondike, and may God have mercy on my soul.

"Money? Manpower? I can get you anything. You tell me what the carpet crap you need. You got it. This is...is...too much. I can barely breathe."

We'd worked our way down half a bottle, but I felt high-tension-wire clear-headed, as if I were drinking cold, Sierra-stream water. Clarity with a capital "C."

Walker pulled a manila folder from behind the bar and tossed it in front of me. "That lieutenant's dad, veterinarian in Tucson, Doctor Mickey O'Bannon. He doesn't normally do cows, but lately he has."

I slid out the papers and thumbed through them: everything from surveillance photos to the vet's kid's grade-school report cards. A little better and a little worse than I could do; but he only had from my phone call and flight there. Remind me never to get on that guy's bad side.

"Lemme guess: Kobe cows."

"They're called Wagyu. Genetically predisposed to Kobe Beef—higher marbling, higher unsaturated fat. Makes them tastier and tender. That and the geisha treatment: massaged, brushed, fed hand-picked sweet-grass, beer. Hell, they're treated better than I am."

I doubted that, but he had a point. No wonder it cost so much. But not "killing" cost.

"Why kill for something you can buy at a restaurant? I mean, a shit-hell expensive, diamond-licking, trust-fund sluts and graying Euro hipsters with potbellies believing their money endowed them with bigger dicks restaurant. But still, just a restaurant with knives, forks, and ketchup."

"His cows weren't kosher."

"Smuggled?"

"Yes and no. Not smuggled *into* the U.S., but once they got here, they sorta did a Houdini. Not sold, not shipped, not anything. Just gone." Walker shrugged. "I pulled every string I had, but nothing doing. Who buys that kinda beef and doesn't make a buck off it? It's un-American."

I thought for a second, then asked, "Doc O'Bannon the last to see 'em?" Walker nodded. "Before or after his daughter's bye-bye?" Walker reached for the file, but I could do it as fast, thumbing through the pages until I found it: "Yup. Looks like his little lieutenant brought home more than a case of the clap from overseas. Shit. So what? What could be so damn important about cows? Who gave a shit about cows?"

Tiny was polite enough not to answer that; instead, he suggested something to eat, so we grabbed the bottle and got out of Dodge, *literally*, heading toward the back of the house and outside to the backyard.

The backyard was just Texas-weird. Two steers were roasting on a barbecue spit, slathered liberally by bikini-clad, over-endowed girls who all looked like the flight attendants and driver Tiny had sent for me. The swimming pool was filled to the brim with pungent-smelling barbecue sauce, and other identical girls floated in plastic boats, plates piled high with beef resting on their tanned and perfectly flat tummies. They'd yank a hunk of meat off and dip it into the sauce they were floating on and chow down, their Euclidianly even teeth dazzling white against the blood-brown of the sauce. Like amatory piranha.

Can't say I'd ever had better barbecue, or as much. Not even the time I audited General Jackson's Rib Ranch Emporium. It was Walker's mom's special, inbred, back-home recipe, so I was told. It was addictive, and I ate more than I should, more than I wanted. Just plain more. Like everything there. Another bottle of scotch, conversation turning back to Lila, but a Lila past. The one Tiny Jim Walker knew best. She sounded like a great girl.

11.

It was Desmond Gloucester's wedding anniversary. His *tenth* wedding anniversary. The "tin" anniversary. Tin? Who thought of that one? One of the original Puritans over on the Mayflower? And why did it not surprise me that his wife divorced him immediately afterward? "You giveth me tin? Thy stuff's on the frontal lawn; I'm callingeth a solicitor." Did we even use tin for anything anymore? Not like we had tin cans, or tin pans, or Tin Men. But I was rambling. Modern gift selection recommended for your tenth: diamond jewelry! Since when did an Oprah-raised, Redbook-in-the-supermarket-checkout-line-reading, I-want-a-separate-bank-account wife married more than three minutes want anything *less* than diamond jewelry? Ten years? She was ready to get a hunk of allotroped carbon that gave her carpel tunnel of the wrist just holding it up. Ten years? It better be set in platinum as well, or "sweetie" wasn't doin' any salami hiding until he manned up. "No rock, no rock 'n' roll."

So, it was Des's tenth with his American wife Patricia, and the Big D had gotten her, dig this, a trip to the dentist. Whoop-dee-frickin'-do. But wait, there was more. On every one of the delightfully understated Patricia's teeth, Desmond overly paid that lucky, lucky dentist a butt-load of dough to implant a diamond, size varying upon the size of the tooth: incisors a carat, on up to a four-carat, F1, princess-cut pink molar. I was sure Patricia was ruing the day she had her wisdom teeth removed. Live and learn.

Also, amazingly, according to my Knicks-loving pal Bennie's DMV super-snooping, it was Rodney and Donna Gloucester's imaginary wedding anniversary as well. Their third anniversary, the leather anniversary. Mother of an Unruly and Vengeful Pacifier-Gnawing God—already into leather so soon. The truly *muy* interesting thing that the Benster found, along with a handicapped driver's license permit pertaining to his scrotal hernia (I shit you not) was that wife Donna consisted of a badly forged birth certificate from Mexicali, two credit cards with $500 limits, and a Facebook page without a photo and only three friends, all a.k.a.'s of Rodney. Donna, for all her no-doubt charms, looked to be as mythical as a Hippogriff with a yeast infection. Good for me; bad for Rodney. What was more, after some digging on my part, I discovered that Rodney had given his spouse-wousy a Craftsman DYS 4500 26-horsepower riding lawn mower for a present. Musta had a leather seat or something. QED: there was no Donna, no marriage, and—most importantly—no deductible. There was only one thing to do: I must convey my felicitations on the happy occasion—with an audit.

Computers in government-sanctioned bureaucracy can be good and bad, rather like a threesome with a mother/daughter tag-team set of nymphos. (What, you gotta ask?) Good in the make-my-life-easier-with-digital-goodness way, and bad in the this-damnable-software-dates-to-the-1980s-and-still-runs-on-DOS-badness way. Extra-credit points to the bureaucrats because they look "cutting edge" and can brag about their bits and their bytes, thus lending a modicum of job security to their already unfireable lives.

Me, I got no problem with computers. According to Harry, in the dark ages pre-microchip, IRS grunts like us needed carbon-copy forms in typewriters, an unending line of signatures on each of those forms, and collated copies for the files, and that was just to requisition a form. Now, I could cut-and-paste a few pertinent pieces of private information, digitally sign my John Hancock, attach e-postage, hit "enter," and ta-da: Rodney Gloucester should be receiving his IRS-sanctioned audit letter by noon the next day. And then the fun would begin because the 1-800 number he'd call at the bottom of the letter led straight to my government-issued phone, line 3. And if he *didn't* call...I would personally visit Mr. Rodney. I kinda hoped he wouldn't call, as I enjoy the *personal* touch.

Ding! E-mail hit my machine: Mr. Aroon. "The aorta eats kumquats." Hmm, highly unlikely—probably. But I've seen that "aorta" do many things before in Mr. Aroon's oddly multilingual hands. Ding! Another e-mail from my boss: "Quiznot blarney." Ah, that made more sense: he wanted to see me in his office. "Over the elevator and through the Constantines to Mr. Aroon's office I go..."

The clickety-clack of two hundred words a minute greeted me as I entered, as well as the somewhat attenuated sneer from Mr. Aroon's sentry of a secretary. But that wasn't all! I noticed, and then was taken aback, that Miss Claudia Faberge Constantine wore atop her bullet-shaped cranium, resting at a rakish angle, a bergère hat: a flip-floppy straw thing with a blue ribbon and yellow flowers. Think of that titillating exhibitionist girl in the Fragonard painting, The Swing (you know, the one where the guy's looking up her dress, and she's lovin' it). *That* bergère hat. Worn by Miss Constantine, who by all paleontological records did not have a girlhood, let alone a childhood, but oozed out from the drum of a mimeograph machine.

"I like the hat, Claudia. Very becoming." Who was I to dash hopes and dreams with the truth? "Gives you a rococo splendor."

Still typing: "I got it on sale at Big Lots. Two for fifteen dollars."

I chewed on that hors d'oeuvre of information, that Rumaki of thought, projecting upon my inner mind the image of yet another hat on Miss Constantine's head.

"The other one's pink."

I would have to wash my brain out.

"I got an e-mail..."

"Mr. Smith will be a minute. Sit. Your audit letter went out, and I put a 'Highest Priority' on it."

Uh-oh. "Highest Priority?" I fully assumed everything I did was monitored by Those Above—or as Harry would say: "Checkin' our underwear that we wiped."—but Constantine helping me? "Highest Priority" meant: You Will Be Totally Frickin' Fired If This Doesn't Get Through. First the hat, now this...What the hell was going on? With all my shriveled and egotistical manhood, I prayed she didn't have the *likies* for me. That's all I needed.

Fortunately, my boss became available that very moment of disquiet, and I hurried into the office looking for sanctuary, normality, and a side of not-so-weird as if I were a full-bladdered seven-year-old having to hold it in.

Aroon Smith waited, standing straight and isoscelitically too tall, holding a seemingly cantilevered hand out. He *never* shook hands. *Ever. "And out of his mouth goeth a sharp sword, that with it he should smite the nations: and he shall rule them with a rod of iron."* You know, Book of Revelations time: dogs sleeping with cats, politicians speaking truth, margarine tasting like butter. My hesitation lasted only as long as it took my self-preservation to kick in, and I shook. And shivered. Mr. Aroon had hands soft as a tiny baby's. Creepy. Disturbing.

"Mr. Douglas..."

I put on a trying-to-be-respectful-boss smile, which, given my creeped-out anxiety, felt more grimace than smile. Still, I tried.

"... have you ever contemplated the reason why the IRS is, under the correct state of affairs and circumstances, considered an ancillary branch of the Federal judicial system?"

I stared for a moment. Judicial system? We took tithes and whomped ass if you didn't pay. We were knights of the accounting round table. Armored in the righteous knowledge that what's yours is mine and what's mine is mine, and don't you forget it. The IRS was *not* the forgiving type. Judicial system? We judged how much you owed us and then made sure we got it. That's all the adjudicating I ever heard of. Mr. Aroon Smith stared back at me, his eyelids closing and opening once, like a lizard's. Obviously, there were more things in heaven and earth, Horatio.

"Judicial system?"

"It's hardly wielded by the rank and file, as they have too much on their plate to begin with, but there is a particular statute—which I leave to your inquisitiveness to look up—that gives the Internal Revenue Service a broad range of absolutional powers, sometimes greater than those of, say, a governor."

And we've all seen those prison movies where someone rushes in at the last second before a prisoner is to be executed with a pardon from the governor, freedom, and a happily-ever-after. I never knew we could do the same. Or how.

"It is certainly something to contemplate, Mr. Douglas. Especially as it reflects upon marital bliss and Mongolian transgressions..."

And with that, I was dismissed, ending up back at my desk naggingly sure that my boss had just fed me an arcane but necessary tidbit. I pulled statutes like toothpicks from my bookshelf of legal and not-so-legal IRS tomes. Mr. Aroon wouldn't have wasted his time with me if there weren't something, and something I looked for. And found.

Interesting. According to the powers vested in me by the blah-blah-blah, I could cut deals. *Sometimes*. If I filled out the paperwork and filed it with the correct authorities in the correct time-frames, and no one could find a bigger crime that outweighed mine. In other, more astrological words, if the planets aligned *just* right, I could be judge, jury, and executioner. Now that could come in handy. I began working out what trumped what. Did drunk driving beat a small deduction falsification? Armed robbery one-better full-blown tax fraud? I see your manslaughter one and raise you two million in back taxes and a seven-year string of non-filings.

I began to dig in earnest, which led me to the IRS Information Centre. Centre with an "re." Swear to the ever-lovin' Virgin Mary of the Cats, it's spelled "re," not "er." Occasionally, we federal sphincter-tighteners have pretensions. Or bad spelling. I never had the nerve to ask, just in case I got stuck with the cleanup.

The IRS Information Centre had every book, record, tax form, computer file, and shoe size of anyone, anything, and anywho that'd ever passed through, been of use, or may be of use to anyone in the IRS since the beginning of time, good till the end of the planet through a fiery-nova'd sun. It squatted, housed in its own separate fugly building, next door to my own, looking architecturally a bit like a bearded circus fat lady: wide-bottomed, thick blocked with an array of antenna on top that made the NSA look like someone had given it a crew-cut. And it was painted robin's egg blue. With blacked out windows. And that was only the outside.

After the usual security prods and probes, the inside revealed a hermetically sealed glass cubical that bathed the IRS employee inside—at the moment, me—with UV light, a diluted combination of chlorine gas, circa Vietnam War defoliant, Afrin nasal spray, and a light jasmine scent. Rumor had it the "phone booth," as we fondly called it, had been "foreclosed" from a tech startup that specialized in space-travel decontamination procedures. I always felt vaguely insulted that my germs, or whatever, were not good enough to enter the Info Centre along with me. But such is the case in government bureaucracy. And then some.

Inside-inside lay the White Room, an audio-deadened space the size of a warehouse that was white. All white. Walls, doors, blacked-out windows (or, in this case, whited-out windows), tables, chairs, lanned and secured computers, even the #2 pencils. White. Matte white so as not to glare. At the white front desk sat Mr. Virgil Valente, custodian/librarian of the Info Centre. He tended to wear white. Look up the word "nondescript" in the dictionary and you'd see a picture of Mr. Virgil Valente. From his every-other-Saturday Super-Cuts-styled hair to the never-smile, never-frown look on his face, Mr. Virgil Valente was bred to nondescription. His voice was subdued with no hint of accent, his gestures and mannerisms nonthreatening and never abrupt. It was like someone in a gene lab spliced together all the DNA taken from a bell-curve cross section of America, the average part, and stuffed it all into Mr. Virgil Valente while in utero. Nine months later out popped Valente, and there he perched, arbiter of data retrieval.

Everything went through Valente. So after a nod toward the desk and a nondescript nod back (I noticed he was Sudoku-ing with an eager yet still nondescript gleam in his eye), I began making out a list, aided by my logged-in white computer, of what I thought I needed in order to bring the weight and soon-to-be judicial powers of the IRS down on Rodney Gloucester. You betchum. The list went on and on, mostly centering on up-to-the-second police cases in the area of Phoenix and how they balanced against my own case.

I never realized that Phoenix rated in the top-ten most dangerous cities in America, according to the Morgan Quitno Awards. Not that I knew who Morgan Quitno was or why they gave out awards for danger, but I could find out his tax status. (In fact, it's a company started and owned by Scott and Kathleen Morgan, and don't get me started about their deduction for five thousand dollars' worth of laxatives and the accompanying cost of Charmin toilet paper and Preparation-H.)

More murders and armed robbery in Phoenix than I could ever imagine. Must be the hot desert air. Whatever. The moment I caught the statistic, I knew I had to get a little lucky with the Rodney. Fortunately, luck and Mr. Virgil Valente walked hand-in-hand at my side.

The key turned on how severe I could diagnose Rodney's tax-fraud situation. Hanging offenses and tax fraud rarely entered into the same conversation, but at least trafficking in clean laundry as yet had not been made a capital crime. I noodled with the various contingencies of false deductions and evasive nonpayment, but could only kludge up minimum time and maximum payback with liens and foreboding encumbrances. I took all my summations and theories to Valente and hoped for the best. Mr. Valente's best did not fail me.

With an almost hushed voice that bordered on a monotone, the information connoisseur pointed out that another option of enforcement could be applied as per sections 7201 and 7206, a small paragraph that I'd never quite noticed before on the definition of "willfulness" and how it related to "cheek." Hey, this stuff, taken in small doses, makes my wang vibrate with anticipation, *honest*. I gotta get out more.

Okay, lemme break it down into bite-sized nuggets. Evasion tax law came in two types: evasion of assessment and evasion of payment. Essentially, are you lying about what's due, or are you lying about where what's due is? Rodney did both, but that wasn't the main point. He did both with willful intent to deceive. But in creating a fictitious spouse for tax purposes (as opposed to masturbatory ones, or just to lie to his longing-for-a-grandkid mother), Valente suggested that Rodney could be brought up on double charges—not only his own, but the person's he fabricated. A loophole, yes, but essentially Rodney Gloucester had legal responsibility for not only his own misdeeds but also those of his wife. Who didn't exist. Sort of the reverse of double indemnity; Rodney got a two-for-one sentencing opportunity via the transitive property of IRS punishment: if A equals B, and B equals C, then A was truly screwed. And with *that*, I could make a totally legal and binding bargain without talking to anyone but my little ol' lonesome. Virgil Valente was a man of genius. I tried to tell him so, but he went back to his Sudoku. It takes all kinds to run the IRS.

***

Feeling triumphant in a two-steps-forward kind of way, I called Devon, boy/girl'd her into a date and time (that night, actually), then picked her up at the appointed hour. We Moroccaned like nobody's business, feeding each other tasty treats and laughing rice all over the table. Something about a woman who doesn't mind Ferakh Maamer smeared all over her face gets me every time. That and her "don't-give-a-damn but you should" attitude, the way her thigh kept nudging up against mine, and the fact that a hole the size of the Marianas Trench gaped in my heart. All that plus a heavy dose of "she's dang sexy" contributed to my drinking more than I should in the hopes of acting more charming than I could. Which led to my bringing her back to Del's for a nightcap.

"Harry told me all about Del's," Devon said as we strolled through the doors, greeted by a blaring rendition of *Fantasy Is Reality* by 4th Avenue Jones. Story of my life. "The mysteries of Del herself, the famous meeting, and affiancing of Miguel and Becky. The works."

"The works, huh?" That Harry, what a joker. "I didn't know he was so talkative."

"You'd be surprised what a guy'll say to a pretty girl." I looked at Devon, she looked at me, I kept looking, she kept looking. "That would be a clue, Mr. Douglas."

"Yes, I know. I'm just figuring out how many 'verys' to use."

" 'Verys?' "

"As in 'very, very, very, very' pretty girl. Or should there be another 'very?' "

Devon hit me with the supernova smile and wrapped an arm around my waist, a head on my shoulder, and made sure I felt very, very pretty girl'd to perfection.

"Not *that's* what I'm talkin' about. You are a smooth-tongued devil, Mr. Douglas."

"Don't I know it? Like butter on a warm sidewalk."

"You have a lot of butter on warm sidewalks where you come from, Mark?"

"In the summertime, it's hard not to." Harry sighted us from across the room while in the midst of what looked to be a head-sketching contest on Wooly Bob's noggin. I sotto voced to Devon: "Try not to stare. It only encourages him."

"McMarkster! Ms. Devon. Come. Sit. Drink. Not necessarily in that order," invited Harry.

He pushed Miguel out of his chair to make room for Devon next to him, and I grabbed a chair from another table and slid it in next to her, then made introductions.

"Devon, this here is Miguel, the affianced of Becky, who's that vision behind the bar." Becky grabbed beers and shots even as I spoke.

Miguel beamed at that. "She's *my* vision."

Harry glared. "And don't you forget it, or we've all vowed to hunt you down and feed your urethra to your anus."

It took Miguel a moment to follow the logic path, then he squirmed, rightly keeping quiet.

I then introduced Wooly Bob. "And the man with the—what *is* that on your head, Bob?"

Bob tilted his dome forward so we could get a better look. Calculations ran about his head like a chalkboard in a mathematician's office. "We're figuring the addition to the gross national product if every taxpayer in America actually paid their correct amount this year."

"On your head?"

"We didn't have any paper. Besides, it washes off."

I could see the lunatic grin on Harry's face, then noticed he was holding a Sharpie. "Anyway, Devon, this is Wooly Bob."

She shook Bob's hand and smiled.

"So what's the final total?"

Harry shook his head. "Don't know. We were just convincing Bob to let us use an arm or two, maybe a buttocks to finish up when you arrived."

"Spare me the image," I protested, knowing it was too late.

Devon smiled around the table. "So this is what tax guys do on their off-hours? More tax stuff?" She eyed me suspiciously. "How come you don't do this sort of thing...yet?"

"I am more well-rounded than my otherwise narrow-minded and blinkered compatriots. I believe there's more to life than just number-crunching and statutes."

Harry shook his head. "Big words from the guy who won the office's annual 'How Much Taxes' pool three years running."

I lowered my head, trying to avoid Devon's gleeful look. "*That* was for *money*."

At that moment, Becky arrived with another round of drinks for the veterans and something for Devon and me. Devon and Becky eyed each other, sort of a sexiness face-off like two hot and steamy wolverines checking out the competition. Becky had the larger square footage, but Devon was no slouch either, and D practically smoldered when she smiled a certain way. I wasn't sure what it was about, but I was smart enough to know not to get in the middle.

Finally, Devon noticed a ribbon tying off Becky's ponytail. It had a gray feather, a blue feather, and a red feather on it. "Blue Birds?"

Together, the two women recited—"Sing, grow, help!"—then laughed, tension broken. Becky bent down and gave Devon a quick hug. "Sisters!"

Devon hugged back. "Forever!"

Miguel looked dumbfounded, then hopeful, "What are the Blue Birds, some college experimental thing?"

Harry whapped Miguel on the back of the head. "You are an ignorant and primitive pissant, Miguel. You're thinking of LUG's or BUG's. Blue Birds is a whole different and younger thing. And wholesome...not that lesbians until graduation aren't. Some of my best friends were lesbians."

Me to Harry: "Were?"

Miguel to Harry: "BUGS?"

Harry turned to Becky and Devon, giving a sitting bow. "I cannot help the men you choose, but I do apologize for them."

Becky went from hugging Devon to hugging Miguel, burying his head in her overly ample amplitude. "No need to apologize. He's cute when he doesn't understand."

Harry and I rock-paper-scissor'd and I won.

"Then he must be cute all the live-long-day."

Becky smiled, oblivious to my comment. "He sure is!"

Devon gave me a smile that promised comeuppance and took my hand. "You know, they send nice little boys like you to Hell for saying things like that."

I squeezed her hand. "They've had a room booked in my name for quite a while. And the bed's got Magic Fingers."

Devon gave me a cute-crazy lopsided grin that made me glad I was sitting down, then took a sniff of the shot Becky had drawn her, then sniffed again. "Herencia de Plata? Blanco?"

Becky lit up. "I thought you looked like a girl who knew her tequila."

Devon saluted to Becky with the glass—"Sing, grow, help!"—then shot it. "Mmm, just like mama used to pour." She took a sip of beer as I looked on in wonder. She cocked an eyebrow at me. "What, a girl can't know her liquor? Don't even get me started on single malts."

Oh, *yeah...*

Harry'd been eyeballing me and Devon for a bit, ruminatively sipping at his booze and nodding his head as if coming to some auspicious conclusion. "You smell of couscous and Turkish coffee. This some kind of a date?"

I shrugged. Devon shrugged. Harry shrugged.

"Okay by me. Not like Marksipad's been gettin' a lot lately. He could use a good humpty-dumpty."

"Thanks, Harry. You make me sound so desirable."

"Hell, son, if I were twenty years younger, blind from glaucoma, and hadn't had any in six months, I might give you a poke myself, provided I turned all gay and everything. Besides, I'm just lookin' out for your best interests. You need all the help you can get."

Devon squeezed my hand. "He's doing okay the way he is, Harry. But I appreciate what a loyal friend you are, and if you ever get glaucoma, I'll be glad to share him occasionally. Maybe Tuesdays and Thursdays."

Everyone at the table snickered, but I was the one holding Devon's hand, so screw 'em.

Becky went off to do bartenderly things, Miguel's eyes following her like hunger. Wooly Bob began a long, roundabout story concerning depilation gone wrong that involved three cans of outdoor bug repellant, a Syrian currycomb, an epidermal sponge, and too long in a tanning machine. The result: a radioactive-red Wooly Bob just in time for his driver's license photo. He flipped out his wallet and passed it around the table to the horror and delight of us all. We were used to it. Devon took it in stride. I liked that about her. I liked a lot of things about her.

Lila's name came up somewhere in conversation, and I froze. I'd forgotten, for a moment, and I felt guilty. And frustrated. Devon let go of my hand and stared at me curiously, with a forensic look in her eye. Nothing angry, simply searching. She nodded, and I got up and went to get another drink. Harry followed me over, gliding on the emotional currents like a hawk. Becky had a shot waiting for me, and I held it in my hand, studying it, the color of the liquor, the droplet balanced carefully on the lip of the glass, ready to fall to one side or the other with a breath. I drank it all down in a gulp.

"Your next move the vet?" ventured Harry, though where he got the info I wasn't sure.

"You reading my files again?" I didn't care and should've known, but I didn't and felt a step or two behind the game. "Doesn't matter. Nothing much there yet."

"You're moving forward. That's all you can do. One shit-kicking foot in front of the other. We could go by and take a looksee at the animal doc, maybe put the fear of God and the IRS into him. I work cheap." He smiled his shark grin. "For friends, I'll even work for free."

I knew I was going to see O'Bannon, but wasn't sure I should use backup. Although in a weird way my quest for Lila's murderer was sanctioned by the powers of truth, justice, and the American way, it didn't make me feel friendly or ready to risk anyone other than myself if it turned bad. And I knew what bad looked like firsthand in that thing.

Harry knew all that well enough about me. "You gotta take someone. Can't huff and puff and blow his house down without someone there to hold your coat. Just plain good manners."

Not like he wasn't right; something in me fought the correct and obvious there. Something small and furtive that wanted to slink below the radar and burrow down in the sand and never come up for air. Something desperate.

Devon waltzed up with a smile. "I'm going. I'm the 'got-your-back' girl the doctor ordered." She turned to me. "So, where we going?"

***

Three hours of flight time, one cramped meal complete with altitude gas, a nice warm Devon sitting next to me, and we arrived in Tucson and rented a metal-magenta Prius—"These things get great mileage," Devon said—and drove out to *We'll Care Well Veterinary Care*. Doctor O'Bannon D.V.M., specializing in exotic animal medicine, theriogenology, and poultry husbandry.

"What's theriogenology?" my sidekick asked.

I didn't know. Maybe something to do with St. Francis of Assisi, or not. Didn't really matter, probably.

Devon and I walked into the vet's office, greeted by a strong, ammonia-cat-piss smell, combined with musty dog scent, barking, a gaggle of chickens that tried to make a break out the open door—"Close the door! Quick!"

A mastiff-sized macaw perched on a coat rack on the left of the entrance swiveled its head our way and said, "Do I know you? Do I know you? Do I know you?"

Behind the front desk flustered an over-harried receptionist who ran from one side of the room-length counter to the other juggling folders and a phone.

Devon glanced over at me and shrugged. Then her eye caught, on one side of the reception area, the cages full of dogs, cats, two rabbits, and a bevy of guinea pigs—all looking for owners.

"Look!" She sprinted over, dodging the chickens like a broken-field running back. "What a sweetie!" She nose-to-nosed a friendly dachshund that licked her cheek. "You're a *good* dog is what you are."

The chickens ebbed and flowed around her legs making an avian ruckus while leaving avian whitewash everywhere. Devon moved onto another cage, that one full of a pitiable terrier that appeared so torpid it could have been comatose.

"Ah, what a cute furball. Hey, you!"

She reached fingers in and scratched the mutt's tummy until the dog raised an eyelid, took a blissed look, and went back to snoozin'. Devon kept cage hopping.

"I need a dog. Let's get one."

"Let's, as in 'us' let's?"

Devon smiled back at me in anticipation, "Sure. Unless you're a cat man. I can do cats, too."

Devon found a bigger cage off in the corner with a bigger dog in it. Or what was left of a bigger dog. Old, with bronchitis—the pile of fur and bones gave a death rattle cough—only six teeth, crazy jibbity-jibbity eyes, mange over the back half of its skeletal body, and a yellow-brown crust on its muzzle that looked like regurgitated liver. Its *own* liver. Devon fell in love immediately.

"*That's* the one! Isn't he a lover?" The dilapidated canine began a long, drawn-out series of coughs punctuated with a sneeze that rocked the room. "Aw, he likes me!"

Fortuitously, the vet's assistant—Zelda, according to her nametag—took that moment to acknowledge me. "Yeah? You coming to drop off or pick up?"

I pulled out my wallet and slithered out my IRS identification, an odd bit of plastic that never failed to make some sort of impression. Zelda's eyes grew full-moon wide and guilty. Good. Always nice to immediately have the upper hand. Gives a man a sense of entitlement, and who was I to fight privilege?

"We're going to buy that dog in the corner!" chirped Devon before I could get a word off in intimidation.

Zelda eyed Devon as if she were booby-hatch insane.

"El Repollo?"

That stopped Devon's headlong charge for about five seconds, then she recovered, intrigued, "El Repollo? What does that mean?"

Zelda, in the long-suffering manner of the true storyteller, started slowly. "The Cabbage." She'd hooked Devon.

"The Cabbage? Why 'The Cabbage?'"

As straight-lines go, it was a lob for me. "Because he smells like old cabbage?"

Devon did not look amused.

"He was one of the Mexico City police department's finest drug-sniffing dogs. Dr. O'Bannon took him in as a personal favor to the mayor when El Repollo was retired."

The dog gave another massive sneeze, shaking the windows of the office. "Definitely sniffed more than he should of. But why 'The Cabbage?'"

I *needed* to know by that time.

Zelda shook her head and crossed herself. "You don't want to know. I don't want to know. Nobody wants to know."

"We're getting him," Devon said. "He's a fixer-upper." She looked at me, "Just like you."

Zelda shook her head but readied a stack of paperwork to fill in and sign and a clipboard to backstop it. I waved my id at her again, lest she forget who the real boss was. Caught between a chance to unload El Repollo and the distinct possibility of shame-faced sins against the federal government, Zelda gave in to her inner criminal.

"The guy at H & R Block swore that my reverse French manicures were a business write-off." She flashed her black-and-wine fingernails like semaphores. "See? My hands are my life."

The phone rang and Zelda froze. Answer? Not answer? Which was right? I nodded my head at the phone, and she gratefully answered it, taking an appointment for a dyspeptic Lhasa Apso as fast as her little words could carry her, then refocused on me. I waited. Zelda's tension built.

"And...well, maybe I didn't really sell my car for only fifty dollars. But I needed the money real wicked. Not that the Doc pays bad, but a girl's gotta take care of things, you know."

Devon scribbled deep into the papers, oblivious of my little conversation with Zelda, but she knew why we were really there, so I figured part of this was "cover" in Devon's world of espionage. And she liked dogs. Obviously a lot more than I knew.

I tilted my head toward the back of the vet office, the nut-clipping, nail-trimming, Rottweiler tail-bobbing medical area.

"I'm not here for you, but I do suggest you try to be more honorable next April fifteenth. Uncle Sam frowns on fibs."

Zelda nodded like a bobble-head.

"It's the doc I want to see. I have a couple of questions for him."

The little furry hamsters in Zelda's head stopped abruptly on their rusty wheel, leaving her completely confused.

"Doctor O'Bannon? He *couldn't* do anything wrong. His daughter died."

"I know. First Lieutenant Gloria O'Bannon. Did time overseas."

"Yeah. Her picture's over there."

A cute but goofy-smiled young woman in army dress uniform, proud of her shoulder board, looked back from the gold frame. Blue eyes, a splatter of freckles. Looked like a good kid. What the hell had she gotten into? I walked over and studied it closer. Nothing in her attitude said "illegal," not that there should be. Still, why her? And why cows?

"I'm gonna just tiptoe back and say hello to the doc. Okie-dokie?"

Zelda, trapped by guilt and a desire to avoid a corn-holing audit something fierce, didn't say a thing.

I went through the heavy, steel-reinforced, self-closing door and got slammed in the face by a two-by-four of animal miasma: dog farts, cat piss, guinea-pig droppings, and bird crap. All animals great and smelly jammed in, yammering away like a zoological orchestra tuning up. A sloe-eyed orangutan wearing a camo boonie hat sat on a stool in the corner drinking from a canteen and flicking its long-horned black fingers at a calico kitten that nipped between the bars of a nearby cage.

A twenty-foot-long reticulated python (I knew 'cause little Marky was a reptile freak growing up and had memorized every kind of constrictor and its length and geographical location) lay coiled on the main table between two vet assistants in green scrubs, one an ex-basketball-player-looking Serbian guy a good six-eight, the other a beach-ball-round, cruelly sunburned woman with bottle-blond hair and three diamond studs to each nostril, and even more to each ear. They wrestled with the python, trying to force a turkey baster down its throat and splash some Pepto Bismol-pink goo into its gullet. The snake refused, trying instead to pass a piece of a vet assistant down as an alternative, its horsey head snapping, its coils looping up, grappling for a hold. However much these two made wasn't enough in my book.

The basketball star glanced up at me: "You're not supposed to be back here."

"Yes, actually, I am," I stated categorically. I learned back in the Marines that bullshit expressed with authority usually passed for truth, or at least authoritative bullshit. "O'Bannon is where?"

The assistants looked at each other, unsure. At that moment, the snake decided to inveigle itself of the advantage and sneak away in the confusion. No luck.

"He's in surgery. Put on a mask," replied Basketball Jonesović, more intent on getting a grip on the python than anything having to do with me, though he gestured to another door with his elbow.

I spotted a box of masks, grabbed one and went through the next door.

Close to a thousand pounds of thoroughbred meat and bone, fileted up the middle with its intestines tabled out for repair like earthworms on a rainy-day sidewalk lay on the operating table, lights blazing down like little suns. One assistant in green scrubs held an acrylic-clear mask over the horse's muzzle, I assume passing anesthesia to the galloper, another checked a Mission Control cart of machines and gizmos that blinked and sputtered and lit up.

Doc O'Bannon in white smock, white hair sticking out grizzled from beneath his surgeon's cap, a sharp, officious nose, and thick-lensed glasses, probed and massaged a link of intestine like a man squeezing toothpaste from a tube.

"The blockage is here. Scalpel and cut."

He held his hand out, a scalpel slapped in, then began slicing into the intestine lengthwise, parting it like a sausage skin, a mass of green and brown silage bursting out in volcanic ooze. The room exploded with the stink of putrification.

"Definitely bad through and through. May have to take out a whole section of this hose."

Collecting the intestinal sewage in a metal pan, it kept exuding out, unstoppable and rotten. At one point, the mass turned black.

"Have the bleeding section now. I'm surprised this horse hadn't fallen down dead a week ago. What have they been feeding the damn thing, peanut butter?"

I watched quietly from the side, the doctor glancing up at me for a moment, then disregarding my presence and finishing his operation, finally stitching the equine up and leaving the final bandaging to an assistant. He then walked straight to me.

"What the heck are you doing in my OR?"

I smiled, realized I had a mask on and he couldn't see my smile, and smiled some more. "Doctor O'Bannon...I want to speak to you about cows."

He stared at me, and I tried to recall if he'd put the scalpel down when he'd finished on the horse. I figured: probably. Nothing I could do about it at that point anyway. He jerked his head toward the door and walked off. I followed.

We walked through the orangutan room—"Hey"—the ape high-fived the doc, then into a side room, O'Bannon's office. Wood bookshelves and big books, wooden desk with a picture frame, family picture. O'Bannon peeled off his scrubs, gloves, and mask and sat down behind his desk. He popped open a mini-fridge and pulled out a bottled water, sucking half of it down before looking over at me.

"You have some cows you need me to look at?"

"*You* have some cows I need to look at."

He had the same features as his daughter, but old and tired. "You police?"

I shook my head.

"F-B-I?"

I shook my head again.

"You're somebody, though."

I nodded.

"Why do you want to know about cows?"

"Because they got a friend of mine killed, and your daughter, too. So...why cows? Who cares so much about a bunch of walking T-bones?"

I watched O'Bannon's shoulders sag, "Why'd you figure the cows?"

"Because no one else does. Your daughter know a Colonel Dax? Or Private Keene? You know, they hang out at the same tapas bar in

Ulan Bator. Maybe hoist a Kumis or two to the red, white, and blue? Decide that, hey, the next big thing would be Kobe Beef?"

O'Bannon finished off the rest of his water in one long nervous swallow.

I kept going. "I know you know something, and you haven't told anyone, but you're going to tell me because you *have* to. Because now you only have your life to worry about, and maybe by now that's not worth much anymore."

O'Bannon surrendered, just like that, and I finally heard the who, what, when, where, and why of Lila having to die.

"Gloria asked me if I knew about animal quarantine regulations, bringing beef in across borders. She told me that she'd met some investors, and she and a couple other army buddies joined up to float a business. Beef in, beef out." O'Bannon began fiddling with a paperclip, bending one end back and forth until it snapped, then he began on another. "Didn't seem like much of a business to me, not that many cows, even if they were Kobe. Still, I didn't see the harm in it."

I eyed O'Bannon, listening to the tone, not the words. A ten-ton weight crushed his recital, needing all his energy to drag it out from under the ruins of his emotions. "But you did find some harm. Somewhere along the line."

"We work with radioisotopes sometimes, with some of the larger animals, especially race horses. Just like in humans: track intestinal disorders, strokes, that sort of thing. It's all pretty mild stuff, but we're required to keep track and follow the rules. Gloria's cows came through here as a quarantine holding station. Saved her some money was what I figured, thinking her old man'd give her a break. Which I did."

"And they were all healthy? No extra heads. They didn't shit gold or anything?"

"No. Seemed fine. Got through the inspections, stayed the quarantine, shipped 'em out like Gloria told me to. Not much to it really."

I led him along like an angler a hesitant trout. "But something happened to change your mind."

"A cow began showing signs of what I thought was intestinal obstruction. Happens more with horses, but cows get it too. So, not wanting Gloria to lose money, I prepped the animal for a full barium

115

enema examine, rolled it into X-ray and took a look. Never seen anything like it. The whole back end of the cow was lit up like Fourth of July."

"The cow was radioactive?"

"The cow was *carrying* something radioactive, stowed up its vaginal cavity, then sewn shut."

"Un-fuckin'-believable. Something was stuffed up its yoo-hoo? What?"

"A sphere of plutonium in a stainless steel container."

"Shi-i-i-i-it. You opened it up to find out?"

"It's not something you find up a cow's vagina every day. Gloria was dead a week later. Carved up by some sadistic murderer."

"What'd you do?"

"Stuck it back up the cow, put in a few sutures and moved on. Now I don't even bother to look when they come through, the money still flowing through Gloria's accounts. I know. I'm the executor. It's a lot of money."

"And no one says anything to you? Ask questions?"

"Not a word. My daughter's dead. What do they need to say?"

"Then why are you telling me if you didn't tell the police before? You like my face?"

"No. Simply think I don't care anymore. Now. And then you come along asking about the cows, which no one else did. And I'm still passing them through, not saying anything."

He shook his head, then shook it again: a man too late to make a difference, too scared to try when he needed to, too out of his league to understand. I empathized a little. I was two steps behind myself, but I wasn't giving up for shit or shineola.

"Where do the cows go from here?"

Before O'Bannon could answer, the sound of Noah's Ark exploded out in the waiting room. Then gunshots. I may not know my Basenji bark from my Catalburun growl, but I damn well connoisseured Lorcin semiautomatics. Another shot. And Mossberg twelve gauges. Someone didn't want me talkin' to the doc, and they'd come to make sure.

Screams; more shots.

"What the fuck!?"

Then shots in the very next room. Two. Two more.

"Kill it! Kill it!"

I knew someone wasn't as fond of snakes as I was. O'Bannon almost yelled, but I shut him down with a look, nodded to a filing cabinet and didn't wait for him to get behind it. I found a set of ceremonial scalpels set in a Vet of the Year Award, chose the biggest and slipped it in my back pocket, hefted a chair, took a deep breath, and busted into the other room like a bull into a china shop—this being a veterinarian's office, perhaps almost an apt description.

One man, dressed casual—jeans, work shirt, gun—screamed, high-pitched and warbling as if he'd run out of air a minute before but couldn't stop expelling more. The python had half the man's arm in its mouth and wasn't letting go. His partner—more upscale in tan Dockers and a Glock—kept blasting the snake, which was deader than a dead snake doorknob. But it didn't let go. That's the thing about pythons. And snapping turtles. And gators. The jaws clamp shut and lock until death and beyond.

The two vet assistants lay on the ground, heads covered and frightened. The orangutan looked on in serene benevolence, a furry Buddha. Me, I swung that chair like John Henry a hammer, and laid out the second man with the Glock and left his buddy to the python. The orangutan held his big black mitt up in space. "High five!" I slapped it good. Who am I to not high-five a friendly Orangutan? I gripped my chair tighter and got ready to charge the waiting room.

"What's happening?" yelled the woman assistant over the python man's screaming, still down on the floor, cowering, snake guts and blood spewed all over her.

"Heck if I know, but I'm going to find out." I looked at the screaming man, then turned to Basketball Star. "You don't happen to have any tranquilizers, you know, for elephants or something?"

Quick on the uptake, he loaded up a syringe and blasted the man, who instantly stopped screaming, his eyes going dreamy, then fell to the floor, his arm still held by the snake, making him look like an opiated kindergartener asking permission from his teacher to go to the bathroom. The two assistants began levering the python's jaws open; the inside didn't look too good: where's Ice Cube when you need him? But by then, I'd already moved on.

And kept moving until I hit the reception area, chair at the ready, and faced five guys with six guns. "Never bring a chair to a gunfight..."

Bits of splintered furniture, the feathers of the old macaw fluttering in the air—the bird, bloodied and with a crippled wing, kept reciting, "Do I know you? Do I know you?"—people huddled with their animals on the floor, trying to root their way into corners and hide under chairs, Zelda the receptionist peeking over the front counter like a kid with a periscope, then ducking down, chickens running around like... er...chickens.

Devon sat wide-eyed, unmoved, staring at me as I came out. Six guns and me holding a chair. A nice rolly office chair with lumbar support and a neck rest, but still not much against guns. I did the only thing I could: I stalled.

I nodded to the back. "Doc's back there, but he's workin' on a horse's ass. Seriously. Kinda disgusting. You might want to wait till he's done."

And then a chicken pecked at my shoe. I looked down, and it pecked again. Definitely trying to tell me something, I thought, and I punted it to the far end zone. The guns boomed, the chicken squawked once and exploded in a hail of feathers and giblets, and I swung my trusty chair, lumbar support and all.

I took the first guy down and let the chair's momentum carry my body into the second guy, who I clotheslined with my opposite arm, right across the neck. I heard the clank as his gun hit the floor and turned to spot it, but my foot hit the remains of that damn chicken, and, as I went for the gun, my legs went out from under me like bowling pins to a bowling ball. I managed to grab the gun, but I knew it was too late.

The tearing of metal like paper, a deep ancestral growl that hindbrained the hairs on my arms upright, the smell of fur and kibble, a flash of bronchial phlegm, and one hundred and twenty pounds of canine muscle and bone flew past me and chomped its jaws on the gun of the nearest man pointing it at me. And swallowed the gun!

El Repollo had burst free from his cage and began tearing up the gunmen like a machine gun nest on Okinawa. Mesmerizing. That dog did things with its teeth and claws that movie special effects couldn't begin to envision. Going from one to the next, barely a touch to the ground, he tore free guns, bit at crotches and even peed a few times to mark his territory. But a last man had him dead to rights from across the room. I put three slugs into the guy, good groupings, and that, as they say, was that. Now I knew what a Mexico City police department drug-sniffing dog did. Seven up, seven down, no hits, no walks, no errors.

Wheezing and coughing, El Repollo shook himself, sweat, slobber, and blood flying everywhere, then lay down and began licking his balls. A warrior through and through.

Everyone looked on in shock. A little awe. A little nausea. And then there was Devon. "You kicked a chicken."

"Damn straight. It was the chicken or me."

"What'd that chicken ever do to you?"

Everyone began unwinding from the floor. Zelda, still behind the counter, frantically 911'd it. El Repollo continued to lick.

"It was an innocent chicken just being a chicken."

"You *did* notice the guns and everything, right?"

El Repollo finished slavering and hunkered over to me, licking my face. "Christ! I *know* where that tongue's been. Get away from me!"

The dog merely flopped over and laid its head in my lap, wanting a scratch.

"See, he likes you. *And* he saved your life. I knew he was the one. Scratch behind his ears. He likes that." Devon smiled, thoroughly pleased with herself.

So I scratched behind El Repollo's ears and waited for the police to arrive. Doc O'Bannon finally peeked out from his OR, seeing the destruction and the men on the floor, and asked if the "coast was clear." Swear ta God, "Is the coast clear?" For one brief shining moment I could see Zelda about to un-receptionist his ass with a double barrel of WTF, as in "what the F were you doing hiding in the back?" or "what the F do you think, we're all dead?"

But then, despite the fact that the office looked like a Kansas Petco after a tornado, despite the fact there were dead and dog-bitten, gun-wielding thugs on the floor and pet owners cowering in the corners, despite all that is holy and grounds for rebuttal in a WTF way, Zelda realized that she still needed to come into work the next day, and mouthing off to the boss probably wasn't going to get her the raise she counted on.

"All clear, Doctor O'Bannon."

With a sound like a quick exhale, the hint of glass, and the thump of screwdriver puncturing a papaya, a two-finger hole blossomed in Doc O'Bannon's forehead like a period at the end of a sentence. A straight line back from the hole led to a similar hole in the vet office front window just between the "E" in "Care" and the "W" in "Well." Which led back to a forgettable-looking man in a forgettable-looking car: Honda Accord, automotive choice of snipers, psychopaths, and eunuchs. The man slowly backed out of his parking slot, looking both ways, checking his mirrors—you know, following the rules of the road. After shooting the vet from one hundred fifty yards away. He didn't look up in a movie moment where we locked eyes, each silently wrestling with the other's will. Nope, he simply drove away quiet as can be. But I *knew* who he was: Juju Klondike.

Zelda probably should've WTF'd it. I know that's undoubtedly what Doc O'Bannon would've asked if he were alive. WTF? And the sounds of police sirens filled the air.

12.

The flight home cost almost double the flight there. After hours with the police—lots of coffee, not enough "eats," a surreptitious call from Juarez that left us in the clear even though the Arizona boys were none too happy about that—Devon insisted on buying a seat for El Repollo, despite his doggie carrier and quite adequate accommodations in the hold.

"If it's so nice, why don't *you* fly down there?" she plied with the Socratic Method.

Who was I to argue with a dead Greek suicide?

The mutt coughed up mucus the whole way and sounded like an asthmatic steam engine. On the plus side, the whiny little brat in the seat in front who kept looking over the back of the headrest and leaking his snotty nose on my tray got the Fear of the Lord from an El Repollo growl. His mother wanted to report the dog to some all-encompassing Animal Control In The Sky, or at least the flight attendants, but I whipped out my IRS identification and mentioned that if *she* reported the dog, I'd report *her*. She shut the heck up right quick (*everybody's* got a guilty conscience when it comes to taxes) and muzzled her drippy-nosed child. Plus one for the pooch. I gave him a piece of his Salisbury steak dinner, and he woofed it down without chewing. I ate his Oreo cookies.

Devon smiled. "We're just one big happy family."

El Repollo farted something fierce.

We touched down in Sacto almost on time, and I nearly herniated a testicle getting the mutt to the curb, where we loosed him to take a whiz on the taxi-stand sign. He then coughed up a gob of green-brown lung juice the size of a cantaloupe and looked for a cat to chase. Or eat. Or something. How do I know what a dog thinks? Then he began sniffing his butt.

"Aw look, he's happy," said Devon, who seemed immune to airplane/airport fatigue. Not to mention long waits at police stations.

I flagged a dirty green-and-white gypsy cab—"Dog extra. Dog extra."—and loaded us in. Yajuke Talmund wheeled out into traffic and began a long dissertation on the scariness of the Burger King king character in those commercials. Nightmares. The shakes. Constipation. All that from a thirty-second commercial.

"But make good double burgers. I like no pickles."

Weaving into, out of and directly in line with the flow of cars, I realized that with Doc O'Bannon dead, Juju's next move would be toward me. How he found out about who I was would be telling. I try not to be too public of a guy. Though I do use Gmail, I don't use Facebook, don't Tweet for shit or money, and chastity belt my router with a customized firewall. But I realize nothing is sacred, or private, anymore if push comes to shove. But the "how" is important. The "how" could tell me lots. Like: Why Juju'd been so sloppy? Why didn't he kill the Doc quietly and messily like Lila? How would they move the cows now? Or is it that they had all the plutonium they needed? Which meant what?

Focusing on the unfocusable, I missed the part where Devon told the driver to head to my apartment. Which he did after going the wrong way in an alley, scraping the side of the taxi against a garbage truck and cursing: "May the Burger King king haunt your dreams!"

On pulling up in a burning miasma of smoking brakes, he gave a gap-toothed smile and demanded "twenty percent for good driving." I paid, simply because I didn't have the energy to face the consequences, then told him to take "the lady" on to her destination and slipped him another twenty. But Devon blithely unloaded the taxi with a magician's assistant's efficiency.

"I thought you'd go back to your place," I said.

Devon shook her head with a pitying forbearance usually associated with nurses to terminal patients and corrected me, "I have to get Polli settled."

"At *my* house?"

The dog let rip with a fart that sounded like a combination of foghorn and dying yak. Smelled like that, too.

"No, no, no...that's *your* dog," I said. "*You* picked it. *You* keep it. I don't have time for a dog. I work nine-to-five. For the *government*. They're very particular about tardiness."

Yajuke Talmund revved the engine: "You go? You stay? Meter running. Double Whopper awaits."

I tried to drag El Repollo by the leash, but the dog applied Newton's First Law of Motion with extreme prejudice. I couldn't budge him.

"Okay—you stay, I go. Ma`a as-salaamah—may the king of burgers protect you."

Off he went, my extra twenty clutched in his fist. Devon clicked her tongue, and El Repollo shambled up to his feet, passed wind again, and wobbled toward my place. I dutifully grabbed the pet carryall, along with everything else and followed.

The dog lapped water from my only salad bowl, the koa wood one shaped like the island of Kauai, while Devon looked on proudly.

"He likes it here. I can tell."

"Devon, I can't take care of him."

"That's okay. I will. You just have to give me your extra key."

Extra key? "Wait, wait, wait. My extra key?"

"Sure. I'll come watch Polli and feed him during the day, and you can take care of him in the morning and evenings."

"I drink. A lot. In the evenings."

"Okay—I can swing by in the evenings, too. I can even fix something for you, if you want. I'm a whiz at French rustic as well as Malaysian and Javanese. I took classes." She volunteered that with the cheer of a candy striper on her first day.

Something did not compute. Give my key to a woman? Get free meals? And I hadn't slept with her yet? No, that wasn't right—went against every code of personal male ethics I'd ever heard of.

"Something's not right here. Why can't *you* keep the mutt?"

"Because you'd never come visit, and it would break his little heart." Devon knelt down and scratched behind El Repollo's ears. "Besides, your bed is bigger."

My bed? At that moment, El Repollo took off like a smelly dragster, straight to my bedroom, leaping onto the bed and crash-landing amongst my pillows. Slobber and drool flew like ocean spray. I could tell it wasn't going to be a good thing. But then Devon came up behind me and put her arms around my waist, pushing herself up against my back in a way that left no doubt she was happy...and as God made her.

"Okay, maybe he can stay here. But I don't even know what Malaysian food *is*."

"You're going to love it. You will be one with the lychee."

Great. A girl. A dog. And now a lychee. When did my life get so complicated?

At that moment, my cell phone started chiming its pipsqueak yelp, and I noticed it was Juarez. Let the games begin!

***

Where did he find these places? Rundown, dirt cheap, little vestigial pockets of yesterday's diners backwatered and forgotten with a vengeful Alzheimer's and torn sheets from the Yellow Pages. Greasy spoons hidden under modern society's rocks until Juarez turned them over, revealing them to the light of day. Ozzie and Harriet funeral homes of recipes gone to die. And there we sat, hopefully as overlooked as the food.

"Tabasco. Gotta put more Tabasco on it."

Juarez had already swimming-pooled his beef hash and eggs, mopping the sides with toast smeared thick with butter and strawberry jelly. He stuck two sticky fingers into his mouth to clean them, then plunged back into his fight with breakfast.

I looked down at my stack of blueberry pancakes and smelled childhood.

"So what'd you find out?"

"Got his name in Venezuela," food-mouthed Juarez.

"Who?"

"Your dog. El Repollo. It means—"

"The cabbage. Yeah, got that already. In Venezuela?"

"Took me a lot of digging into a lot of double-locked, sphincter-tight files. Seems it was a joint Mexican/Venezuelan raid, and the forces of right came under heavy fire, pinned down in a cabbage patch by about a hundred dopers popping up with AO-63s all blazin' away. Like spittin' into a fan. No one coulda gotten out alive. Too many bullets firing too fast. Then the dog went bat shit muther-humpin' crazy and killed all hundred of the poor bastards. Invisible, all teeth and fur. Not one left standing. Not one left alive. El Repollo: the cabbage. He's a legend."

"Is that supposed to make me feel good about the mutt in my house? What happens when he gets a flashback from some bad coleslaw and decides my hair's a little long and it's time to taste long pork again?"

Juarez shrugged, picked up the Tabasco sauce and popped a few drops into his coffee. "Don't look at me. I'm a cat person."

I shook my head in disgust.

"I bet you don't have even a teeny-weenie kitten. You're not a cat person. You're not a dog person. You're not even a person person. You're just a Fed."

He sipped from his coffee and smacked his lips with pleasure. "I like my women like I like my coffee..."

"What, bitter and with a kick?"

He took another sip, "Mmm, spicy."

Juarez pushed a manila folder my way, tracks of spilt syrup slug-trailing behind it. I flipped it open and saw an artist's rendition of my description of Klondike. It was spot on. I lifted it and found a couple of fuzzy INTERPOL shots of him as well, each one under a different alias, short concise descriptions tacked with the shots and possible criminal activities. No one had put two plus two together and gotten Juju. Until me.

Juarez smiled his constipated smile, the one that meant ill will and satisfaction both at once. "It's him. We know him now. I've sent reports to damn near all and sundry from the head of my bureau to every Tom, Dick, and sheriff from Barstow, California, to Berrysburg, Pennsylvania. I have the foreigners on it, as well as the three-letter cloak-and-dagger boys. Plutonium *not* good, so nobody likes Klondike right now. He's the big bad wolf and a half. We'll get him."

I pushed the file back to him and snagged a sausage off my plate, chomping on its juicy goodness but not tasting it at all. "Is that before or after he gets yours truly?"

Shrugged Juarez. "Either way works for me, though probably not for you. Besides, I thought you badass, mo-fo Marines could take care of yourselves. Semper Fido and all that." He snickered at his bad pun, far too delighted.

"Look, I know he's coming. But *how's* he coming? Who's feeding him the inside scoop? And don't say 'Mongs,' 'cause last I checked, they didn't have access to government computers with telephone numbers and addresses of IRS employees. I don't expect the FBI to babysit me, but you should be good for *something*."

Juarez held his hands up in surrender. "Got your phones tapped, your mail read, your e-mail copied, and we have two teams of surveillance escorting you to and from work."

I raised my eyebrow at that last one.

"Okay, *three* teams. Didn't think you'd spot the surfer in the old El Camino. There's a manhunt for the radioactives, and as soon as they turn up, I think you're in the clear."

"You haven't a clue, do you?"

"Not a one, but we're working on it. I may have to buy a vowel though. Look, you're government, I'm government, you know these things take time." He motioned to the rest of my order. "You gonna pack that up in a doggie bag?" He cracked himself up to no end.

I rose, then paused, a thought having struck me with the weight of a sledgehammer on a watermelon. "What if they don't need any more plutonium?"

Juarez stopped guffawing and looked up at me, a hint of intelligence back in his eyes. "Then what do they need?"

Juarez, despite many shortcomings of the humor-related kind, was never slow. "Everybody needs money, yeah? And who has money but needs it laundered?"

***

I finally got smart about flying back and forth to places that the IRS really had no good reason to be going, and I gotta tell ya, having access to one of Tiny's planes could spoil a working Joe like me. Normally, I'd either have to drive all night to root around or jigger up some complicated paper trail that somehow needed my unraveling, as I did to get out to see the late and orangutan-friendly Doc O'Bannon. And that trick only worked once. A single phone call to Tiny's incredibly efficient assistant Zuzu and I was whisking my way back to Phoenix.

Part of the itchy-scratchy idea going on in my hindbrain took advantage of the fact that O'Bannon and Rodney both operated in the same city, a very happy coincidence. It meant that the Mongs and

Klondike wouldn't think twice if a source of money reared its laundry head in their vicinity.

A couple of black-suits of Juarez's persuasion met me at the airport and wheeled me off in a dark-star Ford with windows tinted so black they might as well have been metaled over. I doubted they rolled down. One black-suit was named John, and the other was named John as well. No last names. Feds are a yuck a minute. They'd been "lent" to me in case I needed any surveillance or apprehending powers...or a spiffy car that I couldn't see out of. Despite Eggs Benedict, fresh orange juice, and two espressos on the plane (hey, Tiny could cover me without my having to worry about him), I still had a craving for a nosh, so I made the FBI run me through the Jack In The Box drive-through window for a couple of tacos. Jack makes some great greasy tacos, and I wolfed them down without complaint. John-squared didn't want any. Probably Mickey D fans.

It was fortunate the Fed car had great air conditioning, as the Fahrenheit started soaring early in the day and kept climbing. Dry heat, wet heat—heat is heat in my book, and once it rockets past ninety and heads for a hundred, I'm just looking for a place to curl up and die. The back seat of the Fed car seemed as good a place as any. The Johns didn't secrete a drop of perspiration, no doubt slathered up in deodorant and antiwetness goodness from pointy heads to cloven hooves. I didn't really need FBI help in any way, shape, or form, but as chauffeurs, they couldn't be faulted. So off we went to find Rodney.

The Clean As A Whistle #26 dry cleaners stood right across the street from the Up And At 'Em strip club in downtown Phoenix. Painted bright orange with black trim, it looked like a jack o'lantern with a pituitary problem. I figured it to be Rodney's main hopping-off point because half his credit-card charges were going to the Up And At 'Em—not-so-cleverly disguised as business deductions. Couldn't fault a man for liking titties, even if he did claim them as "operating costs." I would've allowed that for the strippers themselves, but never for the clientele.

Only a fifteen-minute wait and Rodney appeared. Imagine five feet nine inches of toothpaste trying to shove itself back into a tube of immaculately clean Adidas purple-and-gray Phoenix Suns nylon sweats a size too small and cinched tight around the ballooning midriff, yet creased to perfection down the front, and you start to get an idea of what Rodney Gloucester looked like. The prerequisite Steve Nash MVP Nike Zoom basketball shoes (only sold in Canada) weighed down his feet, and he'd shoved an Arizona Diamondbacks cap back-to-front on his head. Rodney sported a retro-70's semi-fro that sprouted out the sides of his cap and padded it up a good couple of inches. I just *knew* there was an almighty bald spot sprouting on the crown of his be-capped head. Made sense. Without waiting for the light to change, Rodney juked-and-jived across the street, waving at approaching cars like a demented crosswalk guard, and finally shimmied to the other side, safe to enter the strip club.

"You guys wanna see some titties?" I smiled to the Feds. "I'm paying."

The Johns shook their heads in unison, and I shrugged, popped the door lock and stepped out of the car, only to be sledgehammered by the heat. The strip club, if they had NASA certified-air conditioning, was looking better and better. At the door, a six-foot-by-six-foot skinhead greeted me with a gap-tooth smile and a cover-charge explanation.

"Cover charge without lunch, no cover charge with lunch. Lunch is fish and chips, but I'm not so sure about what kind of fish...just so you know."

I thanked him and went with the cover charge. Hey, a couple of Jack tacos and I'm good for the day.

Dark in a covering-up-the-blemishes and cold sores kind of way, the inside of the Up And At 'Em was a décor-cross between an early MTV video circa 1982 and a rundown double-wide. The red vinyl booths looked stolen from a Rock Hudson film, while the bar's post-Impressionist cowboy fashion sense had to have been cribbed from a drunken John Ford stupor.

A handful of tired-eyed girls with tasseled breasts and underwear bottoms sporting the days of the week dragged their way through the lunch crowd of bleary businessmen, class-cutting collegiates, and a couple of suit-and-tie lawyer-types who were downing the highballs with gusto.

Up on stage, the featured dancer, a bubble-butted Cuban with bowling ball breasts that looked about as well-rolled, humped the stripper pole like a dog rubbing its ass on shag carpet, all to the beat of Peggy Lee's "You Was Right Baby." An eclectic choice that I could appreciate, if not completely be aroused by. But then again, I was not the professional there. She tossed mirror-practiced *moues* at the customers that enticed dollar bills to the edge of the stage, where she squatted down like a yogi having to pee, rubbing them against her crotch and feigning to do more. All in all, rather more phlegmatic than foxy.

I caught sight of Rodney getting a groin-grinding lap dance at the far side of the bar, the girl knocking her two-sizes-too-fake tits in Rodney's face like fish-slapping in a seal contest. It looked painful, but the Rodster had a beatific smile on his puss, eyes closed for his countdown to ecstasy. I hated to ruin the moment, but business was business and action was action. I fished a fifty out of my wallet—petty cash is a wonderful thing—and windshield wipered it in front of the girl's face.

"Can you grab me a scotch, straight up, and a beer for my friend? Keep the change."

The girl scooted off faster than a case of trots south of the border, leaving Rodney to appreciate his *crotchus interruptus.*

"What the flying fuckarama you doing, you sandpaper dildo? We was conversating!"

I slid into the booth next to Rodney and opened fire, figuratively, of course.

"How do you suppose your big brother Desmond would feel about you having conjugal affairs with a nonexistent wife? Maybe he might think it was a little weird? Kinky? Sad? Incriminating?"

Rodney's jaw dropped mid-curse, a hint of self-preservation creeping into his eyes. "Who you? Poh-lice? F-B-motherfuckin'-I?"

I took my wallet out and flashed him my identification. "Worse. I'm with the Internal Revenue Service." I watched his lips pull the initials out of the words, finally understanding. "And we have a little clerical problem with you."

At that moment, Rodney's lap dancer scurried back with my scotch and his beer, all smiles.

"More dancey-dance, Rodney?" she asked, giving her breasts a quick shake that pile-dove them into one another with a loud smack.

He waved her away, still staring at my credentials. "Later, baby doll. Later."

She hurried off, but I called after: "Don't forget to declare your tips on your ten-forty."

Rodney stared at his beer instead of me, contemplating bubbles, no doubt. Or perhaps his feelings about Max Horkheimer's Frankfurt School of neo-Marxist interdisciplinary social theory. Or maybe he just thought I was going to haul his stripper-lovin' ass to jail. Or worse. Fear is sometimes an IRS agent's best friend. Fear and attention to mind-numbingly boring paperwork. But I digress.

"So, Rodney, I'm going to be straight with you because, well...I like a man who can take ten pounds of titty to the head and not bruise."

Rodney gave a crooked smile as he answered, chagrined, "It's somethin' ya gotta works up to. Can't take no double-G's right off the bat."

I smiled back. "It's a gift, I'm sure. Much like what I'm going to offer you."

Rodney's face took "suspicious" to a completely new realm, the corners of his mouth trying to meet somewhere near the point of his chin.

"You and your brother really think the United States government wouldn't catch your little 'illegalities?' I mean, we fight wars and insurgencies, you know? We're a frickin' *government*, man. What do you expect?"

Rodney shook his head. "Little guy can't make no scratch without someone breathin' down his neck. Ain't fair. I got rights."

"Yeah, you keep believing that, Rodney. See how far that gets you."

I glanced over as the featured dancers changed shifts. The new girl looked like a Scandinavian scarecrow with Parkinson's: all blond and quaking like an aspen. She shook and trembled to Onyx's *Slam*. Don't ask me how I knew that. It's an ugly story.

"Now, don't sweat the meth...everyone's gotta get through the day somehow." I took a sip at my scotch, bad and blended. "Points for transportability and all, but that's not my headache."

Rodney sucked at his beer noisily, a splash of foam clinging to his cheek like a fuzzy white mole.

"So you know?"

"The shit I know, Rodney, would keep your bowels clenched unto your great-grandchildren's generation. But it's not my problem."

Rodney looked hopeful. "Really?"

"Naw, I'll let the Feds try to sort that out...if they ever do. Mouth-breathers." I took another sip and it didn't taste any better. "What I have you and your brother on is a little *converting and concealing income from a specified unlawful act.* The I-*do*-care-about-meth's *profits.* Which means I get to take all of your stuff because you didn't pay taxes."

Rodney jumped straight up. "No you not! You *can't* do that! It's *mine!*"

Not a single person in the bar looked our way; the dancer didn't break a quivering stride; the bartender just kept on pouring. Hardcore. I motioned Rodney back on his fat ass.

"Sit. Drink. Relax. This is your lucky day."

Rodney grumbled, "Doesn't feel so damn lucky." He gulped more beer.

Just then, my cell phone rang: Devon. I gestured to our lap dancing drink-bringer for two more, glared at Rodney—"I have to take this. Have another drink. Won't be long."—and answered. "Hey, kiddo. What's up?"

Devon somehow detected I was sitting in the middle of a strip club, and she just wanted to call to see if I were okay. How could she possibly know that? That was positively supernatural...or freakin' suspicious. I assumed Juarez, but Devon explained she just had a sixth sense about nudity. Her mother did, too, which is how she caught her dad trying out for the lead role in the revival of "Oh! Calcutta!" for their local dinner theater.

I mentioned I was on officially sanctioned Internal Revenue Service business, and Devon assured me she understood. She really did sound like she didn't mind.

"I was just worried for some reason," she reiterated. "And I wanted to hear your voice."

Rodney began to snicker, miming a whipping motion. I glared at him, and he quickly realized making fun of an IRS agent probably wasn't his smartest idea. He gulped beer until he was sucking glass. Fortunately, more drinks arrived with half-nakedness.

"Here you go. Another round," chirped the serving girl, waiting for another fifty, which I gave her. Hey, wasn't *my* money.

Devon asked what I was drinking, and we chatted a bit more about strip clubs, strippers, and stripper poles. I finally mentioned I was working, and she brought the conversation to an end with—"You know, mine are much better"—then rang off, completely dumbfounding me.

Rodney hoisted his glass to me. "Women, can't live with them, can't get 'em to give a good blowjob after you marries 'em."

"Which leads us back to your non-existent wife."

If Rodney were a turtle, he would have snapped his head, arms, and legs tight into his shell. Not being a turtle, he reacted as if I had punched him in the stomach.

I calmed him. "Rodney...if I just wanted to mess you up, I wouldn't have come here to have a drink. As much as I admire shapely parts, I can find my own just fine in Sacramento. No, I came here because I like you. We're going to be best buds."

"Like B-F-Fs?"

"Don't do that, Rodney. You aren't an eleven-year-old girl with an iPhone and her first period are you? Jeez, you're in a strip club for Christ's sake. Show some hair on your balls."

"Sorry." He drank more beer and looked remorseful. Always a good sign.

"You're not the 'smart' one in the family, are you? You're more the 'pick up the dog poop on the carpet' one, the 'set the table before dinner' one, right?"

Rodney chewed his thoughts, not liking the taste, but not knowing how to spit them out. "I'm plenty smart, street smart. You know, the University of Hard Knockers."

"And mismangled clichés. Got it."

"Why you up my ass? I thought we were okie-dokie."

"We are Rodney. As okie as a resident of Tulsa, and as dokie as a misspelled Green Day album." I'd lost the Rodster, which was my intention, so I hurried to the point...finally. "I need your help, and brother Desmond's as well, but I don't think Desmond's going to say 'yes' to me. I need you to pick up the dog poop Rodney and help me convince him."

Rodney looked uncomfortable, squirming in his seat and sending up vinyl farts.

"Des don't like anywho's with a badge, you know. And he don't like me talkin' to him about nuthin'. *He* talks to *me*. Desmond's what you might call a 'particular' fellow—he likes things like he likes things."

I finished my second scotch, wondering why I bothered. Heartburn crept up my gullet with groundswell activity.

"But you're the bearer of good news, the bringer of glad tidings, the messenger who you do *not* shoot. You acquaint me to Desmond, and help me to help you help me, and you'll be a goddamn hero."

"I don't know. Des is not what you'd call a 'forgiving' man. I shouldn'ta even be talkin' with you, if you hadn't caught me all unawares and lap danced. Titties got me all confused."

I watched another girl step up onstage to the tune of Modest Mouse's *Float On*. She brought a wanna-be-on-Dancing-With-The-Stars energy, skipping about the stage and high-kicking with Rockette altitude, if revealing a little more gynecology than precision.

"Titties'll do that to you, Rodney. So what do you say? Take me to Desmond and make nicie-nicie, or do I find him myself and tell him that you corn-holed your tax forms and because of that, both you and him are going to not only lose every single bit of everything, but probably be bunk mates for the rest of forever?"

Rodney downed the last of his beer, his Adam's apple chugging up and down like a fleshy piston, then slammed his glass down with finality.

"Can I get the rest of my lap dance first?"

13.

Rodney enjoyed being chauffeured by the FBI twins. He said it was "classy" and "ostentatious," though it took him three tries and a little help on the last word. I told him he could do it more often if he wanted, but he missed the joke. John and John locked sunglass'd eyes on Rodney with kitchen-magnet intensity. I just wanted it to be over and back in Sacramento. The car wasn't bulletproof, and Juju made me nervous.

Rodney used his craptastic, Chinese-knockoff, GPS-enabled smart phone—"Look, I can play that hedgehog game on it!"—to track his brother's free-floating meth lab. Who knew they had an app for that? We finally arrived, unheralded at my request, out in a desert suburb, tract homes on one side, cactus on the other. An eighteen-wheeler camel-humped a two-bedroom, aluminum-sided fixer-upper on its flatbed. A transportable meth lab: would wonders never cease?

The dynamic FBI duo hustled inside without a knock, yelling their business; warrant wired to a front-seat, HP-portable, inkjet printer—neato—guns at the ready. One of the Johns almost smiled, but caught himself at the last moment.

"I thought we were jus' gonna talk to Des," Rodney said in a little-boy whine. "You didn't say nuthin' 'bout guns and warrants and stuff like that. He's gonna be pissed, and I can't see that working out well for me."

I opened the car door, a knockout punch of hot air blasting me.

"Don't worry so much Rodney," I said. "It's bad for the heart. We're guns and warranting it so it looks good. Gotta keep the respect."

Rodney rolled that around his empty head for a while, then a bright, snaggletooth smile lit him up. "Oh, you keepin' it on the down-low. We all hush-hush, makin' everyone *think* it's a bust when it's not. Smooth as Raisinets."

I shook my head and waited. Shouts from inside the house, then the front and back doors crashed open and a half-dozen lab-coat-wearing women of all colors and persuasions (nothing seemingly on under the lab coats) Olympic-medaled out, racing for some jail-free finish line. They carried trashcan-sized Glad bags over their shoulders, a Hansel and Gretel trail of meth following one of the girls from a tear in the corner.

I waited, door open. Rodney began complaining about being hungry, picking at the corner of his mouth with his tongue. I told him I'd buy him lunch if he shut up.

He grumbled, but agreed. "Can we go to the Jack In The Box? I like the tacos."

Finally, surreptitiously, a figure appeared in the shadows, crouched under the flatbed truck. It looked about, then stood up and began nonchalantly sauntering over to the sidewalk. Dressed in black trousers with cuffs, a white, button-down shirt and gunmetal-gray cardigan despite the heat, Desmond Gloucester looked more like a high-rent art gallery owner than a sleazy-ass drug dealer.

I gave an eardrum assaulting two-fingered whistle worthy of the high school football coach who taught it to me, and Desmond turned, glaring. I pushed Rodney into view and watched his brother's face drop in surrender. Seemed Rodney was nobody's idea of a welcome mat. Defeated by his own blood, Desmond turned back and walked over to the car.

"Slide over," I barked at Rodney, who did, his brother squatting down at the open door but not getting in. He looked at Rodney, who gave a nervous wave.

"He's blood—what 'm I supposed to do? A dickwit, but my brother, and I'd be suspect *numero uno* if he be hacked into pieces and blendered, then fed to my dogs, and crapped out the shit he always was."

Gotta love sibling rivalry.

"It's hot here. Either get in with the air conditioning or head out."

Desmond eyed me, studying my face in a disengaged way, similar to a housewife sizing up how many chicken breasts to buy at the market. I could imagine him calculating odds and prison-sentence numbers, while at the same time looking to gain an advantage. I hoped he wasn't going to sniff me for freshness. Finally, it came down to inevitability.

"What do I get from it?"

"You don't go away to prison for the rest of your life, are hand-delivered into witness relocation with a red carpet and a friendly 'howja do,' and you get to pick the spot. Besides, it's your patriotic duty."

"I hear Hawaii be nice all year round. I like the sun. And they got that surfin' stuff."

"I didn't take you for a swimmer."

Desmond slid into the car and closed the door. The cold air started tipping the scales to bearable again.

"I'm not. But maybe the sharks'd gnaw on my brother. Take an arm, or somethin'."

"You like Jack In The Box, Desmond?"

"They got good tacos."

***

The Phoenix FBI offices looked like the sad lovechild of Paul Troost circa Hitler dinner parties and Max Ernst circa Hitler death camps: sort of monolithic chaos, a Kafkaesque mishmash of cubicles gone wild. Infested with FBI-stamped, color-coded (black), same-suited, cookie-cutter agents bustling about like fleas on a hotplate. And feeb boring. The IRS is bad, but the FBI is worse.

Rodney, seeing a free meal courtesy of Uncle Sammy, had ordered two dozen of El Jack's finest and still had a half a bagful left, occasionally reaching in and pulling out a taco perspiring with grease. Four bites and it vanished. Almost impressive, except for the oil smears across his cheeks and forehead. When he ate, he ate large.

We parked ourselves in a conference room, walls lined with so much technology it looked like a Best Buy on growth hormones: tape decks, DVD decks, Blu-ray decks, a fistful of thumb drives, video screens of all shapes and sizes, a row of computers (all iMacs; good for the feebs), video cameras, web cameras, even camera cameras. NASA never had it so good. My hosts had kindly put chilled bottled water and glasses on a serving tray—very hospitable of them. The two Johns stood at opposite corners against one wall looking like sunglass-wearing bookends.

Desmond cut to the chase: "So, what you want me and my brother to do? And will I need clean underwear to do it?"

I'd already mentioned in the car how the IRS had his balls six ways till sundown, and that between the money laundering *hawla* and the various other particulars, we were looking to put the siblings' asses into the big house of no deductions for longer than their neural functions would stay sound, despite modern medicine's recent geriatric breakthroughs. But...I dangled witness relocation and Des was quick enough to see reason. Besides, it sounded like he was becoming less than enamored of his double-wife situation. "Bitches is bitches, and two is twice as bad." As the poet said: "In the arithmetic of love, one plus one equals everything, and two minus one equals nothing." Whatever that meant.

"You an American, Des?" I asked.

The smart brother cracked the cap on a water bottle and took a swig. "That's a stupid question. I vote Republican, but I'm down with the social agenda of the Democrats."

I raised an eyebrow, then smiled. "Good, because what I'm hoping you and Rodney will help out on will defend the United States against all enemies, foreign and domestic, and in this case, both."

I proceeded to outline the Mongolian Mob and what they were trying to do, as near as I could tell. I left out Juju specifically, but gave the general temperature of the situation: hot to sizzling, with increased chance of bullets. After pointing out that the untimely cessation of Doc O'Bannon and his daughter's bank accounts would force the Mongs to look for some new help in the financial realm, I finished the background, stopping to gauge their reaction.

Rodney, of course, flapped his pie hole first. "No shit? Radioactive whoo-hoos? And I thought mad-cow disease was trouble. I ain't eatin' steak no more."

Desmond and I exchanged beleaguered looks. I commiserated with his Sisyphean boulder of a brother, and he took it stoically, the eternal sacrifice.

"You want us to step in 'n offer our services so you can hide-and-seek the money."

"It seemed a skill set suited to your expertise. Trying to get someone on the side of the angels would take too long and require too deep of a background, which takes further time. I don't believe we have time. I think they're looking to run some large sums before they do whatever it is they're trying to do. You're my shortcut."

Desmond took another sip and contemplated. Rodney only saw palm trees and hula skirts. "So we can pick any island in Hawaii? Somethin' on the beach maybe?"

"You know how much a beach house costs, Rodney?" I asked, watching greed warring with a Do Not Go To Jail card in the Rodster's eyes, the greed taking the first hurdle in the lead.

"A lot. That's why I'm askin'. This thing you want sounds dangerous," he said, rolling the last word around on his tongue and adding checkbook zeroes to each syllable.

"More dangerous than a cell with a serial rapist named Gunther who specialized in overweight thirty-year-olds who formerly ran dry cleaners?"

Rodney parsed the sentence with difficulty, his face telling the slow story of comprehension, finally dawning with a frown of consternation. "You threatening me?"

"Rodney, I don't have to threaten. I'm the IRS. Now be a good boy and keep quiet while your brother thinks this through."

Rodney did as I suggested, even if he wasn't too happy about it. He sulked, reaching for a bottled water, then putting it back.

"Gunther?" noted his brother.

"Something about the colder climes of Scandinavia brings out the sodomist in some criminals. Don't know why. Maybe it's any port in the storm during those overly long winter nights. Akvavit's only good for so much."

Desmond thought a moment more, then made his decision. "Any way we can do this clean in the end? You score your bad guys, and we float away in the fog?"

"That's the way I'd like it, but I can't guarantee it. The harder you sell it, the easier it'll be for me. You screw me in any way, I'll bullhorn your contribution from on high—make the burning bush look like a scented aroma-therapy candle."

Desmond threw his hands out, palms to me. "No need to get all cracker-in-the-hood on me. I understand the situation. We may not see eye-to-eye on the legalities of some things, but no one blows up my country. After nine-eleven a bunch of us began sliding cake towards various paramilitary motherfuckers in need of capital to fight the good fight. Least we could do."

"Criminals for Democracy. I never knew."

Desmond gave a "what can you do?" shrug.

"Okay, your heart's in the right place. Good," I said. "Then here's what I'll need from you, and here's what you'll get from me. First, though...can you keep your brother's yap shut during all of this? One peep from him, and we're all going down."

Rodney was about to protest, when Desmond cut him short. "We'll bring Mama in."

Rodney looked like someone had reached down his throat and turned him inside-out, so shocked was he by his brother's statement. "Not Mama! No! Des, you know what happens when she gets involved."

"Rodney, you need...*guidance*, and Mama do that. We fuck this up, we're screwed in every hole possible. Not going to happen with Mama around. She can stay at your place and keep an eye on things."

Rodney began shaking his head back and forth. "Shitshitshit! Not *my* house. *Your* house."

"Got Patricia at my house. Mama don't get along with Patricia," Desmond said. "I think it's a pheromone thing."

"Mama don't get along with nobody. It's a fucked-up attitude thing. You puts her in with me, I'll be dead in three days. Probably take my own life, slit my wrists or take the Drāno." Rodney put his head in his hands. "You recall what happened last time?"

The turn of conversation fascinated me. "Do tell what happened last time."

Desmond glared at me. "Don't get him started."

"Can't help it. It's my nature."

Rodney looked up, purgatory in his eyes. "She...she gave me a bath. Said I smelled, and she gave me a bath. Then..." Rodney choked, snatched a bottle of water and gulped half of it down. "Then she came along with me on a meth run, and when she didn't like the attitude of the cooker, she took him by the ear, pulled down his pants and spanked him. I've never been so embarrassed in all my life."

I turned to Desmond. "True?"

"That's Mama. She's real rigorous."

Rodney couldn't contain himself. "You *can't* bring her in! Please, Des. I'll do *anything*!"

Desmond put a hand on Rodney's shoulder, one brother to another, "Sorry, Rodney, I gotta. She's the only one that can keep you straight."

Rodney broke down in tears. It's a sad, sad day when a big mean criminal is afraid of his own mother. Of course, I hadn't met Mama yet.

***

As the sun set slowly into the West and the lights popped on all over Sacramento, I lugged myself back to home, sweet home. It'd been a long and oddly reassuring day, but I was as glad to get back to my apartment, slotting the key into the lock without giving it a second, or a third, thought. Mistake. Big time.

A fetid blast hit me as I opened the door, followed by a fetid dog zooming chest-high and droolish, big, meaty and full of unrelenting momentum. Physics is a bitch and always in heat. I whipsawed a leg around out of reflex, but that only put me Leaning-Tower-of-Pisa off balance when El Repollo hit, slamming me backwards in a gymnastically ill-conceived tumble of man, dog, and stank.

"Polli! Don't do that to Daddy! He's had a hard day at the strip club. Ogling all those naked breasts can take a lot out of a man."

It was a setup.

Volcanic dog breath hosed my face, the mutt squatting on my chest like a cardiac arrest with psoriasis. The panting increased, bringing with it the odor of leather. Couch leather was my guess. *My* couch.

"Devon...a little help?"

A sharp whistle and, unbelievably, the hulking monster skittered off me and ran back inside. It reeked of more than just unbathed dog; it smelled of heavy trouble for yours truly. I rolled to my feet, unsuccessfully tried to brush off the dog hair and went into *my* apartment.

The smell of garlic and butter filled the entry, and when I peeked into the kitchen, I saw Devon in an apron, shorts, and a halter-top cheffing at the stove. Cute is as cute does, and she was workin' the cute somethin' fierce.

It was *definitely* a setup. But it looked like a tasty one.

"What's for dinner?"

"Paella—my grandmother's recipe." Devon grinned at me as she stirred a wooden spoon around a saucepan—firecrackers of flavor filling the air—then brought it over for me to taste.

"Your grandmother was Valencian? Funny, you don't look Valencian." I blew on the spoon, then licked it. "Wow, that's a little bit of all right with sprinkles on top."

Chomp! El Repollo leapt high and bit off the head of the spoon, swallowing it in one gulp. Devon and I both looked at the dog in awed amazement as it hunched on the kitchen floor, wagging its tail furiously and sniffing about for more. I tossed it the handle and the dog munched it up as well.

"Good thing you have more spoons," Devon said, giving me an I-do-more-than-just-cook smile.

"Good thing I have more fingers."

El Repollo grunted, then coughed, then farted, then ran twice around in a circle and trotted out of the room. "Does he need a walk? I don't mind losing spoons, but spoon-filled piles of crap all over the house is where I draw the line."

Devon pulled another wooden spoon out of the middle drawer, an obvious sign of domestication and internalization of geography, which somehow weren't worrisome.

"And what line would that be, Mr. Douglas?"

"The one in small print at the bottom of my contract that says, 'No smelly, drooling, spoon-eating dogs crapping all over the house.' It's right above the 'Beautiful women can cook for me any time," and right below the 'Nothing happened at the strip club; it was work' lines."

The ding of a timer, the smile of a smug woman: rice was scooped, paella was poured, dinner was eaten, dogs were locked in the bathroom with nary a noise (except for what sounded like El Repollo scarfing down either a stick of Mitchum or a roll of toilet paper, possibly both), and bliss was blissed.

Dessert was even better. Strippers were not even a part of it. Well, not much.

By the hollow hours of latest night, the time between the ache of discovery, soft skin, and tongue-touched epiphany, and the drowsy moment, legs tangled, sheets thrown off, then gathered up to tuck tight, there came the Libra-balance of yesterday's possibilities and tomorrow's bright scratching hopes. A tick of time trapped in the amber of natal excitements and calm afterglow. Devon squirmed back against me, a Goldilocks-just-right heat coming off her long, lean back. We fit in too many ways.

"So this is it?" I mouthed into her hair as it dusted my face in strands of soft finality, my breath tasting of peppermint and moisturizer. "The rhyme and reason, the lost, found, and the flurry?"

"As 'it' as it can be, which is pretty 'it' if you ask me. I'm definitely liking the 'it,'" teased Devon as she wriggled, making talk stop again.

It definitely was "it."

Sunrise brought El Repollo in all his stanky get-up-and-go-or-I'm-doing-it-on-the-rug glory, laying a cross block across the bed and rudely interrupting the beginning of another sleepily instigated "it."

"Baby needs a walk, sweetlily-dee. I'll make coffee if you take Polli around the block. He's a three-bagger: two plastic and a big grocery bag. He likes paper, not plastic."

Snorting into my butt while trying to burrow under the covers, El Repollo knew how to spoil a moment with two periods and an exclamation point.

"Christ! Is this my future—at the mercy of a dog's incontinent intestines? 'Out, damned spot! out, I say!' "

The dog simply began gnawing on my pillow with big saliva-y bites.

"Ignorant canine. Next you'll be telling me the mutt has an aversion to Moliere and Yeats."

I rolled out of bed, drafty and scooting on my underwear in record time, as El Repollo eyed my "tidbits" a little too hungrily. Jeans and shirt, running shoes, three bags, and a chain improvised for a leash (Devon's invention), and me and doggy-doo-doo were ready to roll. Then I looked back and saw Devon curled up in blankets and dream, and took a moment to inhale, slowly and desperately, then shook myself free.

"C'mon, mutt. Let's do the do."

Outside, my block, all apartments and condominiums and silent preparation for the day, caught the rising sun with orange'd windows and symphony'd sparrows all cacophonous and chirping. El Repollo sniffed an azalea bush, lifted a leg, then began a steady stream that would have shamed a race horse. It smelled of asparagus and wooden spoon. I waited...and waited...and waited, trying to look nonchalant and devil-may-care, despite the fact there was no one else around. I dreaded the outcome of his upcoming ca-ca.

And still the stream streamed. The azalea dropped. Footsteps coming down the sidewalk, and El Repollo growled a back-of-the-throat, cavemen-heard-this-in-the-dark growl. Juju Klondike strolled up easy as breathing. Or *not* breathing.

My quick snapshot glimpse of him in the Honda in Phoenix, freshly shot Doc O'Bannon lifeless nearby, didn't do his nondescriptiveness justice. Klondike was forgettable in so many ways. His shoes were Target-bought specials, mud-brown lace-ups with worn heels that hushed as he moved in them. His socks matched, also brown, stretched taut against his calves, which peeked out under the cuffs of his beige Dockers creased from recent ironing. They rode high on his hips, pockets jangling from keys and an abundance of change. A black leather belt, two extra holes punched into it, as if Klondike's weight had varied recently, was cinched tight. Tucked neatly into his pants was a brand-new, short-sleeved, button-down dress shirt, also beige, with thin purple striping, one collar tip slightly askew from even. Clean shaven to the point of pinkness, he neither smiled nor frowned, had eyes the color of overcast skies, and side-parted hair neatly cut just below his ears. He could have been a dentist, or an H & R Block accountant. Perhaps a middle school vice principal. Nothing particularly out of the ordinary. Neither old, nor young, he was as blandly dangerous as a cup of coffee laced with strychnine and fat-free hazelnut creamer. If it weren't for the seriousness and intent of the man, it would have been laughable. But if there was anything Juju Klondike wasn't, it was laughable.

He stopped a few yards away, careful, and staring at me with deep-sea, taken-from- the-depths fish eyes. "I have not been paid to kill you. Yet."

His voice, high and squeaky like a cartoon mouse, surprised me. Disconcerted me. Scared me a little. El Repollo took a charge at him in no time, one second at the azalea, the next yanked to the end of the chain, just a handbreadth from Klondike, who had calculated well, never flinching.

"Dog's jumpy until he takes his morning dump. I'd stay upwind. He's a melting pot of digestive surprises."

I calculated my odds if he pulled a gun. Nuthin' from nuthin' leaves nuthin'. Best bet: dive behind a car and hope he killed me quick.

"The fecal habits of your animal are of little interest to me. I have never owned a pet myself, and I doubt I ever will. No, I came to ask if you wished to pay me my normal fee," he said.

I wrapped the chain twice around my wrist, El Repollo not coming to heel, just growling and taut and pointing at Klondike like a furry guided missile.

"Pay you? If I could pay you to kill yourself, you'd have a deal."

"That's funny, isn't it?" Klondike flicked the imitation of a smile, a brief second, then gone, all lips and no teeth, just the barest corners of his mouth. "But you misunderstand. There are those I kill, and those who hire me. Those I kill have no need to know who I am. Those who hire me do. There is no in-between. You are an in-between."

"I've found life to be a series of mitigating circumstances. Get used to it."

I recalculated and realized that if he drew a gun, and I threw myself right at him, I'd probably die instantly, but there was a small chance the dog might tear Klondike's throat out before he could re-aim. A thought full of mixed blessings, but a better conclusion than my previous one. I kept thinking.

"I do not think my present employer would appreciate that there was an onlooker to my, er...appointed rounds."

"Clever," I said, hefting the three bags and further thinking. "You are the cunning linguist. But I'm not sure my own boss would agree to that sort of thing. He's a stickler for forms and regulations. A fatal flaw, I know, but what can you do?"

"Fatal flaw. Yes. You are clever, too."

Klondike wiped his palms on his pants, not a good sign. I brought up the bags, covering the chain around my wrist as offhand as I could, then dropped the leash and dove behind the parked car, an old Mercedes, fortunately—El Repollo flew at Juju Klondike's crotch like a Guatemalan hooker seeing a fifty-dollar bill and no cops around.

I grabbed my keys from my pocket and levered one around the edge of the Mercedes wheel, popping the hub, slicing my forefinger in the process, but not giving a damn. I had more blood to spill. Coming up from my crouch, I took the far corner of the car and saw Klondike, El Repollo, jaws clamped to his groin, screaming a high-pitched, dog-ears scream and beating on the animal's head with one fist, trying to pull a gun from beneath the back of his shirt, but being shaken too hard by El Repollo to be able.

I rounded on Klondike with the hubcap just as he locked onto the grip of his pistol, and Babe Ruth'd his hand as he brought it up, sending the gun meteoring through the air and down the street. A SIG P226, I realized. Odd the things one notices in those split seconds between a blink. I ran for the gun, El Repollo growling louder and louder, Klondike screaming louder and louder. When I'd scooped it up and turned, Klondike was gone, and El Repollo chewed on a wad of inseam and zipper, flecks of blood still spattering down. Up the street, down the street: no Klondike. The man was a ghost. A crotchless ghost, but a ghost. I figured if he'd had genitalia like the rest of humankind, El Repòllo'd be munching on scrotum tartar and happily waiting for it to pass. Luckily for Klondike, he didn't have any. Yeah, lucky guy.

I patted El Repollo on the head and let him lick the blood dripping from my finger. They say dog saliva is antiseptic; there was my chance to prove it. Then I snaked up the leash and turned to finish our circuit of the neighborhood.

"Come on Polli. You've earned your poop today."

14.

Aroon Kumaar Vijah Smith—fingers steepled before his horse-long, reenactment-of- the-Battle-of-Plassey face, eyes peering over the top like hyenas on a sweltering Serengeti day—sat in sway in his chair, waiting for me to contend with his query. His tie fiercely glowed Orange Crush, which distracted me from the question: "How will you contrive a union between the Mongolian syndicate and your two criminal siblings without losing the reins of control? You have forewarned the Gloucesters. Will they not go to ground?"

"Desmond's too smart to try that, and Rodney's too dumb. Plus, they're both terrified of their mother, and I got a phone call from her promising they'd follow my design to a 'T.' I'm terrified of her now, too. She sounded like a transsexual Attila the Hun with anal fissures and a propensity for eating babies, raw."

My boss cleared his throat, a sound both industrial and feral.

I quickly added, "Mama Gloucester's the real power, her husband Xerxes, now deceased under mitigating circumstances. It seems he was found *in flagrante i*n a dumpster with an underage Thai ladyboy named Wang-ho. Seriously, you can't make this weirdness up. She oversees various Gloucester 'areas of interest' from her run-down, second-floor apartment in the poorer part of Phoenix. Says she 'ain't movin' fer Jesus or freeways.' And that she wished we'd just 'get off her mole-encrusted ass and let her do what she does.'"

"She sounds formidable. So she will not be receiving witness protection with her sons?"

"Doesn't seem like it, but it's up to the Feds and Mama Gloucester, I guess. As long as she doesn't move in near me, I'm all right."

That didn't seem the real topic of conversation, so I waited, unsure where Mr. Smith might go. I hardly needed to wait at all.

"You won't get a second chance, you realize."

Call it telepathy, paid informants, a backroom deal with Lucifer, whatever: how did my boss know about Klondike and me? He knew I knew that he shouldn't know; he gave a flash of a carnivorous smile and cleared his throat again, a bit of explosive Presbyterian pastor with a tendency toward flicking the garbage disposal.

"It was unexpected, my meeting. There doesn't need to be a second chance because I'll be facilitating the FBI in dealing with the problem," I told him. As I said, stretching the truth comes easy to me.

Klondike butchered Lila, and we had a big, fat, red circle on our calendars to have a little get-together, just we two, maybe a couple of drinks, some old-school barbecue, his head on a platter. The usual.

Smith stared at me a moment more, the pupils of his eyes contracting to pinpoints, almost disappearing, then he pushed an envelope over to me, no writing, just the manila.

"You'd be surprised who I went to school with. Butchers, bakers, and candlestick makers. Even State Department personnel at arcane levels of the bureaucracy with cryptic job descriptions." My boss meticulously squared the knot on his hideous tie. "Everyone needs to do their taxes, it seems."

I picked up the envelope, knowing that whatever lay inside was worth more than gold, silver, and Las Vegas sex.

"There is a doctrine of international law called 'immunity from prosecution' that allows an accused to avoid judicial process for criminal offences. There are two types: immunity *ratione materiae*, in which immunity is granted to people who perform certain functions of state. The second, immunity *ratione personae*. This is an immunity granted to certain officials because of the office they hold, rather than in relation to the act they have committed. In that envelope are both."

Carte blanche to murder and get away with it. Or pretty much anything else as well. Da-a-a-a-a-amn.

"I thought that was just for ambassadors and hoity-toity hotshots like that. Special-plates people from foreign climes."

"Yes, that's a common misconception bolstered by too much television. In fact, it can be assigned to anyone, given the proper antecedence. I hope you appreciate the complexity."

"It's...unforeseen, but definitely appreciated."

"Good. Remember: she was *my* employee."

And with that, I walked out of the office in paper armor and legal mumbo-jumbo, safe in the knowledge that if I somehow lived through it, I could not be prosecuted for the execution of Juju Klondike.

***

Del's Bar looked like happy hour at the Alamo: lots of drinks, lots of pretzels, lots of automatic weapons close at hand on the tabletops and leaned up against chairs. I'd sic'd Harry on Devon, deputizing him as the Babysitter from Hell, complete with a couple of AA12 shotguns (and I quote from the project manager of the thing: "There's no way that anybody within two hundred yards can face this weapon and survive it," kind of shotgun). He took his trust seriously, having robed her head-to-toe in Kevlar and a San Francisco 49ers football helmet—disturbingly erotic to me for some reason—as well as shepherding her to the IRS offices for the day, then bringing her to Del's before handing her off to me for the evening watch.

Wooly Bob preferred the nonlethal weapons approach—"It's wa-a-a-ay more holistic and better for your karma"—having a bandoleer full of Taser X3 multishot stun guns strapped crisscross over his chest. He fiddled with the yellow-and-black handles, whipping one out in a quick draw, then holstering it again.

"Range-adjusted, dual laser sights, independent fire-control system with up to a fifty-thousand-volt range. I know. I tried it on myself. Whoa, what a rush!"

No one in their right mind allowed Miguel within ten yards and a spit of a gun, even the toy ones housing a Wii controller, so he made do with two baseball bats and a golf club—a nine iron. Even Becky was holding, having hauled out Del's formidable double-barreled sawed-off, laying it on the bar in portend of things to come. Miguel kept trying to seduce her with nauseatingly sweet nicknames and abject begging into giving him a quick feel, but engagement or no engagement, Becky knew that love was never having to say, "Don't point that thing at me!"

The other patrons of Del's took it with mixed enthusiasm. Many nursed their drinks as far as humanly possible from our table. A few walked in, took one look, and walked back out again. A Good Samaritan called 911, but we set him and the cops who arrived straight, buying them all a round. For icing, a trio of personable, leather-clad bikers joined in, hauling out their Smith & Wesson .357 Sigs, slapping them down on their table and getting into the spirit of the thing.

All in all, a well-fortified bar.

"So, Marksketeer, what's next? Me and the Dev already hit the Macy's at the Downtown Plaza Mall for lunch." Harry lifted two boutique shopping bags from beneath the table, then placed them back under. "And were thinking of taking in Ann Taylor and Getta Clue tomorrow."

I lowered my head into my hands. "Shopping? Do you really think that's the safe play, Harry? I got a doubly-crotched psycho-banana gunning for me, you know?"

"Who's going to follow your girlie into a dressing room, other than me?"

Devon backhanded Harry on the shoulder. "He didn't. I wouldn't let him. But he checked every stall before I went in it and chatted up all the clerks. He's a doll."

"Got a few phone numbers, too," Harry said, looking smug and wizenly sassy. "And some underwear someone left behind. A *thong*."

I knocked back a shot of tequila, three more full glasses lined up, three upturned, pyramided and done. Devon leaned over and tried to kiss me to make me feel better, but clanged her helmet into my nose, forgetting she was wearing it. "Oopsie." She unstrapped and gave it another try, to tongue-tingling success. When I surfaced for air, I noticed everyone staring. At me. And Devon.

"What, like you all didn't see this coming?" I gave a game show presenter's two-handed point at Devon. "Look at her, for God's sake. Like I had a chance."

Not a peep until Becky brought out a congratulatory round of drinks, kissing both me and Becky in *mozel tov*. And she wasn't even Jewish. "It's about time. I was going to have to invite my younger sister to town and introduce you."

Younger sister? Yabba! I smiled at Devon, knowing which side my bread was buttered on, and buttered good. High-fives around the table and we were all lovey-dovey. Except for the fact that a nutso psycho-eunuch and a bunch of hopped-up Mongolian mobsters were none too happy with yours truly.

We drank with gusto deep into the a.m., no one particularly wanting to broach the night and anything terrible it might hold in its shadows and empty moments. My cell phone vibrated, and I fished it out on the second try—Devon's hand being squeezed into my pocket quite comfortably on the first try. A text from Juarez: "Coast clear."

Seemed my tax dollars—correctly deducted, I might add—were working overtime.

I stood, offering a help-up to Devon, who looked muzzy enough to eat. "Time to skedaddle."

She smiled at me, then came straight up and into my arms. "I like skedaddling."

Miguel had inched closer and closer to Becky's shotgun all night, finally reaching out to touch it, when: BANG! Harry spanked his palm on the table like, well, a *gunshot*, sending Miguel three feet in the air, legs pedaling like something Hanna-Barbara used to animate. When he landed, he'd lost all motor control, collapsing to the floor, everyone in the bar laughing their asses off. Becky gave him an I-warned-you glance, then bustled around the bar and helped him up, crushing his face into her comfy-parts.

"Did the big bad Harry scare you?"

Miguel nodded, perhaps more for the rubbing than the consoling.

"Don't worry, sweet chunks, he's going...*now!*"

Harry got the message, holding his hands, palms out, high.

"Was a mosquito on the table. Anyone would've done the same," he claimed, but proceeded to exit, stage left, like the rest of us.

Waves, hugs, and "goodnights" exchanged at the door, Devon and I walked ourselves out of Del's and into the FBI-entrusted moonlight.

"Home, James," Devon said.

"Who's this 'James' you speak of? I'll sic El Repollo on him if he doesn't keep his hands off you."

Devon snuggled into my shoulder, a strand of hair catching across my lips. I tried to blow it out, but it stuck fast. I let it lie.

"You like the doggie now, eh?"

"He's grown on me, like prostate cancer or weevils."

We negotiated the car—I checked the backseat, just in case—and struck out for my apartment. Home. Devon lolled back, a secret smile touching her lips, Kevlar still tight on her. Which gave me an idea.

"So, when we get back, could you keep the helmet on?"

"O-u-u-u, kinky..."

***

Rodney's head looked humpback whale-huge, like an encephalitic on steroids, all crusty nostril, black-headed cheeks, and balloon eyeballs. It almost put me off my cup of coffee.

"You need white stuff?" asked Juarez, holding a carton of half-and-half out to me.

I shook my head, still studying Rodney. "Does he have to shove his face that close? Can't you tell him to back off, give it some air? Nothing suspicious here."

Juarez eyed the image of Rodney on one of the four video monitors hung on the wall of the trailer, cables and wires snaking about the room connecting to computers, RAID enclosures, and various other high-tech monitoring equipment. Welcome to state-of-the-art surveillance heaven, starring Rodney and Desmond Gloucester, each outfitted with their own minicams, mics, and earpieces. Sort of the law enforcement version of a vlog. A webcam "Cops."

Rodney couldn't stop staring into his brother's pinhole camera and fiddling with the micro-mic fastened to his collar. "Can you hear me? Testing: 1, 2, 3. Testing."

Whap! Rodney's Mama slapped him upside the head, sending his earwig flying across the room.

"Mo-o-o-o-om! Don't do that!"

He ran to get it, stuffing it back into his ear. It was the first time any of us had seen Mama Gloucester, a formidable initial view, to say the least. A freeze-dried husk of a woman, like a potato left in the cupboard too long. With a face that looked like a hollowed-out umber gourd and crazy onionskin-marble eyes, she stood Jack-and-the-Beanstalk tall, seriously—gotta have been close to seven feet in bare feet, and she wore Worx hiking boots at the bottom of her black jeans, black dress shirt, sort of a pituitary freak version of classic Patti Smith crossed with disco Grace Jones. Neither son was over six feet. But who was going to ask her about that little genetic disparity? And she was tough as a pregnant piranha, showing no mercy to her own offspring. Probably worse for her enemies.

I took a swig of my coffee. "Good coffee. Didn't know you feebs had so much style."

In the b.g., two other FBI agents monitored various wavelengths and fiddling with countless knobs, clacking on various keyboards. A third FBI agent manned the espresso machine, pulling shots for everyone who needed one.

"The NSA loaned it to our department. I think they want to go independent and turn a profit. They're offering to sell it to us. This first trial run is free, so have as much coffee as you want."

"You're a generous man when it ain't your dime."

I held my cup up and he topped it off.

"A saint's what I am."

One of the monitors caught movement, and we spotted our Mongs. Looking like a historical reproduction of the steppe plains of Eastern Asia, a bunch of natively dressed, high-booted, leather trouser'd (baggy at the leg, tight at the ankles), fur-lined, silk sashed, weird hatted—we're talkin' beret with a high pyramid sticking out of the middle—half dozen little guys, none more than five feet six, rushed into the room.

Desmond and Rodney were completely nonplussed, Rodney even snickering. "They look like them little Ewok guys from the Star Wars movie." Slap! Mama Gloucester hit him across the back of the head again. "Well, they *do*!"

The "little Ewok guys" pulled AN-94 Abakan assault rifles from under their coats, all fitted with GP-34 grenade launchers.

"Okay, I can dig it." Rodney again.

Juarez glanced at me. "The Mongs don't fool around, do they? That's enough muscle to make cheddar cheese out of everyone and still have time to break for lunch and a quickie."

"They seem determined to express their arm-bearing rights, as well as intimidate the shit out of anyone in a hundred-yard radius. Mission accomplished, I'd say."

At which point Mama Gloucester pulled from out of God knows where two of what looked like plastic paint cans—quart sized—with an upside-down bell and seemingly a half dozen, maybe less, mechanical pencils shoved into the top. Sort of a miniature satellite, pre-orbit.

Juarez scratched his earlobe as if trying to kick-start his brain. "Okay, Mr. ex-Marine. What the hell did she just raise the ante with?"

I analyzed the screen, a splinter of memory nagging at me, then gelling into a thought. "Huh...well, what do you know? Italian antipersonnel mines, I'm pretty sure. Valmara Fifty-nines or Sixty-nines...not my specialty, really. Twenty-five-, thirty-meter blast radius. Basically, will turn everyone in the room to humus, twice over."

Tightass whistled. "Gotta love the Italians for sheer overkill."

"It's an art."

Before anyone could get trigger/detonator happy, a diminutive woman dressed in a Blumarine business suit, shuffled in, her presence dominating the situation. She looked fragile as a hummingbird, and deadly as a cobra, an odd combination immediately acknowledged by all.

"Hump my balls and call me Fido—that's Erdenetungalag Antioch herself. Jeez, you IRS boys don't fool around. In person."

Erdenetungalag meant "jewel clear" in Mongolian, like the light through a perfectly cut diamond. Crisp, transparent, pure. Barely four feet nine, Erdenetungalag Antioch gave the impression of being taller, perhaps closer to nine feet rather than five. It was a trick of the light, perhaps, or an optical illusion. A kink in the space-time continuum. A fault in the fabric that glued truth and lies.

Her soldiers lowered their rifles, and Mama Gloucester lowered her land mines. The two women nodded to each other: one a giant, one a pigmy, and both scarier than a doctor's report of uveal melanoma. I was glad to be out in the electronics trailer and not in that room.

"We need the Gloucesters in the Mong gene pool, and here we go," I reminded Juarez.

"Let's hope they stay in the gene pool and don't get bumped into the food chain."

I leaned into the cantilevered mic on the table, keeping my voice low so as not to startle my Gloucesters too much with my sudden aural presence.

"Okay, guys...remember: just be cool and make the money deal. Nothing else."

I could see Rodney about to respond to me, when Desmond punched him in the arm, covering his brother's start with, "I'm Desmond Gloucester. I've been led to believe we can collaborate."

Erdenetungalag looked at Desmond as if he were an interesting bowel movement she'd just had, getting ready to flush it.

"Belief is fickle thing." She looked to Mama Gloucester for clarification. "Do I talk to him, or you?"

Mama Gloucester gave a brittle smile. "My oldest. Why don't we begin with him, and if there's anything you find confusing, I can step in. We do what we must for our children, yes?"

Erdenetungalag eyed Mama Gloucester, then sucked her front teeth. "I not have children. I never let a man touch me that way, even husband."

Mama Gloucester's smile grew bigger as she toyed with that thought. "You know, I never thought of that. Perhaps in my next life." She turned to Desmond. "Speak your piece. I have errands to run."

I could see Desmond trying hard to control his reflexive abeyance to his mother, coupled with his anger at his authority being usurped. But he was the smart one, so he managed.

"My brother and I got a sort of Swiss banking here in the states. Money in, money out, no muss, no fuss."

Erdenetungalag nodded. "I become aware of your facilities recently. I had man killed in Hyderabad. Before he pass, I learn person can live without their hands and feet for long time before dying of blood loss. He gladly explain workings of your services."

Desmond nodded, controlled, but I could see a small twitch. "Ah, Johnny Ashok. I'd wondered what happened to his ass."

Erdenetungalag shrugged, like a snake slithering, "Consider it 'interest' on account. Now, tell me please—how you find out about me?"

The room went stone silent, and I knew the moment I'd contrived had arrived with bells on and ammunition at the ready. I whispered very, very slowly into the Gloucester's ears: "Just say one word...'cows.'"

Desmond, taken by surprise, blurted, "Cows?"

The six Mongolian soldiers instantly snapped their rifles up in clockwork precision, pointing them two to a Gloucester.

Shit, shit, shit.

"Stay cool, guys—try to smile," I coaxed, mellowing like Wayne Newton.

Rodney sweated bricks, starting to fart from anxiety; Desmond carved a smile onto his face with pure nerve. Mama Gloucester couldn't hear my advice, but already ran three steps ahead, looking bored by the situation.

"Cows. Plutonium. Cash. We killed a veterinary assistant...so we're all even here. Amazing how people who see the insides of animals all day have no nerve when it comes to seeing their own."

I turned to Juarez. "Oh, my. She's *good*."

He nodded. "Remind me not to get on her bad side."

"Ever think it might be too late for that?"

Erdenetungalag and Mama Gloucester locked eyes and lasered seven kinds of hell at each other in ninja-feminine-felonious-no-uncertain-terms. Finally, the little Mongolian woman flicked her hand and the rifles snapped down.

"It would seem none of us die today."

Desmond slumped slightly. Rodney let loose with a flatus that sounded as if an outboard motor and a broken muffler had a baby, then covered his mouth as if he had burped.

Mama Gloucester took point, offering to introduce Erdenetungalag's money to the system in any denomination she cared to pursue. The Mongolian leader thought for a moment, then fished a USB thumb drive from her pocket and held it out for Desmond, who roused his courage before taking it.

"I would like that held for me until further notice."

Desmond assured her he would. "Anything we gotta know to get it ready for afterwards?"

Erdenetungalag simply swept out of the room, her little Mongolians following in her wake like heavily armed murderous ducklings. Mama Gloucester slapped Rodney upside the head again.

"Mom! What was that for?"

"Acting unprofessional. What did I tell you about eating fast food and not taking your Maalox?"

Rodney looked chagrined, then farted again.

I leaned back in my chair and put my shoes up on the computer ledge. Juarez eyed me with anal-retentive, perspective-buyer's remorse.

"I did tell you this is the NSA's?"

"Yup, and you'll get a better deal if it's a little scuffed up."

Juarez tried on his "long-suffering" face, then discarded it for a smile. "Your people did good."

"Maybe. Have to see what's on that drive, and if we can go from point A to point B and grab us the plutonium." Another loud fart broke from the speakers. "Gotta do something about Rodney's irritable bowel as well."

Juarez slowly hunched up to his feet, gave a full-body stretch and smacked his lips together. "One match outta do it."

15.

"You want to eat at a 'meat and three?'" she asked.

Devon and I rolled through town in my car thinking of dinner places, trying on this and discarding that, but her suggestion made no sense to me.

"What the heck is a 'meat and three?'"

Still, with her dressed in read-a-dime-in-the-back-pocket-tight jeans and a filled-up T-shirt with a picture of a chimp wearing a Che Guevara beret and bearing the logo "Viva La Evolucion" on it, confusion was my middle name.

"You know, like a Cracker Barrel, where you get a main course, the meat, plus a choice of three side dishes?"

"Cracker Barrel? What's a Cracker Barrel?" I seriously wasn't following that conversation.

"You are *so* not where I come from." She patted my shoulder like she would El Repollo. "Restaurant. Country cooking. Greatest chicken and dumplings in the universe."

"JR's Texas Bar-B-Que's pretty okay. You can get lots of meat and as many threes as you want." I was *really* starving all of a sudden. "And there's room and lines of sight for our friendly feebs."

"They still behind us?"

I glanced in my rear-view and caught sight of your basic black Buick, descript in its nondescriptness. Tightass wasn't taking any chances with me, and I felt comfortable that when the chips were down, there'd be witnesses to my demise.

"Yup, slow and steady like always."

Devon aimed a dangerous smirk at me like a high-powered rifle with telescopic sight.

"Think they peek when you're doing all those temptingly horrible things to me in the dark?"

"Doing to *you*? If I'm not mistaken, it was a deliciously naked female who shall remain nameless that used the French vanilla coffee creamer to—"

157

She slapped a hand over my mouth with fearsome quickness, then motioned her head toward the roof and rest of the car, mouthing, "Are we bugged?"

"Who cares? They're feebs. It's not like it's going up on the Internet."

Devon adjusted her seating, "A girl's gotta have standards. And mace. The two go hand-in-hand."

I glanced over at her. "Good to know."

"I'm like a puzzle box, an onion and a thesaurus all rolled into one. It keeps me mysterious."

I could just imagine what the FBI made of all that as they kept tabs and shuffled audio files from office to office. Perhaps they found it good practice for the cryptologists. Or the shrinks. Or both.

"Are you a *hungry* puzzle onion thesaurus with a cherry on top?"

"Ravenous. Cherry and all."

From the back seat, in the dark, unbeknownst and all, I heard the snick of a safety being caught back on, then Harry piped up, "Me, too, Mark-in-the-box."

Seems my girlfriend's babysitter was taking his job a little too seriously.

God save me from those who wanted to save me: militant evangelists, evangelical militarists or God Herself.

***

Juarez brought me the news later that night, *personally*. No phone call. No intermediary. Knocking and curses got me up from my nice warm bed with my nice warm Devon, and my ugly, farting, slobbering, snoring but warm dog. Dragging on my trusty gray sweats, I wandered in the dark, lifting my biggest carving knife, the Thanksgiving turkey one, twelve inches of Damascus steel, from my knife block, bringing the two-prong carving fork along as well. Never know when a body'll need a good two-prong carving fork in a fight; should be standard-issued military, if you ask me.

More knocking, and my bleary brain finally recognized the knuckles: Juarez's. Not a good sign.

"What, did the Starbucks kick you out for over-flashing your FBI badge? They don't take kindly to that."

Juarez marched in without a "hello, how's your warm bed doing without you in it?" I noticed two feebs standing outside the door, protective duty, and he noticed the carving set in my hands.

"I'll take a thigh and a wing. And coffee if you got it."

I stared at him in incredulity and wonder: man had a lot of nerve asking for coffee at a time like that, turkey past midnight I understood, but coffee? Especially since grinding the beans would wake Devon. But, after putting down the knife and carving fork, I did it and found out something extremely useful, both good and bad: Devon could sleep through bean grinding with will and forethought, not to mention without the need of earplugs.

Tightass and I settled in at the kitchen counter and sipped our java, passing the half-and-half carton back and forth like two kids with bowls of cereal.

"Mmm, good coffee. You roast your own beans?" he asked, savoring his mouthful, rolling it around on his tongue before swallowing. "Kinda nutty."

I glared at Juarez, then shrugged. "Yeah, I cook my own beans. You come to compare air roasters to drum roasters now? Whether a burr grinder is *absolutely* necessary for a savory cup, or can you cheat with blade? *You're* kinda nutty."

Juarez took another sip, then, "He killed everyone."

I sipped, knowing he meant Klondike and knowing I didn't want to know but had to. "Everyone where?"

"Came into the ER at Sutter General, got stitched up from whatever your doggy did, then proceeded to butcher every single person on the first floor of the hospital. He had some sort of machine gun, like a Rheinmetall MG Three or something that he had in a duffel bag. Don't know how he got it in, but just as the doctor finished, he pulled it out and blew a Holland Tunnel in the guy's stomach, then mounted it on a gurney and began wheeling through the corridors, hunka-chunking everything in sight. Nothing but red walls and the glitter of intestine and brain. No one survived, and if he wasn't in a hurry, the alarms blaring and cops racing in, he looked like he was going to take the elevator and start on the second floor."

I poured another cup for myself, then Juarez.

"You know this how?"

"Security cameras everywhere. Nothing pretty. Nothing hopeful. Everyone dead." Juarez started to take another sip, then stopped, putting his cup back down. "Sacto police want to declare a curfew and have already blockaded the roads in and out tighter than a constipated porn star. One of the officers first on scene lost it. Had to be taken away in cuffs. Klondike's not going anywhere."

I nodded, thinking, calculating, knowing the answer in the back of the book already. "He doesn't really want to, does he? We finally know what he looks like, so he has two choices: kill me, then vanish..." Juarez waited, "...or kill everybody. Everywhere."

Tightass poured more cream, then stirred, the white clouds swirling clockwise, a mini caffeine hurricane in a cup. "You think he might try that?"

"Kill everyone? I wouldn't put it past the sick-ass freak. It's what he does, so why not? But I think he'll come after me first. And I don't think anyone's going to be able to stop him before then."

Juarez dumped a heap of fake sugar into his cup and stirred some more. "Mongs first?"

"That would seem the logical order. Haven't a clue yet, but the Gloucesters only arrived. I'm waiting for the clickety-clack of virtual criminal activity before I make an assessment. It's an IRS thing."

I chewed my lip, tasting the slow drip of coffee and the tang of salt. I was sweating.

Juarez downed the rest of his coffee and stood, a tightass look on Tightass's face. No one needed to say a thing, but we both acknowledged it in some John Ford Western way.

"You get some sleep," he said as he headed for the door. "I can let myself out."

And he did, the lock clicking in place after he'd quietly closed the door. Leave it to the feebs to have a key to my place. I'd have to remember to change the locks...*after*. For the time being, a warm bed called with Circean seduction and dog breath. Lucky me. Klondike waited for morning.

***

Back in my still-felt-stolen cubical, a memory's hint of Lila caught me by surprise, a strand of remembrance, a recall of laughter and smile. "Don't you worry kiddo. I will do unto them so damn Biblical, people will start their own tax-exempt religion around it."

"Talkin' to yourself's one of the telltale signs of loop-the-loopism, Markgilla Gorilla. And not very 'suit.' I would think less of you if I didn't already hate suits with a stern and undying passion."

Harry wheeled up in his office chair like a drag racer to the starting line.

"You call me a suit again, and you and I are going out behind the woodshed and having words."

Harry swiveled about on his chair. "You don't do redneck very well do you?"

"I'm learning," I replied, mousing a spreadsheet into view on my screen and eyeballing a column of expenditures brought to my attention by a smalltime squealer looking for reward money. Seems his sister-in-law wasn't declaring her eBay income to the tune of $20,000 a year in refurbished toaster-ovens, of all things. I guess a girl's gotta have a hobby. I tracked her indiscretions, then noticed that her brother-in-ratfink also owed back taxes, so I sent a request for a reward check, then promptly took a lien against it. No matter what, work never stops at your happy-go-lucky Internal Revenue Service. You can't afford to, and neither can we.

Harry scratched at his thigh with bug-bite satisfaction, then readjusted his pants leg, revealing he was packing something in an ankle holster. I raised eyebrows in askance, and he smiled, "Just a little bit of heaven in a most unexpected place."

"How'd you get by the detectors?"

Harry pulled a double-edged military knife out from under his cuff. "Ceramic, one-hundred percent. One of them super-industrial Okinawan companies that are on the no-import list."

"You have a friend, no doubt."

I picked up my favorite imaginary Sharpie and scribbled a nonexistent post-it reminding myself to absolutely *never* get into one of those conversations with Harry ever again, really, really, really, swear to God.

"Flies 'em in on his route with DHL along with fugu and single-distillation sake." He hefted the knife, rapidly chopping air with it. "A lot of sushi chefs use these things for slicing fish, I guess. Makes a handy-dandy holdout. Could cut a cunt hair without scratchin' the poonie. Course it takes a steady hand."

"And a willing heart. No doubt you have cunt-hair-cutting volunteers bangin' on your door all hours of the day and night."

That was my life: listening to Harry and having a psycho-assassin trying to kill me. It was a sad testament to my social skills. But then there was Devon; that was in the double-plus column.

My cell rang, a "withheld" number flashing up on my screen, and I figured that had to be a Gloucester. I stared down Harry, who nodded, lock-stepped to my thought process.

"Man oh Manischewitz. Go to it."

It was Desmond. Seems the Mongs'd begun funneling funds in and around his circumstances, through the laundries and back out the other side. Major big amounts. Government-in-exile sponsored amounts. Desmond couldn't keep the avarice out of his voice. "I put a bleed valve in there to nibble a million here and a million there—no one'll know shit."

I glanced upwards, hoping God would hear my pleas, knowing full well that the Gloucester brothers were my own penance for something or other.

"Desmond, remember, you're the smart one. That money's not yours to spend."

A bleat of whiny incredulity popped into Desmond's response. "It's *illegal*, man. You gotta give me a taste. What they gonna do, call the cops?"

"*What they gonna do* is find a nice quiet warehouse somewhere and start punching teeny-tiny holes in your body with a watchmaker's screwdriver until you look like an oozing pin cushion, then when the blood's nice and slick, they'll take out a little jar, the kind kids collect fireflies in, only the bugs fluttering around behind the glass are these interesting little creatures called bot flies. Now, they come in a wonderful bunch of varieties: there's the horse-stomach bot fly, the sheep-nose bot fly, and guess what, there's even a human bot fly. In your case, these human bot flies will rub their eggs off into all your bleeding punctures, and the eggs will shortly hatch into maggots that will burrow inwards, eating all the way. Getting bigger and bigger, crawling around munching your insides. I even heard of a case where one ate a whole chunk out of a guy's brain before he died. Screaming. I doubt it's fun."

Harry, who hadn't gone, smiled his ruthless amused grin. Silence on the end of the line.

"Besides, Desmond, we here at the IRS have to follow *all* the money, tracking where it goes. You pinch a piece, we'll just track it to you, and then the F-B-I'll get wind of it and all bets are off."

I heard Desmond clear his throat, then clear it again. "Okay, I hear you 'bout the do-not-disturb. I abide your wishes."

"Abiding's good, Desmond. Now, I need all the account info you have."

"Copied it on another thumb drive and FedEx'd it to you. Seemed safest that way." I liked Desmond's thinking: hide in plain sight. "I sent it overnight, next morning, on your plastic."

Cheap-ass criminals. What was the world coming to?

"We'll get to it then. You keep your head down. You may think you're a big mean criminal, but these Mongolians really are. And they don't like their dance partners doing the cha-cha with someone else."

Desmond hung up. I guess he didn't like the cha-cha.

"I like your use of descriptive narrative there. Had me all tingly. You could write best sellers, I bet," Harry said, enjoying it all a bit too much. "So criminals are really stupid. Film at eleven. What else you got?"

I'd been tossing an idea around, playing pickle with it, just back and forth between my frontal lobes, and I needed another set of eyes. "Why three military people? I get that the lieutenant's father was a vet, so they needed her to get the plutonium past customs and launder the money, but why the other two?"

Harry scratched the bridge of his nose. "Someone needed to get the radioactives out of Mongolia, I would bet. A paper pusher or string puller over in Ulan Bator."

I nodded, having come to the same conclusion. "They have people on-ground here. What do they need the third G.I. Joe for?"

"I make it the private that's the odd man out. The looie's dad's the vet. Gotta be the colonel did the fuzzy-duzzy with the plutonium trail out of Asia. What good's a grunt?"

"Maybe to do grunt work?"

"Think Markaletto. The Mongs don't have grunts in Mongolia? That's like sayin' Wal-Mart ain't got knocked-up checkout girls. Why an Army boy?"

We went round and round, throwing out ideas and grabbing them back when they splatted. Wooly Bob wandered over and tried his hand at various hypotheses, even going so far as to contemplate an association between our third soldier and the grassy knoll, but after a minute or two of hearing Jimmy Hoffa, Judge Crater, and Kermit the Frog all tied into a web of intrigue, we cut him off and sent him back to Wooly Bob Land, a cubicle of such veganly holistic power, none of us dared enter.

Miguel knew enough to lay low. The kid was learning. Soon-to-be domesticity agreed with him.

But why a private? I began computering Private Keene's tax info, then his bank info, then his info info. I even pulled a digital copy of his second-grade report card from Eagle Ridge Elementary, Rio Rancho, New Mexico—so-so, but an "E" for effort—before I was done. A life of bytes and decimal points.

One thing stuck out: when Keene's tour finished, *permanently*, his body didn't fly home to Rio Rancho, New Mexico, didn't pass Go, but did collect $250,000, then landed in Muscat, Oman, the Mideast. Odd place for a Southwest kid to end up, but maybe desert was desert. Or maybe not. Maybe Private Keene wasn't as dead as everyone thought he was.

By the end of the day, I'd turned over enough financial rocks to find six dummy bank accounts and a long line of transactions that totaled in the millions. Interesting. The private went from dead grunt to live liaison. But for whom? The next day Desmond's thumb drive came FedEx and answers began to rear their ugly little answer-y heads.

***

"So why don't you want me to go to your place? You have whips, chains, small latex figurines of all fifty-six signers of the Declaration of Independence in the bedroom that vibrate and glow when they're switched on? Or did you paint the walls some horrible green-and-yellow mixture that looks like something Repollo coughed up after eating too many Big Macs?"

In fact, Devon and I were heading over to her apartment to pick up some of her things, though she'd been hesitant to allow me to go upstairs with her.

"You got another guy stuffed up there for while I'm at work?"

"Laugh it up, Mr. Humor-pants, but Lars is quite useful when I'm bored, and he doesn't try to be funny like some people I know." Devon stuck her tongue out at me, and I clacked my teeth together, miming a bite.

"No one really names their kid Lars though, do they?"

"If he's six feet five with the body of a god and Norwegian they do," Devon said, then gave a sexy shiver. "Mmm, like having a fjord in a can."

I lost it on that one, laughing until I hiccupped. "Fjord in a can?"

"It's a girl thing." She snuggled across the seats and hugged me, and I hiccupped and drove. "But if it will make you feel better, you're like a braunschweiger sandwich in my brown bag lunch. With mustard."

I wanted to kiss her, but driving took precedence. I saved it up for when we stopped, as per her directions, in a most unexpected part of town: Rancho Murieta, one of the wealthier spots in Sacto, average net worth a tad lower than $1.35 million. I knew that because, well...I worked for the IRS. A six-story, deluxe mondo-expensive with marble in the bathroom and caviar in the fridge-type of condo/apartment complex, a doorman at the front. I glanced over at Devon, who diligently didn't look back.

"Nice place you live in." I said.

"Really? You know how it is, you get so used to something you don't even notice." She grabbed her purse, then the door handle, trying to do a Houdini from the car as fast as possible. I snicked the locks down.

"You locked the doors, Mark. I can't get out if you lock the doors. It's something about structural engineering."

"That's the point. So, this place you live. Seems mighty pricy for a magician's assistant to afford. Is there a Sugar Daddy or drug connection I don't know about?"

Devon didn't want to talk about it; I knew because the little spot between her eyebrows scrunched up all squinty and ridged. Finally, she frowned, glared at me in a threatening but cute manner, then gave up the fight.

"It's my grandmother Burgundy Suncloud's place."

I opened my mouth, then closed it, then opened it again, then closed it.

"She...well, she was big in the Sixties."

"Big in the Sixties?" I queried, truly knowing I was going to enjoy it, but at the risk of whama-whama felicity if I pushed too hard.

"She pays for this place with royalties from a couple of Jimi Hendrix's songs that were left to her in his will. She'd always been the sexually adventurous black sheep of the family. No racial innuendoes intended." Devon got it all out in rapid fire, jilting along the words and racing for the end.

I turned the whole nugget around in my thoughts for a moment, then smiled. "So, do I get to meet granny? This is *paella* granny, right? She of the Valencian recipes?"

Routed, Devon gave into my cheerful inevitability. "Look, I love her a lot, but she's freaky-deaky with a capital deaky."

I gave Devon a soft lip-to-lip, just a brush of consideration, then gone. "I can handle deaky. I'm a little deaky myself."

Another hug, and off to grandmother's house we went, only to be welcomed with hallucinogenic opulence: black light illuminated artwork: Albers, Rileys, and a Wesselman, looking very Oppy and Poppy. There were a couple Reinhardt statues and an Oldenburg something or other in a corner. A stack of Marshall Amps humped an entire wall, a rather familiar-looking Strat plugged into them. A grand piano hung from the ceiling like the Spirit of St. Louis at the Smithsonian. Huge gumdrop-colored pillows in lieu of furniture ramshackled the floor, incense and peppermint filling the air, with a six-foot-tall hookah sitting smack-dab center living room. Propped on a pillow in full Ustrasana Yoga Pose (hey, I once audited a guru), Devon's grandma Burgundy Suncloud in tight black leotard and loose pale skin. Her hair spread Rapunzelesque across the pillow behind her, shock-silver.

Devon dragged me toward a hallway off to the back, no doubt her room was there, but I didn't want to seem rude. "Don't I get to meet your grandmother?"

"We've met before, no doubt, many, many times."

Devon's grandmother uncurled from her pose like a jointless marionette, effortless and gravity-defying. She dusted off her thighs and shook her shoulders out. Stepping across the room, she kissed both my cheeks, then cocked her head to one side and stared at me. For a while.

"Any idea what's going on?" I asked Devon.

"She's interpreting your aura," she replied in an I-told-you-not-to-come-in tone of voice.

"Good to know, because I wasn't sure I even had one."

Ms. Burgundy Suncloud snapped into focus again. "Reminds me a little of Roger McGuinn's aura, sarcastic and thoughtful. But you have a violent shade of red at your core, tempered by the deep blue of sorrow. I see a long enshackling on the Dharmacakra. It will be a lively series of lives for you, I'm afraid."

"Lively is good, yes?"

"Sometimes. Would you like some Chinese takeout?"

She glided across the room and picked up a dragon-stitched kimono and slipped it on, then pulled a small gray cat out of the sleeve, looked at the feline for a moment, then put it back into her sleeve.

"Chinese is good, too. Have any kung pao chicken?"

"Of course. What dharma-fearing Buddhist household wouldn't order some?"

I threw an arm around Devon's waist and followed her grandmother toward the kitchen. "I love to meet new people."

It wasn't until much later, after a stomach-stuffing dinner with lots of soy sauce and MSG, some semi-heavy petting in Devon's room just to see if we could, and one quick toke on the hookah, that we headed back to my place, Devon's suitcase stowed in the trunk. Devon ran her fingers up and down the back of my hand, just a gentle reminder of things to come and a job well done.

Unfortunately, my phone rang and the end game began with a sharp enticement from Harry.

"Me and the Woolster just found out where the hinky money is coming and going, and it's kinda weird."

16.

I knew the feebs watched us, but I also knew Juju waited out there, somehow, somewhere, so I didn't feel comfortable leaving Devon alone at my place. Instead, I took her with me to the IRS offices to meet up with Harry and Wooly Bob. She didn't mind and produced a pillow from her suitcase. "You have nice pillows, Mark, but *this* is a Soba Gara Makura buckwheat-hull pillow. It's like putting your head on orthopedically endorsed breasts."

I could but accede to her cushional comfort. And the image of orthopedically endorsed breasts. Not to mention I was a fan of buckwheat pancakes.

Harry'd bivouacked in a conference room, snagging a wall-screen to plug his laptop into so we could all play connect-the-dots together. Devon curled up in a corner on an office chair levered back to recline. I'd found a fleece-lined paisley poncho in the rain closet, next to a left sneaker and a Jetsons lunchbox, and between that and her super-pillow, she'd nodded off immediately. Harry and Wooly Bob kept their voices down, but I knew from my midnight coffee grinding with Juarez, it didn't matter. My Devon slept on.

"I fiddled with the thumb drive your money-laundering Phoenix woo-hah gave us." Some Excel sheets flashed onto the screen, zipping past with speed-reading velocity; we all absorbed it with years of IRS drudgery gone reflex. "At first, I tabbed big chunks of dough coming in from overseas and that's about it. I sniffed about a bit, just testing the urine for territorial rights, but got stuck somewhere in the Canary Islands. Bob then gave it a whack."

Bob glowed with late-night defoliants and skin moisturizer, like some sticky-gooey mystic of the digital realm. He clattered the keyboard a bit and a tech-map of the Mideast sprang up, Internet mainframe touch points iconized from city to city, a trail of bytes leading one to another.

"The funds bounced all over Africa, jumping north to south, then east to west, going from bank to trader to under some Bedouin's camel-hair mattress. Swear to God. Finally, I tracked it down."

"To Muscat, Oman," I threw in, causing Bob's face to drop something terrible.

"If you already knew, you could have saved us a lot of time," he said.

"Didn't know. Just a lucky guess."

Harry threw a glare my way. "New York is a lucky guess. London, another one. Muscat, Oman, is like pulling a squid out of your anus—nuthin' nice or lucky about that, and the beak always hurts."

"Something me and the feebs were looking into. But it needed verification, and I wasn't sure we were going to get it. Until now."

Wooly Bob ran his palm across his greasy scalp; I could hear a squishy sound. "But that's not all we found."

"The 'weird' stuff, I take it."

Harry gave a Harry grin of predatory satisfaction. "You'll never lucky-guess where the money went from there."

"Believe me, I'm not going to even try," I conceded. "Weird is why I came down, girlfriend in tow." We all looked over at Devon, who slept along pretty as a snoozing peach.

Harry nodded to Bob, who flicked a few more keys, and the lines of digital trace moved from the Mideast across the Atlantic, did a do-si-do in and around Chicago, and headed straight to the account of a Dr. Wilcox Tobitt, Board Certified Plastic Surgeon...Beverly Hills.

Weird is as weird does, and that was weird.

"Plastic surgeon?"

Harry and Bob both nodded.

"Beverly Hills?"

They both nodded again.

"Huh. That's something I wasn't expecting. We've got Mongs, cows, plutonium, Mideastern money, and now...plastic surgery." I teased a cuticle between my teeth. "Fuck 'em. Maybe they're giving everyone new faces or something. Doesn't matter. I take it you fine-tooth-combed this quack's finances?"

Harry lazily reached over and one-handed the keyboard, bringing up the full fiscal records of said M.D. "What can I say—he's a Beverly Hills plastic surgeon. He rakes in the bucks and his accountant plays fair with the taxes. Nevertheless, he's been wired money to do two dozen surgeries, unnamed, that aren't cheap. And that's where the Oman money ended up."

"Twenty-four surgeries? But where's the plutonium? Are you *sure* this is right?"

Harry shook his head with disenchantment. "Sure as I am that as I get older my bowels will become more and more inflamed and nodules will appear on my prostate like pimples on a fourteen-year-old potato-chip eater. The data's right, but what it means...haven't a hint."

"Anyone need a tit job or a rhinoplasty?"

Harry fingered the bridge of his nose. "I kinda like my hooter. It's got character. And my bazooms are just fine, thank you very much."

Bob looked offended. "I believe elective surgery, although a person's right to choose, is a barbarity against the beauty of humankind. I believe we are as we are and should not try to alter that with a knife."

The man had no hair. What the hell was he going on about?

"I guess it's up to me and the FBI to have a chat with the dear doctor and see about those two dozen surgeries he has scheduled. Maybe they just all want to look like Semitic Michael Jacksons or something." I did my worst Michael Jackson impersonation, which was pretty much the same as my best Michael Jackson impersonation. " 'Billie Jinni is not my lover, she's just a girl who claims that I am the one!' "

On that off-note, I collected a groggy Devon, and we all left the offices to each our separate hours of late-night. Tooling back to my apartment, I began calculating Mongs and Mideastern surgeries, adding up the columns and carrying the two. Something didn't jibe, and I couldn't even make a guess as to what, but I was going to find out. You betchum in spades.

Unlocking my door, lights poured out from inside as I swung it open. I clutched Devon and whirled her around, shielding her with my back and trying to body-walk her away, but she kept squeaking half-asleep protests. I hadn't left the lights on.

"Mr. Douglas. Is that who is out there and is you?"

Not a voice I recognized, but with a heavy British accent and a dab of something else. Couldn't be good, but then, it wasn't Juju, so maybe it wasn't Armageddon with a soprano. I looked back over my shoulder and there stood Lawrence of Arabia in full cloth of gold robes and headgear, with Moss Lipowa sunglasses (had a supermodel I once audited; claimed 'em as a "business expense," $3,800 a pop) jacked over his eyes. Standing in *my* doorway. That I had to see.

"I'm Mark Douglas, and you are?"

"Sheik Kamal Issah bin Saqr Al Khaimah, known to my friends as Louie."

He held out a hand, and I took it. Strong, a little fleshy, a good grip, and ultra-wealthy smooth, as in daily manicures with goat placenta lotions and nubile young nubiles for each finger.

I motioned to the quickly awakening Devon. "Devon Pontac."

Sheik Louie gave a small bow but did not shake. "I am delighted to meet you, Miss Pontac."

Sleepy, but still my Devon. "I'd be delighted if I knew what I was being delighted about."

The Sheik ignored her and turned back to me. I sensed some gender-challenge issues, but I was no shrink; I just audited them for the IRS. Mr. Robe salaam'd me gracefully. "I hope I am not intruding."

He'd jiggered my lock, gone into my home, and nonchalantly waved it off. Not by me.

"You're in my place, and I didn't invite you, Louie. Any reason why I shouldn't kick the crap out of you and then call the police to come donut-break you?"

Two large sides of beef dressed in Savile Row suits, again with the sunglasses, stepped up behind the Sheik. "I felt, considering the gift I am offering you, that it would be better if my presence were not readily known. To anyone but you, of course, so I took some liberties to ensure that."

"I go in when I find out what this is about, if that's all right. It's been a long day."

If the goons were going to pull guns, I thought I could give Devon enough time to run by going straight at them. After that, I was hoping Harry'd get all nasty in return...after my much-wept-at burial, of course.

Sheik Louie cleared his throat, and the two hunka-hunka-threatening loves backed off.

"I have been ill-met in my introduction. I, who is me, have flown from Tabuk with a message to give you. At the behest of Lila."

Ah, the magic word. "Inside."

We all pushed in, and I whispered Devon to the bedroom under the guise of sleeping, knowing she'd have 911 at the speed dial, ready to scream.

"That's one of the many things I like about you." I ran my fingers down the small of her back, perfect and inviting. "You have a way with an emergency call."

She gave me a quick kiss and disappeared into the other room. I could imagine her warming up the bed, skin to sheet, and wished I were in there with her helping to warm it up.

I turned back to Sheik Louie, who parked himself on my couch, proper but relaxed. His bodyguards stood on either side of the room, stone, immaculate. They still hadn't taken their sunglasses off. I waited.

"I have a diamond encrusted penis," he began without preamble.

Devon popped out of the back room. "Really?"

The Sheik did not look over at her but continued to speak to me. "Would you like to see it? Or pictures? I had a professional photographer do a whole series of before and after images. The lighting is quite exquisite."

I motioned Devon away, and she shot me a long-suffering look, then a smile. I shooed her back one more time. "Don't get your hopes up, sweet stuff. If it's a new fad, I'm not sure I'm *ever* going to be hip." I then turned to the sheik again. "I don't think I need to see it or the photographs. Why would I?"

"It is a sight to behold. All of them Marquise cut and studded beneath the skin of my shaft in various designs and beadings. I like to say they are 'ribbed for her pleasure.' Ha-ha." Laugh a minute with Sheik Louie. "It is not an uncommon procedure, though I believe I have set the record for most carats per penis."

I was in the middle of a dick-measuring contest and I hadn't even realized it.

"You must be very proud. But you'd mentioned a 'gift' and 'Lila.' I'm not sure if you realize, but she was killed."

The Sheik bowed his head. "That is why I am here. You are her *Muntaqimu*, yes?"

"What does that mean?"

"Avenger. Someone of God who takes justice upon the unholy," he explained.

That pretty much summed me up, for better or worse. "Yeah, I'm whatever that is. You knew Lila?"

"I had the utmost pleasure of that acquaintance. She was a rare and delicate flower of womanhood." And for the first time I saw emotion from the Sheik. Just a flicker, like a glimpse beneath a veil.

"She was all that. And what does your jeweled Johnson have to do with her and me and the price of oil in Saudi Arabia?"

The sheik momentarily grew flustered, taking, of all things, a can of chewing tobacco from out of his robes, Chattanooga Chew, grabbing a chaw and packing it in his cheek, calming down with the action.

"I use a particular doctor for the surgery. One who gives excellent results and who I trust implicitly."

"I would think you'd have to, considering where he's wielding the scalpel."

Sheik Louie grudgingly nodded. "It is a very personal thing. But not one I am ashamed of in any way, and in fact am willing to discuss it with anyone who wishes to know more."

I'll bet you do, I thought but only smiled, hoping for him to get to the point.

"I have a second cousin with...*unsavory* business associates. Still, family is family, and when he'd asked me recently about my surgery, I regaled him with the specifics as well as the name of my doctor."

The pit of my stomach went squelchy. I could not only taste my dinner, but my lunch and breakfast as well.

"My second cousin, it seems, booked surgeries with my doctor, who called to thank me for the recommendations."

"Plural?" Not liking where it was going one bit.

"Twenty-four surgeries. But unlike mine, these are in the scrotal region."

And the bile rose hard up my throat. "Dr. Wilcox Tobitt."

The sheik looked about to spit. I handed him an old Ronald McDonald Coke glass I used to collect pennies. He dribbled tobacco juice in it and frowned back at me.

"You know?"

"Peripherally, and no specifics. Is your second cousin the type to be on the No Fly list?" The sheik nodded. "And his associates?"

"Distasteful zealots who believe that history is better left unlearned. Or ignored altogether." He piled another chunk of chew under his lip.

Too much information, and none of it good. "The surgeries? Do you know?"

Sheik Louie let loose with a long sigh. "They are having their testicles removed. One apiece."

Deus ex Lila's ex. I suspected I finally knew what the plutonium was for. Damn.

***

Six FBI shooters, Juarez, and I, all making a little nicey-nicey visit, after an eight-hour trek—the feebs *always* abide by the speed limits—to our favorite Beverly Hills plastic surgeon. Devon wanted me to bring her back something from Rodeo Drive, like the entire Gucci store. Juarez wanted to bring Tobitt's head back on a barbecue spit. I had other ideas percolating in my noggin: nasty underhanded ideas; my specialty.

"You think we really needed a backup of six, Juarez? I mean, he's a plastic surgeon. What's he going to do, give us an overly aggressive tummy tuck?"

I knew Tightass worried every time I mentioned his name, unsure if I'd use the "Tightass" moniker or not.

"Procedure. Homeland Security got word, and now they're breakin' wind trying to paperwork us to death. Besides, it's two-dozen terrorists. My six are point, and we'll pick up more before we go in from the Lala branch." He offered me an official FBI jacket. "I got an extra if you want."

"Sweet of you to think of me, but I'm good with my official jeans and T-shirt. Besides, I don't think I have the short sides and back look to pull it off." The buzz of my cell phone stopped my Juarez-baiting. "That you, Harry?"

Seems Harry'd found some more links in the money-go-round, leading from Dr. Tobitt to Oman and back to a small Mongolian barbecue restaurant in Sacramento. Surprise, surprise.

"Keep a few tabs on the place and root around on the owners. I think we both know what's going to turn up, but we might as well make sure."

Harry laughed and hung up. From Ulan Bator to Muscat to Beverly Hills to Sacramento to Lila; round and round and round she goes, and where she stops...I'll be there.

Parking in Beverly Hills was nonexistent, especially when it was on the FBI's dime and they wouldn't spring for a paid lot. We ended up five blocks from our building, having to use our feeb permit on the windshield to make sure we didn't come back and find the van towed. Wouldn't that be a bitch?

Juarez phoned the locals, who waited in place outside of a brownstone-and-glass, two-story office building. It had its own private drive, both front and back—ritzy-titzy. Dr. Wilcox Tobitt's offices took up the top floor. Juarez positioned his windbreakers around the building and took four of his hand-picks from our trip up with us. He carried warrants up the wazoo, packin' for bear, clam, and whale. I was supposedly along for the ride, but he and I knew better: he'd do his federal thing, and I'd do whatever it was I did. Repeatedly.

Downstairs was all ferns and soft lighting. The elevator cooed open, and we marched in like Sherman lacing on his boots before Atlanta. One of the windbreakers hit the "2" button and away we went. The elevator doors opened again, and we were greeted by gazongas. Huge, bouncy gazongas. The best money could buy.

"Hey, hi! You coming out or in?" said the twenty-something, silicone-augmented blonde in short white shorts and a scoop-neck T-shirt that looked like a big top tent straining to contain the elephants. Terminally perky with an orthodontically correct smile and an indoor tan that no doubt had no lines, she all but bounced as she talked, giving all of us in the elevator whiplash simply from proximity.

Juarez couldn't find his tongue, mouth or breathing, so I stepped to the fore: "Out."

"You going to see Dr. Willy? He's the best *ever*." Hefting her bounty for all to get a closer look—I heard a strangled gulp from one of the feebs behind me—the laws of fluid dynamics threatening to overturn, Miss Bigger-Than-A-Breadbasket chirped how much we'd like him. "Would you believe I used to be a B-cup? Now look at me...double E all the way."

With tight pants and tighter smiles, we exited the elevator, swiveling back over our shoulders to watch the short white shorts ping-pong away, doors closing and gone. When we looked back around, greeting us were an even bigger pair of gazongas—so large, in fact, it seemed insurmountable for the receptionist to type on her keyboard, let alone see her monitor. It looked like a Photoshopped porn site come to life, some secret Japanese Hentai cloning lab. I heard a smothered "mama" from behind, same guy, but took no note; that was Juarez's territory. We needed to talk to Tobitt, and no amount a breastage was going to stop us.

"Is Dr. Tobitt in?" I asked, slathering on the sweetness.

With a husky, trained voice, Doris—I read the nameplate—returned, "You don't have an appointment. Are you here to sell something? Dr. Tobitt usually discusses samples and enhancement technologies after hours. If you leave your card, I can arrange a day and time for you."

Juarez shook his enhancement stupor off and charged forward, flipping his ID out, "Agent Juarez, F-B-I. Please tell your employer that we have some questions for him. And we'll need your patient records as well."

Doris didn't faze. With a rack like that, she'd probably dealt with more thermonuclear requests than mere government mortals'. "Our records are confidential, as you know, and I'll see if the doctor has a free moment."

As she reached for her phone, Juarez slapped his inch-thick warrant in front of her. "This is a warrant, as *you* know, and you better start showing me records and getting the doc's butt out here pronto, or there's going to be a real need of plastic surgery."

I looked over at Juarez with a gimme-a-break look, then turned back to the receptionist.

"Doris, your boss may be in something bigger than he's used to," I said, giving a meaningful glance at her abundance. That got a sliver of a smile. "Seriously, my friend brought a dozen F-B-I guys 'just in case,' and in this case, it's one of those 'five dead, anchorman' kind of things. Did you book surgery for two dozen men of Mideastern persuasion recently?"

That got her attention quick, and she went all serious. "Yeah, we did. Testicular replacement procedures. Not something you see much of unless there's cancer. I thought perhaps it was for religious reasons or something."

"Something like that. Could you call up when the surgeries are scheduled? You'd be doing everyone a favor, even if the warrant says you have to."

She began typing, an extraordinary method that entailed somehow reaching *around* to access the keyboard. Quite fulfilling to watch.

At that moment, the doctor himself came out from back, white surgical coat and movie-star good looks gone decrepit, rather like George Clooney at seventy-five and only getting gigs on the reunions of ER anymore: full head of hair plugs, nose chiseled to perfection in a Fifties's way, jaw ennobled, and chin cleft, with skin so tight his forehead looked taut as the top of a snare drum. I could catch capped teeth behind his stretched grin. Only his eyes showed their unadorned years. And his pack-a-day voice. "Doris. What's going on?" He caught Juarez's credentials and began to back up.

"Dr. Wilcox Tobitt?" Juarez went all G-Man precise. "We have a warrant to search your premises and records. Can you please take us back to your office so we can talk while my people begin?"

The FBI agents started to fan out.

"I...what's going on? I'm as legal as the Book of Judges. I don't even use Botox, let alone monkey pituitary glands. That's all mumbo-jumbo anyway. Now sea-slug venom has its merits, but I go through the correct channels."

"It's the testicular replacement procedures, doctor," Doris lobbed to him.

"Damn. I knew they were too good to be true. But Sheik Louie is one of my better customers. Have you seen his diamond encrusted penis?"

"It *is* a doozy," Doris added.

"Some of my best work. I have excellent pictures of the before and after," the doc said, lighting up with pride.

Juarez begged off. "We have more significant things to discuss, doctor."

Dr. Tobitt shrugged and led Juarez and me back to his office. "Each to his own, but *I* think it's pretty significant."

Tobitt's office was a shrine to celebrity surgery. Every inch of his walls was covered in eight-by-ten signed glossies of the rich and famous, the rich and infamous, the plain old rich, and even a few poor and famous. Every one of the photographed beamed with more-than-nature-made-them perfection.

The doctor sat down behind his desk and turned business-like. "So, what do you want to know?"

Juarez, wary, "No doctor-patient privileges?"

"Screw it. I'm too old for that. If you've got a warrant, they must be bad guys, so what's going on?"

I could suddenly see the pit bull-young doctor who'd forged himself a plastic surgery temple here in Beverly Hills lo those many years ago.

"You can probably figure that Mideastern and F-B-I add up to no good in a 'civil rights don't mean shit' kind of way."

Tobitt nodded. "I'm a vet. Screw 'em all."

"We need to know when those surgeries are scheduled, and what they entail."

Tobitt opened a drawer in his desk and pulled out a five-times-normal-size plastic cutaway of the male genitalia. He deftly snapped the scrotum apart and popped out one of the testicles.

"Easy as pie. Go in, snip-snip, grab the testicle and replace it. Happens all the time for guys with cancer down there. It's called the Armstrong procedure these days. It's the only sure-fire remedy with the chemo."

While Juarez nervously took the plastic testicle Tobitt had thrust into his hands, I asked the million-dollar question. "But these men don't have any cancer, do they?"

"Nope. They're doing it for some other weird purpose. Which is beyond me. They want artificial testicles put in for no medical reason."

He began rummaging around in his desk again, finally coming out with a heavy lockbox, the metal thicker than on any I'd seen before. He opened it up and pulled out a perfect metal testicle.

"Here's the sample they gave me."

It was warm to the touch, and I froze inside.

"Please put this back in the box and close it up doctor," I declared quietly. Juarez's feeb antenna twitched at my words, and he looked over, concerned and expectant. "We'll take this with us. Agent Juarez, if you would."

Tobitt handed the box to Tightass, who gladly handed the plastic testicle back.

"Just hypothetically, Dr. Tobitt, would anyone be able to feel the difference if you put an object other than this particular one in?" I asked.

"You mean like do a little ball-and-switch," Tobitt replied, cracking himself up. Juarez and I looked governmental, and he cut himself short. "Well, if they were the same size and shape, and basically the same weight. But you gotta remember, none of these guys knows what a fake ball feels like in the first place, huh? I could put a tangerine in there and tell 'em it's good to go, and they'd have to believe me. And there's the initial swelling right after the surgery. Seriously, who's gonna know?"

I smiled, and Juarez looked confused. "What kind of recovery are we talking about?"

"Oh, it's pretty much an out-patient thing, though I wouldn't be jumpin' on any trampolines for a couple of weeks. One ball's not a big deal, but two is a whole rerouting of the plumbing."

I patted the lockbox Juarez was holding. "Doctor, if you could keep your schedule on these surgeries, the United States government would be very thankful."

"No problem."

17.

The FBI did a real number on that metal testicle, and, as I suspected, its outer skin was certified, grade-A, momma's-little-helper plutonium. The insides were typical plastic explosive with a cell-phone-triggered charge. A dirty body bomb. The biggest nightmare in all the government's big paranoid nightmares. Able to slip through millimeter wave portals without trouble; no airport security could detect it unless they were absolutely looking for it, and even then...probably not. It did double duty on an airplane: it took down the plane, then irradiated the rescue workers who came to clean up after the crash. Radiation poisoning was monstrously ugly, painful, and slow. Undetectable, any man passed on the street could bring death. Once word got out, it'd be a panic.

I gave Juarez my nasty ideas of what to do, and he ran with them. Identical metal testicles were built by the feeb engineering boys, but instead of bombs, they were transmitters. We'd surgically implant homing devices into the terror cells and track them back to their dens. They could run, but unless they cut their own balls off, they couldn't hide.

But calculations done on the theoretical amount of plutonium the Mongs had brought into the country showed twenty-four golf balls barely put a dent into their stash. We needed, desperately, to grab the rest before someone else came up with another unpleasant use for it.

Harry dogged the restaurant's financials, and we bull's-eyed its certainty as headquarters and base for all things bad Mongolian. Then Miguel of all people added a tidbit about trucking and food delivery. Seems he'd once been a restaurant busboy during high school, and among his other duties had been packing the produce and canned goods in from outside when the haul came in. He mentioned that well-run restaurants scheduled deliveries like clockwork—same days each week so they could keep constant calculation on what they needed and when, never too much, never too little. Wooly Bob danced the numbers and found oblique trucking runs coming into the restaurant, and from those we tallied the plutonium deliveries from Arizona. Perfect match.

We simply needed an invitation to the party.

***

"Stop screwing around, Rodney. Put Desmond on the line, okay?"

The idiot had answered the phone and was pretending, in a lopsided Mexican accent, that he "no hable Inglés," only he kept repeating, "no burrito English." What a riot. Always nice to work with professionals.

I waited a moment while Rodney grumbled, then handed the phone to his brother. An announcer play-by-played in the background; they were watching the game, same as me. No doubt beered up, if Rodney's hilarious Hispanic was any indication.

"It's Desmond. What up?"

"What up, Desmond, is your brother's a moron."

"You jus' figurin' that out? He's got ass fo' brains, and he don't ever wipe. Why you callin'? I'm watchin' the Rams get backdoored by the Chargers."

I heard the gurgle of beer going down his throat, amplified by the phone. Something similar to a toilet flush with benefits.

"So far, you've been the model of helpful, like Betty Crocker with a record. But now I need one more thing." I took a swig of my own beer. The Chargers were threatening to score again.

"Not like I have no choice. So, what'chou need me to do? And I don't dance." With a hint of stereo echo, I heard the Chargers score via TV and cell phone. "Dang, that was a sweet pass."

I agreed. A bootleg right, then a quick flip to the tight end who rumbled and stumbled over the goal line. "No dancing required, just eating. I need you to tell our lovely friend Erdenetungalag Antioch—"

"Say that bitch three times fast." The fizz of another beer opening.

"Tell Erdenetungalag Antioch that an extra payment came through. One more than was supposed to, and now you're stuck with six hundred and fifty thousand dollars in cash, and that you want to bring it to her."

"Why not send it like all the rest?" he said. "You know she's gonna ask, and I don't want that midget oriental snapper mad at me."

Desmond had a point, but I had an answer. "Tell her it's extra, and if she doesn't want it, you'll keep it. Tell her to send someone to come by and pick it up."

"Seems easy. *Damn!*" The Chargers had just successfully onside kicked it.

"Except she won't have anyone pick it up. She'll want you to come to her," I added, watching the Rams coach hold his head in his hands, his team a bunch of overpaid slackers. I knew the feeling.

"Why not? And where I gotta go? And why won't she have someone pick it up?"

The Chargers ran for twelve yards.

"One, she doesn't trust you and this extra money will confuse her. She'll think you're up to something."

The Chargers passed for seven more yards.

"Which I am."

Chargers with an incomplete.

"Which *I* am. Two, you're going to come to beautiful Sacramento to dine at a no-star Mongolian barbecue...all you can eat."

Chargers with a nice draw up the middle for fourteen.

"Rodney'll 'preciate that shit. He eats like a Pit Bull with the tapeworms. And don't ask about his dumps. They're *Alien vs. Predator* dumps."

I refused to think of what that entailed.

"Just tell her six hundred and fifty thousand."

"Yeah, yeah. Got it. Now can I watch the game?"

Another touchdown.

***

No one appreciated the amount of brute-force paperwork that went into making a legal law-enforcement raid. Sure, on television it was a piece of birthday cake with candles: one phone call and the next thing everyone had their guns drawn, busting down the door with a sledgehammer. Not a friggin' chance. There were days and days of triplicate forms, warrants, D.A.'s to mollify, and judges to good side get upon. Logistics ensued. Who had priority? Obviously the Feds, but the locals weren't going to acquiesce like a roofied Girls Gone Wild; they'd want a pound of flesh, grilled, medium-rare before they went along peacefully. Then there were the preliminary scouting reports. The lay of the land. Who went in? Who came out? What time? How long? And *everybody* had to get a copy. One would think the digital age streamlined this grunt crap, but quite the opposite. Mazes of forking e-mail trails went from computer to computer and bounced back again in electronic hailstorms. Sometimes a computer went down. Crash. Sometimes a server went down. Boom. The course of true government hardware rarely ran smooth. Or updated. *Ever.*

Juarez lived for this miasma of administration. His heart raced, his hands grew sweaty, his pupils dilated. Forget heroin, bookkeeping formalities were the drug of Tightass's choice. He'd boast of his managemental prowess, having Power Pointed the whole operation, then wrapping the forms, photos, and surveillance video into one big computerized presentation package. Just click to run.

Glad I didn't have to do it.

The boys and I cross-checked our money flows and kept tabs on all the players. Not a whisper on Juju Klondike, though. The police's manhunt came up nil, but they refused to give up. They wanted Klondike, and because of that, the feebs had free run of the Mongs. I wanted them to get Klondike, too, but my primitive hindbrain knew better, constantly starting at every noise. He was coming for me, and if I lived past the raid on the plutonium, something or other was going to have to give.

El Repollo stayed by Devon's side, the mange clearing up with his more refined diet—same thing we ate—though his gas never relented, and Devon stayed locked up in my apartment, a couple of Feds standing watch and Harry lurking. Harry lurked like no one else. He had graduate degrees in lurking and post-grad dissertations on skulking. Even I didn't always know when he was around. Disturbing at best. Nevertheless, if I didn't know, good chance Juju Klondike didn't either. Or at least that was the master plan.

The Gloucesters flew in with instructions, date and time, when to head over to the Mongolian Restaurant, $650,000 FBI-supplied dollars in tow. Human nature's a commodity, generally predictable and always useful. Erdenetungalag Antioch might deal in illicit radioactives and treat obstacles, human or otherwise, with .45 caliber bullets, but she was vaguely human, so I could forecast her responses to a certain extent. Curiosity over the money insisted she ask the Gloucesters for a chat, which ensured Erdenetungalag Antioch would be at the restaurant, which then established the FBI's raid. Like a game of solitaire, the cards fell, stacked and finally broken open.

Juarez and I decided to sample the delicacies of Mongolian barbecue, keeping an eye on Rodney and Desmond, as well as Erdenetungalag, giving the go-ahead for the agents to storm in and do their agent-y thing with guns drawn, vests on, bullhorns blaring, and all that macho jazz. I went along on sufferance, but Tightass understood that there was no rest for the wicked, and I'd give him hell if I didn't ride with. Besides, I'd called *shotgun.*

We briefed at the Federal Building, the only place that held a conference room big enough to handle the crowd, not to mention they offered refreshments. Desmond looked nervous as a baitfish waiting to be cast into a school of barracuda. Criminals did not ordinarily volunteer to sit in a room packed with armed and slavering law-enforcement officers. He kept glancing from wall clock to door, taking short breaths and licking his lips over and over.

"Don't worry, Desmond," I said from the end of the table. "If you did try to run, you wouldn't make it two steps before forty guys drew and fired in unison. Be quite an abstract work of art against the far wall, I bet."

He growled but said nothing.

Rodney, oblivious as always, stuffed his face with ridged potato chips—sour cream flavored—and clam dip, washing it down with repeated Diet Pepsis sans napkin wiping, his face smeared with mung. When he spotted a platter of deviled eggs, he grinned like a barfly at a new bartender, and inhaled half the plate hasty-pasty, shoveling eggs in conveyor belt fashion. The FBI agents gave him a wide berth, preferring to drown in bitter coffee sweetened to the point of colloidal suspension and TastyKake honey buns. They liked their sugar rushes with a little kick.

Juarez, with digital visual aids tossed on the wall screens on every side of the room, ran down the play-by-play, drawing X's and O's for everyone, footnoting their placement and duties. When he'd finished, I felt like I'd just gotten done cramming for my SATs. Tightass grinned, all smug and self-righteous. The feebs filed out to prepare for later that evening, while Juarez and I sat down with the Gloucester brothers for a fourth-quarter chat.

"We'll be in there at another table, so stay chill and look for us to give you the three, two, one, go," I instructed, trying to keep it as simple as possible for Rodney's sake.

"But we'll get dinner, right? I like that stir-fry crap," he asked.

He scratched behind one of his ears, digging in with a finger until I began to worry he was going to either draw blood or strike oil. We sat staring while it kept up for a minute, then Rodney realized he was the object of scrutiny.

"I gotta itch, so I itch. No fightin' the itch."

On that the security of America rested.

Desmond beady-eyed me all rat-in-a-pet-store sniffing a snake, "Why you need us there if you gonna be there, too? Not some caught-in-the-crossfire bullshit goin' down is there? We done what you told us to, but it don't seem sensible to walk into a shooting arcade."

"We need Erdenetungalag Antioch, mama Mong." Juarez spelled it out like letters on a Scrabble board. "Without her, none of this means a thing. Without her, no plutonium. She'll come out for you, so you'll be there. Then it's goodbye Phoenix, hello somethin' somethin' somewhere."

Desmond nodded. "But they'll know it's us."

"You'll be in a galaxy far, far away by the time they get around to even giving you a second thought," I said. "You know all this. What's up?"

Rodney clam-fisted a couple of granola bars, stuffing them both in his mouth at once. Desmond's long-suffering eyebrow raise said it all: *any chance you could shoot him for me by accident?*

I looked at Juarez and he at me, and he sighed, then shook his head.

"Sorry, Desmond. No can do. Genetics and the law tie our hands. But I know of a good assassin you could hire," I said.

Both Desmond and Juarez looked away, obviously not finding it as funny as I did. Or as cavalier. Maybe I needed to rethink my comedy quotient, or my life expectancy. Whichever came first.

***

I watched a black-leotarded Devon fold herself into origami shapes, tucking herself in and out of a black box with a mysteries-of-the-Orient-red dragon painted on the front that couldn't have been more than two feet on any side. Somehow, she managed. A multitude of possibilities ran through my brain, and when she glanced over her shoulder at me, it was obvious she knew exactly what I was thinking.

"Naughty-naughty. Mr. Douglas. Do I get all hot and bothered when you're plunging through ten-forty forms like an Acapulco cliff diver?"

"Don't tell me your lip didn't quiver when I talked Schedule C in bed the other night."

I trowelled mayonnaise and mustard on a couple of slices of wheat bread, built a solid layer of turkey bologna, topped with paper-thin cuts of purple onion and tomato, iceberg lettuce, pepper, jalapenos, and a splash of wine vinegar. And a dab of peanut butter hidden underneath to add crunch. El Repollo sat on my feet, looking up at me with eat-the-world eyes, tail wagging like a scythe. I heard a low, B-string rumble come from his stomach.

"It was so sad, I was ready to cry." Devon refolded herself into another pretzel, then back in the box.

I raised the knife high, ready to slice. "You sure you don't want half?"

Devon looked out from that tiny little box, a cute mouse from a hole. "Are you kidding me?"

I chomped into my creation, munching happily. "More for me." A drip of mayonnaise clung to the corner of my mouth, and I had to backhand it, licking it clean.

Fingers first, then forearms, then shoulders, then leveraging herself free, followed by long, long legs, Devon slithered out of the box, finally satisfied. "You always hungry before going off to play cops and robbers?"

I stopped mid-swallow, a piece of lettuce dangling from my lips; her words came out less than playful. I gulped it down. "I can't trust the FBI to get it done, Dev, so I'm going along as brain trust and babysitter. I get paid overtime, too."

Devon bent straight over, palms to floor. "Well, as long as you're getting paid for it. You could use a new couch and towels in the bathroom." There was the smile in her voice again.

I brought my sandwich over and crouched down for an awkward face-to-face from between her ankles. "Spoken like a true double-jointed interior decorator."

I ate my lunch and marveled at Devon's...*flexibility*.

"Who gets moments of snottiness about her number-one auditor going out into the big bad world with a bullet-proof paper vest."

"It's in triplicate," I added.

She unfolded, standing straight, top of her head to my chin, looking into my eyes. "I know you can't go all your life with pieces of broken ghosts following after. She...she needs you to say good-bye, and if that's with blood instead of tears, then that's what you have to do. You walk around wounded by loss, now wound 'em back."

I ran my palm down her cheek, then cupped her chin and kissed her. "Wow, you're yummy *and* deep."

"And you taste like bologna and peanut butter." She kissed me. "Only for the discerning palate."

I set the plate down and put hands on her waist, appreciating how tiny she felt, completely out of proportion to how I felt about her. "It's something I have to do."

"I know. That's what I just said."

"Would it matter if I promised to let Juarez get hit by all the bullets?"

"Nice of you to offer. Just keep your head down."

We kissed again, then my phone buzzed.

"Liftoff time."

I shoved the last of the sandwich in my mouth and grabbed my sweatshirt—always fashionable at an FBI raid—patting my pockets for my keys.

"Am I forgetting anything?"

Devon quirked a grin at me. "Your breath?"

"Secret weapon. I'll call when we're done. You stay inside, no answering doors. Harry's...Harry's off duty tonight."

Devon blew me a kiss as I headed out, El Repollo snuffling at her toes. "It's just gonna be you and me big guy." El Repollo gave a hearty fart, then wagged his tail vigorously fanning the pong fumes. Devon held her nose, "Mark! You have to do something about Polli's diet. No more six-dollar teriyaki burgers for him!"

"What could I do? He was buying." And with that I closed the door and double locked it, heading off to meet and greet.

***

Genghis Khan's smelled like Rooster Sauce armpit and fried rice mixed with date-expiration meat. A glorified back-alley dive transported to mini-mall status by its location and city clientele, it neon-signed its existence with big bold colors and a second "h," which flickered in the wind. Relentlessly open for lunch and dinner seven days a week, including holidays, it boasted a "B" health rating in sanction.

A surly teenagette Mongolian greeter posed near the front door under a framed and pin-lit photograph of Mongolian President Nambaryn Enkhbayar in all his baby-faced glory. With badly dyed blonde hair and bottle-tanned skin, the greeter chewed rabidly on a toothpick and sported enough tatoo'd midriff to be mistaken for a Thai hooker, bumping people to their tables whenever she damn well pleased.

Part fast-food drippings at the all-you-can-stand buffet, part plastic-packet soy sauce, two-to-a-customer table settings, part half-full no matter the time, Khan's held court to a spectrum of hungry, running from shabby, dime-saving civil servants to lost tourists who wanted a taste of the "Orient."

Constantly welcoming as he went, Paul Antioch flitted from table to table wiping them down with a soiled cloth that would embarrass a bar rag. He didn't stand on tiptoes more than five and a half feet tall, with thin, lank, seaweed hair that had already begun the mid-life exodus from forehead to nape, leaving nothing but balding watershed behind. And moles. He had a connect-the-dot head of moles ranging from freckle to quarter-size, an archipelago of precancers time-bombed for melanoma, if something else didn't get him first.

Something like the FBI.

I pestered Juarez. "So, you're buying, right? I mean, it's an F-B-I shindig. You should buy. It'd be a business write-off that way. Make sure you keep the receipt."

Juarez dipped his Asian-style boat-spoon into his fried-wonton soup, sprinkling extra crunchy bits on top. "No one's going to pay for dinner. We're raiding the place as soon as Erdenetungalag Antioch makes her appearance."

"But what if she doesn't come until dessert, and the server brings the check? Do you grab it, or do I? Are we going Dutch to the arrest?"

I bit into a fried shrimp puff after dousing it with hot mustard and ketchup, the tang of fresh batter and sweet-juiced seafood dappling my tongue. Juarez wouldn't even get the tab for his own open-heart surgery—he'd find a way to stiff the doctor for leaving a scar.

"Not going to happen, so why worry?"

The hard-at-work-but-still-pleasant waitress, dressing in what I took to be traditional Mongolian garb (jeans, black-and-white wingtips, and a Buck Owens T-shirt) whirred by, Juarez's Coke and my iced tea placed on the table, two bowls full of uncooked sliced meat—chicken for the miser, lamb for me—set before us.

"Have you been here before?" she asked.

Juarez looked questioningly at her. "I don't think so. Do you think I have?"

The server, not to be sidetracked by Hell, high water, or Juarez, boldly took that as a "no."

"Okay, then just take your bowl of meat to the serving counter over there and pile on any vegetables you want. I suggest you put the broccoli on first, as it tends to roll off otherwise, then follow the instructions on which sauces go on top: like soy sauce, or garlic sauce, or Genghis Khan's Special Sauce. Take the whole thing to the non-English-speaking chef over at the genuine Mongolian Barbecue Grill, gotten from Mongolia, where he'll stir fry it to perfection, dump it back into a new bowl, and then you come back to your table, where there'll be rice to eat it with."

"Genghis Khan's Special Sauce?" I smirked to the waitress who smirked back, looking more and more like a late-night bar hopper and mojito slammer by the second.

"Don't ask...but it's good. Stay away from the Tien Tsin chile peppers, though, unless you like tongue-flaying hot—it's a trick to sell more drinks. And a word to the wise...the sprouts are a day old, so they're a little soggy."

"Thanks. I hate limp sprouts."

"Me, too," she said with a wink, then wandered to the next table of business-suit businesswomen, all with Hershey chocolate bar-sized business phones Panini'd to their ears, to repeat her spiel, word for traditionally non-Mongolian word. Even if Juarez ditched paying, I was going to tip her something.

Behind her, heading toward the back, Rodney and Desmond, just coming from the fry-line, Rodney's bowl heaped high with meaty vegetable gooey goodness, Desmond's helping, less gluttonous—he looked more constipated than hungry. They sat at a Paul Bunyan wagon-wheel-sized table with four of Erdenetungalag Antioch's busy bees, who all dressed in bad-guy black turtlenecks and loose-fitting black sweaters, *de rigueur* for the up-and-coming soldier/henchman. The heavies drank Cokes and kept their backs stick-up-the-ass straight at attention, even sitting down, sure sign of ex-military. That and their Chinese knock-off military boots, laces untied like gangsta Mongs in the hood. At their feet, equidistant between the Gloucester boys' chairs, parked the messenger bag with $650,000 in it.

Paul Antioch buzzed around the dining area, obsequious and toadying until the cows came home, ate some hay and fell asleep. "Hello! Welcome to Genghis Khan's! Welcome, welcome!" But still no Erdenetungalag.

"So, ready to barbecue some veggies?" I asked Juarez, who clearly wanted the show to start already. "I see some cilantro with your name on it."

Tightass grumbled and shook his head. "She'll be out, and I don't want to be standing in line when she does." He picked at a shrimp puff, dipping too much hot mustard on it, mouth-afire, and gargling with Coke while trying to breathe through his nose. "Damn."

"Puts hair on your chest."

"Sure, who doesn't want more of that?"

Another couple gulps and Juarez caught movement at the far side of the room: Erdenetungalag Antioch arrived. Like a jade Hindu goddess in miniature, swathed in flickering green silk with emerald earrings and a predacious stare, she Pai Gow'd about the tables, curving straight toward the Gloucesters in a bodhisattva tranquility, but at the last moment turning to her husband with a snarl.

"Wipe tables again—they look like poodle shit! And mop bathroom stalls. They still have vomit all over floors."

Paul Antioch bowed to his bride and hurried to do her bidding, muttering curses and prayers under his breath, and looking as if he hoped for a quick and complete heart attack but knowing with his luck it would be a lingering aneurysm. He'd never escape his wife in this life, or the next.

Desmond caught Erdenetungalag's approach, wary and ready to lie, while Rodney bent face-deep into his rice bowl, shoveling into his mouth with chopsticks, unmindful.

"You need to try your bowl, Des. This stuff is really something," G the Younger said.

"I glad you enjoy our cuisine, Mr. Gloucester," Erdenetungalag said, sliding into the empty chair as her four troops swiveled about in surveillance. "We very, very pride ourselves on authenticity and taste."

A limp sprout dangling from the corner of his mouth, Rodney smiled. "I gotta get one of them barbecue grill metal things at my place. I could eat this all day."

Erdenetungalag reached over and flicked the hanging sprout from Rodney's mouth with an exceptionally long, vermillion-painted fingernail, then wiped her hands on her napkin.

"I not think you find one anywhere else in United States. It...*special*."

I looked at Juarez, who was trying not to look at the other table so hard his eyes popped like hardboiled eggs. "How sweet, small talk. Next we'll be hearing about the weather in Ulan Bator and parts unknown."

Desmond caught Erdenetungalag's eye and tapped the moneybag with his foot, the pregnant thump of fullness heard. "Didn't know what to do, so I brought it. I asked around; you aren't someone I need to get on their bad side."

"We in the preliminary dance of our association. Better to be safe than sorry," Antioch suggested. No one made a move for the money in any way, just letting it anchor the conversation.

I took a sip of my ice tea, crunching a cube between my teeth, then putting the glass carefully down next to my soup bowl, a final moment of dinnertime calm.

"You ready to rain fire, brimstone, and the whole judicial process down?"

Juarez puffed air out between his lips like a horse, fished his cell phone from his jacket and speed dialed.

"Now's good," he decreed into the phone, and that's when the bullhorn outside detonated, and forty FBI agents hit the restaurant from every conceivable angle like black-suited battering rams.

The surly teenagette greeter popped her toothpick from her mouth and ducked into a fetal position behind the entrance door, yelling at the top of her lungs: "Don't kill me! I give head!" Survival instincts at their finest.

Erdenetungalag Antioch reared up at the crack of attack, four foot nine and hoisting the biggest frickin' revolver ever, a Pfeifer Zeliska .600 Nitro. Twice the size of her head, it fired rifle bullets. Her first shot took an ex-fullback FBI agent through the body armor, puncturing it like jabbing a nozzle into an oilcan, tearing a hole in and out of his shoulder and spinning him around, a screaming propeller. It simultaneously knocked the Mong Queen backward, across the floor on her ass. Two more shots bucked her up against the wall, where she braced herself. Even so, she made an imprint in the paneling at her back every time she fired.

At that point, in a feature film, everything would begin moving in syrupy slow-motion, a graceful tango of violence and horror orchestrated to some classical piece of music or operatic aria that juxtaposed beauty with repulsion: blood and bodies, bullets and crying, all colliding between the pulse of one heartbeat and the next. In a movie, the Mongolians would fire round after round, miraculously missing everyone and the FBI'd shoot straight and true.

Of course, it didn't really take place that way. First, it happened fast. *Real* fast. Fast as a cough, people dying before they even noticed it. And it was not only color-corrected, paintbrush-pretty blood that flew, but chips of marble-white bone and slushy gray brain. The smell of scalded meat, ruptured bowels, and tangy fireworks spangled the air, while screeches and screams, despairing prayers, and no mercy rose louder and louder, cacophonic, layer upon layer upon unending layer.

Like an eclipse of the sun, comforting daylight, then nothing but darkness, the Genghis Khan's Mongolian Barbecue light-switched from family smiles and lovers touching fingertips under the tables to a slaughterhouse of fulminant and sesame oil.

Second, neither the bad guys nor the good guys shot particularly well. There were simply more good guys to begin with, and anyone left standing at the end hadn't been standing at the beginning.

We kicked the table over and ducked behind it. Juarez pulled a Glock 23 pistol from his holster. I couldn't legally join in the brouhaha, so he slid me his backup piece, a Glock 27. He might be a tightass, but he certainly wasn't a *stupid* tightass: rules were fine, but survival was finer.

He yelled for surrender. He got a fusillade instead. Suddenly little Mongolian mobsters boiled out of the back rooms like maggots from a sick dog's turd. Each hefted well-cared for Heckler & Koch Mark 23s with, of all things, suppressors. Seemed a damn strange time to keep things to a minimum, what with all the bullets flying, the people screaming, the bullhorns blaring. Maybe they got them on sale: "Buy one, get a suppressor free."

Bullets popcorn popped around the room, cracking and clacking. The side of a Mong's face turned hamburger, but he still kept firing, until another shot took out his knee and he crumpled in three distinct movements, like folding up an ironing board.

A group of FBI agents sought refuge around a potted fichus bush, comm-ing one another on their sleeve radios, even though they stood shoulder to shoulder. From their tenuous vantage, they took turns sighting on scrambling Mongolians and exchanging short bursts of fire as if warming up for an FPS game on their Xboxes.

All through the barrage, Paul Antioch, coming out from the back, continuously glad-handed and greeted, immune through determined salutation to any and all injury. Kinda weird to me, but he pachinko'd around, being missed by both sides in utter lack of red shirtism. What, no one watched Star Trek? Red Shirts? Instant death? Forget it. He finally ended up near his wife, who began berating him in her native tongue, Mr. Antioch's smile slowly curving farther and farther down until it drooped like a Fu Manchu mustache.

Rodney and Desmond crawled under their table, their four dinner companions blazing away above them. Bowls of rice and Mongolian barbecue rained down with each shot taken, covering them in sprouts, stir-fry, and soy sauce. Desmond whipped himself around, desperate to find a safe haven, while Rodney kept eating the puffed shrimp appetizers, dipping them into a pool of hot mustard and ketchup that'd fallen on his brother's shoulder. "Hey, they're *really* good. Have you tried one?"

Juarez kept on his cell phone, guiding the base camp of agents still on the outside. It didn't seem to be following the plan; the Mongs should have given up by then. Instead, they'd hunkered behind tables and sideboards with caches of ammunition, suicidal in defense, refusing to give up, and basically blazed away to the end.

"Oh, crap! Everyone down!" I yelled, unbelieving of what I saw coming at us.

One of the little Mongolian dumbasses had a rocket launcher— RPG for you role-playing gamers; no doubt where this guy got the idea—*inside* the restaurant, screaming something completely incomprehensible, then letting rip! Like a comet in a fishbowl, the thing contrailed out of the antitank gun, flew right by everyone who'd long before face-firsted it to the floor, then blew the entire side wall out of the restaurant, revealing a lot of stupefied feebs, who suddenly dove for cover and opened fire themselves, cutting down the now-rocket-less launcher of rockets.

That lit things up. But it got worse. Another bozo had an even dozen weapons strapped and cinched and shoved about his body. Every time he ran out of ammo for one, he'd grab another and continue firing. Juarez was getting frustrated. Finally, the idiot accidentally blew himself up reaching for a grenade he'd shoved, gangbanger-style, into his pants, Juarez unprofessionally yelling at the top of his lungs: "About frickin' time!"

I wormed my way along the tables, trying to angle toward the back exit, figuring that if anyone made an ollie-ollie-oxen-free for it, that'd be the way. Scrambling under tables, past terrified patrons who found out in wide-eyed high definition that television and real life weren't actually the same thing. Hands pressed to ears, faces to floor, the adults prayed fervently for takeout next time they didn't cook dinner. The kids looked on in fascination. I winked at a tow-headed six-year-old who winked back, then was grabbed by the scruff by his father, who cradled him under his arm like a football.

Feebs fell like mowed grass on a Saturday afternoon, their Kevlar hopefully doing its Kevlar job. If not, the butcher bill'd be higher than a Deadhead at a Further concert. The Mongs simply refused to put down their weapons and surrender in an orderly fashion, and the hits just kept on coming. Knees shattered, heads exploded, they seemed intent on taking as many people with them as possible. And they were doing a good job of it. But why? This wasn't their Jihad. They simply brokered the deal, made massive amounts of cash, and stir-fried some vegetables.

Erdenetungalag Antioch forefingered her iPhone's touch screen with a politician's continuous jab, either calling someone extremely important, or app-ing her DVR timer for the next rerun of Hannah Montana. Don't we all just love young Miley Cyrus in the midst of a gun battle? Done with the call, she fired two more shots, both hitting deadeye, then made a break for the back exit, her little henchlians ratcheting up the barrage. *This* was why they fought: Queen Mong's safety. Like a beehive or chess: protect the queen.

Not on my dollar.

Erdenetungalag moved and fired, moved and fired, her husband Paul, saprophytic lung leach that he was, trailing behind, bowing and greeting the whole way. I rounded the barbecue grill and rose up, Glock two-handed and aimed dead center on Erdenetungalag's green-sheathed heart. No time to raise her own heavy metal gun, she cried out—"I love you but this *business!*"—and threw her husband into my line of fire, then ran like a weasel for the back. Paul Antioch grabbed my gun, wrestling with it. I fired, fired again, but the little mollusk lampreyed my hand, forcing miss after miss. As Erdenetungalag ducked out the exit, another Mong grabbed me from behind. I kicked out, connecting with Paul Antioch's marbles, and he grunted, going down, but still able to crawl dutifully after his wife. Wrestling back and forth, my arms pinned like turkey wings, I leveraged up against the railing of the altar-sized hunk of metal grill and monkey-barred my attacker flat on his back...*onto* the grill. The sizzle and scream were equally loud and ear piercing; the smell of the *other* fried white meat filled my nostrils. I'd *never* eat Mongolian barbecue again. With a burbled sobbing, the Mong let go and slid from the grill. I starting-gunned after the Antiochs, ducking just as another flock of bullets zigzagged in my overall direction.

The kitchen in the rear looked like William-Sonoma meets Sam Peckinpah: bodies and kitchen equipment strewn about in pools of blood, oil, and cooking sherry. FBI, Mongolians, blenders, ladles, chef's knives, and guns, meat cleavers stuck in different cuts, skewers with fingers and onions, a salad of body parts and last-breath dressing. No one back there was alive, nothing moving. The Antioch's footprints, tracks of gore, walked back to the delivery doors. I followed.

They either waited on the other side of the doors, in which case, they had me dead to rights...emphasis on the dead, but that meant they were in eye-line of the feebs out there. Or they'd managed an escape route, feebs or no feebs, and were living to fight, or smuggle, or stir-fry another day, plutonium notwithstanding.

Who knew there was a third choice?

A two-handed pistol stance, like the cops on television use, and the cops in real life are supposed to use, puts the gun at nipple height, usually shooting straight across, give or take a head high or a crotch low. A one-handed, hip-hoppin' gangsta stance, with gun canted to the side and arm waving crazily to the beat of sampled R&B from better bands than you are Gunga-Din, ranged...well, wherever it damn well pleased, but again, usually chest height and shooting in that general vicinity. Eyes look eye-ward in the normal case of looking. It's the way our furry monkey ancestors were built, and so were we.

Running out into a possible gunfight, pistol held high in heroic fashion, simply put me exactly where, in the course of evolution, both ocularly and weaponry, a bullet could do its best to perforate my body like a hole puncher does paper. Not a good thing. I found getting higher than the eye-line, or lower, gave a moment's confusion to a shooter's brain, for the fact that it wasn't expected. Of course, a moment's not very long—shorter than a "sec" and longer than an "instant"—so geography only accomplished so much, but I had a gun, too, and with a little luck, everyone else stood where they were supposed to in the course of human events.

I darted out the delivery doors cockroach low and scurrying as fast as my little legs could carry me. Outside I expected FBI, dead or alive, Antiochs, dead or alive. I got a little of both. The FBI, as one, raised their guns, sighting down on me. I raised my hands, "You shoot me and Juarez is gonna be pissed at the paperwork," and they changed their aim, back to the ten-round championship fight going on in the middle of the parking lot.

Erdenetungalag Antioch and her husband Paul wrestled each other, clawing, scratching, slamming heads, gouging eyes, pulling hair, spitting, biting, and basically having a knockdown drag-out brawl in front of everyone's eyes. Erdenetungalag's mega-pistol had been knocked to the side, a feeb hooking it with his toe and soccering it away. Oddly, they screamed at the top of their lungs, "I love you!" while pummeling each other, drawing blood or biting an earlobe.

I circled the main event and asked the FBI squad leader what the heck was happening.

"Don't really know. She came out the back door blazing, then he coldcocked her. Then they went at each other like two cats in a burlap sack. He's crying that she doesn't give him enough attention and she was going to leave without him, and she's yelling that he's a spineless jellyfish, but he's *her* spineless jellyfish."

"Funny how the pressure gets to different people differently, though it's good to see that theirs is a relationship founded on a solid base of adoration and contempt. Barring meeting an attractive cellmate with a desire for being a 'prisoner with benefits,' I can see them making it to their golden anniversary eventually. Unless there's a lethal injection beforehand."

The squad leader grunted, then grunted again in the direction of four of his men, who waded in to break up the tussle and apprehend the Antiochs. It took another four guys, as both Erdenetungalag and Paul were stronger and dirtier fighters than they looked. Cuffs on, being led back to a van, the Antiochs continued their fight with nasty taunts in both English and Mongolian.

Juarez strolled out to scrutinize the capture. "So, where's the plutonium?" he asked Erdenetungalag, who promptly spit in his face, the glob tearing down his cheek, and laughed. "It gone! I got rid of it already, and it gone. You screwed now, Mr. F-B-I. You want, you make deal with me."

Paul Antioch began keening, "What about me? What about *my* deal? You can't let me go to prison if you go free! My heart would break into a thousand pieces and cry every night!"

Erdenetungalag growled at her husband. "Keep it zipped. We have lawyer coming."

I motioned my head, and Juarez followed me off to the side, while the Antiochs were bundled into the transport.

"So, anything inside?"

"We took out every last one of the Mongs...*none* of them gave up. Then I sent the lab boys in with Geiger counters, and other than the normal background clickety-clicks, no sign of it."

We walked through the wall-less side of the restaurant. the patrons already herded out the front, all giving statements and napkining bits and pieces of bodies off themselves. FBI techs hauled the bodies of the dead out that way as well. Two guys in full-orange Hazmat suits waved metal wands about. The Gloucesters sat at a righted table chatting with an FBI agent, Rodney still stuffing his face with scrounged stir-fry remains, while brother Desmond seemed worse-for-wear, rubbing his cheek over and over as if something were on it, but there wasn't.

I eyeballed the room, trying to put two plus two together and get a fissional mass. It *had* to be here somewhere. Juarez and his team had canvased, searched, turned stones over, and there couldn't be another place to stash the radioactives without the FBI getting wind of it. But with so little left standing in Genghis Kahn's, the chances of it being stashed anywhere seemed nil.

"Anybody else want any?" Rodney'd gotten up and heaped more pre-fry into his bowl, leaving a trail of spouts that'd slid from his vegetative mound behind, then went to the Mongolian grill—I didn't have the heart to tell him what else had recently been cooked on it—and began self-serving. When he caught Juarez and me staring, he shrugged. "Hey, all-you-can-eat is all-you-can-eat." Juarez shook his head, at a loss to answer without cursing, no doubt.

The hazmat techs kept Geiger-ing, bodies kept being hauled out, Rodney finished cooking, then went back to his table, a gleeful, hungry expression of delight on his face.

"Hey, Juarez," I said. "Didn't you cut the power and gas before hitting the place? So there'd be no explosions? I mean, no explosions *you* caused?"

Juarez called an agent over and double-checked. "Yeah, right before we came in we cut everything. Why?"

I'd already gotten down near the grill, sesame and soy sauce goo sopping the knees of my pants, sniffing and staring, and seeing no burner on. Not even a pilot light.

"Juarez, remember that testicle bomb we found at the plastic surgeon's?"

He stood over me, confused, but steeling himself in the official FBI manner to never show it. "Yeah, what about it?"

"It was warm to the touch, right? And it only had a *little* plutonium in it. Do you think that a *lot* of plutonium'd be a *lot* hotter? Like, *grilling* hot?"

Juarez grabbed me away from the grill and screamed for his lab techs. The two *squints* hurried over at a waddle, holding their lab gear before them like they were holding their dicks to a urinal. They hadn't checked the grill because, well...it was a grill, and too hot to touch.

"These instruments are sensitive and cost more than my pay grade," the taller of them explained.

One pass over the grill, two passes over the grill, and the Geiger counters clattered like hail stones on a car roof. The hazmatters wrapped their hands with towels and manhandled the top of the grill off. Underneath, radiating heat like the center of a sun, we all saw what two nuclear bombs' worth of plutonium looked like.

Rodney stopped chewing in mid-forkful. "Did that shit make my food radioactive or anything? It doesn't taste like it." He took another bite. "Tastes okay to me."

One of the lab guys explained that there was nothing to worry about; these big chunks were blocked out by the two-inch-thick-steel grill surface, which turned the radiation into heat...lots and lots of heat. But we all needed to stay well away now that the top was off and alpha, beta, and gamma rays were spewing like hot oil. At least until they took care of the bare plutonium and put it in The Box. They'd brought a lead-lined suitcase kinda thing, which they plopped the shiny, thermonuclear metal into, snapping the latches shut with Hiroshima finality.

Rodney continued eating. "Okay. Just checking."

Idiot is as idiot does.

I found our waitress in the front parking lot chatting up an FBI agent who took her phone number. I handed her a twenty. "Great service, but I'd look for a new job tomorrow, if I were you."

She nodded. "That's okay. I was thinking of going back to school anyway."

18.

Life to me often seemed a series of word problems, none of which had a right answer. Sometimes an answer *looked* right. Or sometimes an answer wasn't *wrong*. But I'd yet to see a life question that actually had a bona fide correct solution. And I'd looked. Repeatedly. With a magnifying glass and the back of the book open. No go.

The FBI jetted the plutonium to wherever it was that plutonium was jetted to for safekeeping when it wasn't being used in the warhead of a missile. Probably Boca, or Buffalo, somewhere like that. Side note: was it my imagination, or did many of the great hellholes of our nation have names that began with the letter "B?" Barstow, Birmingham, San Bernardino (okay, it *ended* with a "B"). Although Newark was the exception.

The Antiochs and their whole Mongolian mob empire had been thrown into the court system with reckless abandon, deep-end only. The Gloucesters, Rodney munchin' on fortune cookies, depositions in hand, met and befriended the United States Marshalls' office, ready to begin their new lives, in their new locations, somewhere, no doubt, in a city whose name started with a "B."

That should've been enough. But it wasn't. Juju Klondike had his own *final solution* for the problem, and that didn't have a happy ending for me. Or anyone else I'd ever known. Would know. Or ever *thought* of knowing. There lay the bug under the Persian rug; the fly in the topical ointment; the one bad apple that spoiled the whole bunch with extreme prejudice. There was no right answer, but there was *an* answer.

Sitting at Del's, already on my third tequila and beer, I contemplated the inevitable. Lila sat beside me and no one else, which was probably a good thing, as Lila was still dead. Though dressed very expensively, which she rarely did with me. Nor did she need to. I did most of the talking, but she kept up drink-for-drink, so I didn't feel odd exhibiting one of the classic signs of alcoholism. When she did speak, it was always about the same thing, so I guess she was a ghost after all.

"So *they* killed me?" she finally mentioned after putting on another coat of lipstick, mopping it on her napkin, then tossing down a shot with mechanical precision. "And you found them, like I knew you would."

I sipped beer, trying to remember if Lila looked like that or only looked like I remembered her...a difficult paradox even without tequila and beer. "Juju Klondike killed you; the Antiochs...well, *Lady* Antioch...hired him."

"So there's still unfinished business." She smiled with a Lila-full-of-life smile that somehow faded the moment it left her lips, then tumbled to the floor, later to be swept up with the peanut shells, pretzel crumbs, and balled up napkins.

"There's *always* unfinished business kiddo." I contemplated that third shot, unable to decide to drink it or to call it a night.

"I wish I could have met her. She seems like someone I'd like." Lila reached over and drank the shot for me. Or at least the glass was empty. Same thing.

"I hope one day you'll be able to," I replied, knowing she knew that I knew that it wasn't a slip of the tongue or mangling of a phrase.

Lila shook her head, not a hair floating out of place. I guess being dead does that to a person. "You never used to be religious, Mark."

"I never used to be so tired, either."

Lila downed another shot. "It gets better, I think. Eventually. Or so they tell me."

"So *who* tells you?" I quizzed, curious, but not that curious, figuring that tidbit was on a need-to-know basis.

"You know, the usual suspects." Kinda the way I figured. "But that isn't really important, is it? It's once this is over, really over, that you have to begin to forget all of it."

I drank that extra shot then. "How am I supposed to do that? Or even want to?"

But Lila'd vanished, was never there, only the empty shot glasses, the beers, and my growing haze. No spirits other than those of eighty proof, no afterlife, nothing but a guy getting drunk in a bar all by himself.

Becky looked over from across the room, but I shook my head. I'd had enough.

***

I woke the next morning with a vague head and slow eye, which eventually, after orange juice and oatmeal peppered with blueberries, picked up the pace. El Repollo, stench and all, galumphed in, looking like the Fenris wolf with a hangover, plopping his big droolly muzzle down on my feet. I gave him the rest of the oatmeal, straight out of the pot, and hoped it would stopper up his flatulence like a big fiber-and-roughage cork. Only time would tell. And my nostril hairs.

No Devon. When I'd come back the night before she was gone. Laying low, like the doctor ordered. I missed her. I didn't know where she'd gone, but I hoped she wasn't as lonely as I was. Juarez mentioned something about feeb protection, and I didn't ask any more. Tightass loosened up on that thing, but we both understood the game. What I didn't know couldn't hurt her. But it could hurt me. A lot.

People who killed people for money didn't usually hold grudges. They murdered witnesses, executed obstacles, and assassinated turncoats, but grudges didn't pay. Too many complications, and those that lived by taking other people's lives didn't like complications. Or so I'd heard.

But I'd seen Klondike in person, mano-a-eunuch, so that made me a witness. I'd been standing between him and one of his targets, since deceased, so that *might* make me an obstacle. No one ever called me a turncoat. Vegas had the odds of his going after me at twelve-to-five, with an over-under of two days. Not the best probabilities for me. If I didn't want to end up in the ground, I desperately needed to alter the chances.

FBI surveillance helped about as much as a thong on a fat person—too little, too late. If Juju and I danced, by the time the feebs cut in, one of us'd already be polka'd. I needed to know where Juju'd be at a certain time so that I could meet him before he met me. The question was always *how*. Formal, engraved invitations had gone out of style except in the cotillion set, and I didn't know his personal cell number, nor were we Facebook buddies. That left the curious coincidence of him and me bumping into each other by accident. I wanted Klondike to know where I'd be so he could meet me there, only I didn't want him to know he knew that I knew that he knew where I'd be. So I simply counted on Juju's expertise: assassins needed to be one step ahead. It was a matter of my choosing which step he'd be ahead of.

The Mongs who killed Lila, mister *and* missus, were locked up tighter than an orthodox virgin, so I took El Repollo to my poor dead friend's place to give a final tour before closing the door on it forever.

I stood there on the doorstep, the dog snuffling around, slobbering on the stoop and occasionally scratching at a hock, then gnawing on its paw, worrying it like an Iowan on a cob of corn. The police tape was gone. I still had my extra set of keys, weighing them in my palm as if scrying to see what my future would hold. Not a peep. I slotted the master into the groove and turned it in one motion.

Klondike waited for me behind that door as I entered and knocked me good with the butt of his gun. I hit the floor hard, rolling end over end before righting myself and looking up at the barrels of a Stoeger Condor over-under twelve-gauge shotgun. Not a great point of view, lemme tell you—if the first don't get you, the second definitely would. Messily.

"Call the animal off," Klondike squeaked to me, the gun not veering for an instant. I looked over and saw Polli hunkered down nibbling on a paw again, completely uninterested in the proceedings.

"Seems my dog doesn't think much of you as a threat anymore," I said. "Once bitten, twice bored."

The assassin squinted one more time at my mutt, calculating, then El Repollo cracked off a monster cheek trumpet that sounded like a bullhorn having a bowel movement, and Klondike turned his attention back my way, motioning me to stand.

"I have waited a considerable time," he said as he gestured me into the living room, a navy pea jacket a size too big, draped over him. "Eight hours, twenty-two minutes. But I am used to waiting a long time. Eventually, waiting leads to doing."

"How very Zen of you," I said, not much else in my arsenal. "I bet you and the Dali Llama get along like karmic gangbusters."

There I was, standing in the middle of what once was Lila's place and now only ghosted her memory, the psycho who'd sliced and diced her salivating to do the same to me. My dog of doom lying on the floor doing nothing. Seemed all too hopeless. Just one teeny-tiny thing—killers think they're good at killing because they kill. That's because the neurological Jiminy Cricket in their forebrain was stillborn; that somehow made them skillful. It's as if the baseball rules suddenly stated only midgets could play: there'd be no Babe Ruth, no Willie Mays, no Hank Aaron. They'd have lived and died, but they'd have never played baseball. And the midgets would think they were good. Most people don't kill. For moral reasons, for legal reasons, for just plain reasons. But what if they *did* kill? Who's to say how many Hall of Fame murderers simply never played the game?

Most killers are midgets who think they're All-Stars.

Juju stood me in the middle of the room, shotgun steady toward my chest, slowly reaching for a KA-BAR knife and a hacksaw he'd stuffed into his inside coat pockets. I stepped back across Lila's floor safe, couch still pushed aside, and he stepped to follow me. He whistled a thin rendition of Cher's classic *Half-Breed*. An odd choice for an odd creature.

I finally commented. "Eight hours, twenty-two minutes...long time."

Juju placed the hacksaw and knife on a coffee table, tidily squaring them up like place settings.

"Patience is a virtue."

"True," I answered, then stomped my foot down hard on the floor—once, twice, again. "But eight hours, twenty-two minutes isn't nearly as long as sixteen...."

Harry rose up out of the safe, holdout ankle gun in hand, Harry-grin bigger than I'd ever seen it before. "Man, I could use a drink."

Juju whipped around to face Harry just as Wooly Bob called out from the central air duct, the muzzle of a rifle sticking out through the grating: "Uh-uh-uh, Mr. Eunuch."

With an actor's timing, El Repollo trotted up to stand beside me, a hackle-raising growl in the back of his throat. I patted his bear-sized head.

"Good doggy."

Klondike froze, caught between Harry in front, Bob high and to the side, and me and Mr. Bitey behind. I picked up the KA-BAR. I *liked* KA-BARs. All Marines like KA-BARs.

Just then Miguel grunted and spilled out of a kitchen cabinet, a Taser in one hand, a roll of duct tape in the other, spilling a two-liter sized Coca-Cola bottle he'd filled with pee all over the floor and himself—"Oh, damn!"—imprints of cans on his ass. We all stared, even Juju. "Hey, I have a nervous bladder."

I knew I'd promised to keep Miguel out of harm's way, but really, I needed him, and I didn't let him have a gun, and I only promised to keep him away from the Mongs.

Harry spit on the floor, then pointed out to Miguel that, "You were supposed to clear the cans out of the cabinet *first* Miguel." He spit again. "Swear ta God, that boy was born without half his brain, and the other half has gone missing."

I grabbed the shotgun out of Klondike's hands and caught him with the butt, shattering his nose into mush. It felt good. He howled and came at me, but Harry kicked him hard on the knee, sending him to the floor. I pointed the shotgun at the killer, situations reversed. A moment of betrayal passed Juju's eyes.

"What, you think I'm going to go one-on-one with you? You're a mad-dog psycho dickless wonder. Best thing to do is put you down. Just because you don't have any friends doesn't mean no one else does."

Like I said: most killers are midgets who think they're All-Stars.

My bang-squad buddies had camped out the night before, rationed and ready, waiting for Juju and waiting for me. Bad guys weren't the only ones with patience. And no one ever expects the other guy to get there first.

Wooly Bob slithered from the air duct, no doubt aided by his hairlessness, then righted himself and tromped forward, 30.06 Springfield at the ready. Hardly the holistic gun of choice; I'd have to ask him if deer hunting fell under the heading of environmentally sound. I wasn't complaining.

Miguel held his Taser in front of him like a sword, but we had given him that for show. He would have been useless in the clinch with Klondike, but he was razzle-dazzle with duct tape. After Christmas-wrapping the killer and propping him against a chair, we all looked around, the smell of fear, sweat, and waiting in the air. It was almost over.

"Juarez bring the fun and games?" I asked Harry, who nodded toward the bookshelf. A familiar thick-sided box sat on the second tier, right next to *Huckleberry Finn* and the *Iliad*. "Then I guess we're all set."

"So, we bring him in now?" asked Miguel, duty done, mission accomplished, Boy Scout badge at the ready, still rubbing the can imprints out of his ass.

Harry looked at Miguel, then over to Bob.

"Anyone for Del's? I'm buying...but you guys have to pay."

Confused, Miguel worked his jaws, eager to comment, but Wooly Bob grabbed his arm and steered him out.

"We'll catch you later, boss man. Don't stay long or Harry'll be too far ahead for you to catch up, and you know how much fun that isn't."

Harry held his hands up, all innocence and blamelessness, "Not my fault I'm alcohol retentive. It's genetic. Besides, that's the least of our worries. We have to pick Miguel up a urinal cake. He smells like piss."

And just like that, they left.

Klondike stared up at me, still not saying a word. I smiled, then stepped over and picked up the box on the bookshelf.

"So now what happens, Mr. Douglas?" Juju asked, but with barely a whisper, his eyes scanning about the room, pinballing from end to end. "You caught the big, bad bogyman. Do you really think I care about going to jail? And capital punishment is a complicated joke with barely a punch line. By the time they get around to it, I'll probably be dead of old age. So now what happens...and do you really think I'm concerned about it?"

I placed the box on the side table and fished a key from my pocket.

"You killed my friend. You shouldn't have killed my friend. And right here. Right in this room."

"Are you going to kill me for that? Are you going to do to me what I so longingly and slowly did to that beautiful but helpless woman? Are you going to murder me in hot spurting blood with tears and cries?"

A nasty piece of work, Juju Klondike, but then, so was I.

"Actually, I thought I'd have *you* do it."

That made him laugh big, air-gulping piccolo hoots, head thrown back, mouth wide open, finally gasping out. "You have the most implausible sense of humor, Mr. Douglas."

I unlocked the box, grabbed one of the objects inside snake-quick, and shoved it into Klondike's mouth and down his throat, holding his broken nose closed and clamping his jaws shut before he even knew that tomorrow was over. He struggled and gagged, but I held tight with all my might, his face turning tear-pink, cheeks quivering, throat throttling hard, trying to vomit up what couldn't be vomited.

Anyone who'd watched as many bad science-fiction movies as I had as a kid knew that a "rad" was a unit of measurement of radiation, and that if the human body absorbed enough of them, it would either kill a person or turn them into a horrible, slavering, mutant monster that destructively rampaged through various model-built miniature cities. Nowadays, as the new CGI effects had updated the old analog effects, the "rad" had been replaced as well by the "gray" (Gy) as the unit of measure of absorbed radiation dosage. No need to get into the technical details, which involved joules and kilograms of matter—usually human tissue—but suffice it to say, the more grays, the more death. For some reason in modern bad science-fiction movies, the gray did *not* turn a person into a horrible, slavering, mutant monster anymore, it only killed them. Horribly.

When Juju finally caught his breath, the prototype testicular bomb that Juarez had Santa Claused me after much begging, pleading, and threatening on my part, was swallowed and resting uncomfortably in his stomach, confusion in his eyes.

"What?" he gasped, sucking in air and puckering his mouth, trying to get the taste out.

I took an old-fashion flip phone from the box and hit a number on the keys.

"The people you worked for. They stole a whole bunch of tasty plutonium. Then they sold it to some fanatical idiots who made little dirty bombs out of bits of it. C4 wrapped in a shell of radioactive material with a wireless detonator at the core. Rather nifty. You have one in your belly right now, working its way through your sensitive intestines, glowing softly and dousing the rest of your soft inner tissues, organs, and gooey parts with alpha, beta, and gamma rays. Lots and lots of them."

Klondike began squirming and desperately flexing his arms and legs, but we'd taped him almost as good as a UPS box. He tried retching, but without a finger down the throat, it's a hard one to pull off, even if he were a fashion-model bulimic, which he wasn't.

I opened the floor safe back up and booted Klondike inside, forcing him fetal, his fingers trailing against the sides behind him, unable to do more than rattle against the walls a little. He was *that* snug. I placed the cell phone in his taped hands. To add insult to icing, El Repollo ambled over, lifted a leg, and let forth a long stream of ammonia piss all over Klondike, splattering him golden. The dog *definitely* was growing on me.

"I figure you have two choices," I continued. "You can wait here until the FBI arrives, and I'll probably call them...oh, after a drink or two at the bar. By the time they get here, manage to open the safe, take you back to headquarters, listen to what you're babbling about, *believe* what you're babbling about, get a doctor to *confirm* what you're babbling about, then finally get the bomb out of you, either through surgery or good old-fashioned crap passing, you'll have absorbed so much radiation you'll start dying like a Hiroshima victim before the sun rises. And I hear that's a bitch."

I finally saw fear in Klondike's eyes, and that was all right by me.

"Or, you can manage to not drop that phone I gave you, flip it open, and hit the dial button, which is set to speed dial a certain wireless detonator, which will explode that dirty bomb from inside your warm, bloody body. Not nearly as painful, I would guess. Either way, you're not my worry any longer."

"You're lying!" he shouted, arching up as far as he could just as I slammed the safe door down on him, catching his head with the swing in a satisfying manner.

"Why the hell would I lie?"

I'd brought the envelope with the two types of immunity papers—immunity *ratione materiae* and immunity *ratione personae*—in it, and tossed it on top of the safe door, then turned, grabbed El Repollo's leash and left Lila's. It didn't make up for anything, but I knew she'd sleep better at night, if they slept at all in heaven. Knowing Lila, probably not.

Dog and I stepped out onto the street, while I pulled my own phone out, calling Juarez, who answered on the first ping.

"Hey, Daniel. Juju Klondike is duct taped and ready back at the crime scene like we figured he'd go. You might want to come by with some men, a good locksmith, and a doctor."

A sudden thump, a jump to the ground like a baseball bat hitting a softball, then nothing. I could imagine little confetties of Juju splattered inside the safe.

"No need to rush though. In fact, you might want to stop by Del's first. I'll buy you a beer."

***

Harry managed to dump me off at my place; miracle of miracles, for once I was one ahead of him and messy drunk, with a loud vigor to continue. He didn't even give me much Harry shit about it. Devon stood in the doorway, El Repollo snuffling behind her, looking newly bathed. She and Harry manhandled me to the couch where I rallied, hoping to get another beer, or whisky, or anything to throw down.

"You gonna be okay with the Markallen here? He's had more than an awful lot of scotch. Even by our standards."

Devon shooed him back out, then ER'd me with a blanket and pillow, pulling my shoes off and fixing hot cocoa. Hot cocoa? I only had hot cocoa when I was stuffed-lion-toy little and my stepdad had "conventioned" his way out of town. My mom used to make it late at night when it rained, and we'd pull a big chair half in and half out of the sliding door at the back of the house, snuggling into the chair, a flannel comforter wrapped around us, and I'd drink the cocoa piled high with marshmallows while we watched the rain come down.

I took a sip, the Head & Shoulders-smelling mutt laying his snoot up against my chest and whipping his tail back and forth across my foot. Devon stood over me, looking down, waiting. I took another sip, then I reached up for her and cried. And couldn't stop crying for a long time. She held my hand the whole time. Just that.

When I finally finished, I took another sip of cocoa....

19.

Juarez received a full-fledged, hoity-toity, pin-on-the-jacket, picture-in-the-paper commendation for the apprehension of the Antiochs and their barbecue-happy gang of plutonium-smuggling, cow-irradiating illegals. Yup, not a green card amongst them. Jurisdiction became a bit sticky, but the Mongolian government acceded to the Share and Share Alike Doctrine, happily taking the leftovers after the U.S. of A. dealt with them. Tightass basked in the glory of being top-dog feeb, almost going so far as to buy breakfast for me when I saw him again.

The testicularly deprived suicide bunglers—ball-bombers? scrotum exploders?—with the swapped wireless trackers a jock-itch from discovery, GPS'd their whereabouts crystal clear no matter how they tried to hide or confuse their trails, and in doing so, pointed digital fingers to their various terror cells about the country. The FBI and Homeland security rode in like John Wayne in a smoldering birch-bark canoe: the terrorists and their anti-American handlers met the mailed fist of freedom, taken like rabbits in a snare, then vanished to some Guantanamo-ish holding facility who-the-God-knows-where for further interrogation. Still, dumb is dumb, and I didn't think they'd get much from them. They'd volunteered to get their nuts cut out and replaced with a bomb. Not a rocket scientist in the whole dang bunch.

Private Keene, lately late, then lately of Muscat, Oman, jumped ship on a ship heading for parts unknown, until Interpol flagged him doing the soft shoe through customs in Phnom Penh, Cambodia, declaring it a business trip, and hauling 96,250 in unmarked Rials stuffed in a Hello Kitty overnight bag. Questions pending his arrival back on American soil. I bet he wished he were still dead.

Juarez and I hunched on badly stained wood benches at an all-you-can-eat breakfast corral called the Gobble M Up Café that touted inch-thick buckwheat waffles and pancakes in the shape of Panamanian turkeys as their specialties. Trays and trays of bacon swimming in gelatinous grease tag-teamed by sausages, scrambled eggs, fried potatoes, grits, and gravy also snorkeling in lard, lined up behind. Lemonade barrels stood on end, along with military industrial complex-sized coffee makers that gurgled out java hot as the center of the Sun. The kaleidoscope of empty plates heaping up grub whirled by as I toyed with my eggs, contemplating whether to eat them or use them for skipping across ponds.

"Level with me—the FBI puts out a weekly bulletin about restaurants like this, don't they? There's no other way you could find so many cheap dives by yourself. It's statistically impossible and still get any work done."

I tested the coffee, still molten.

"It's a gift I've always had. I'm like a dousing rod for bargain-basement eats. If it's under a tenner, I'll find it."

He shoveled from his mound of drippings, fat and pork, alternating between fork and toast to scoop the breakfast mulch from plate to mouth. Primitive man in all his nascent glory.

"So what happened with Klondike? Or, what didn't happen?" I hadn't heard a word for a week, then came the breakfast invite. I wondered.

"DNA confirmed the bloody connect-the-dots inside the safe was in fact Juju Klondike eunuch killer for hire, wanted from Hell and back. Hazmat crews cleaned the spore up, and my superiors worried about terrorist dirty-bomb attacks until I casually let drop Klondike's relationship with the Mongs. I then casually let drop your immunity papers all signed, sealed, delivered, and somehow magically appearing right on top of the detonation. Fancy that. I got promoted on the spot. Seems no one likes red tape, *especially* my superiors."

"Nice of them not to arrest me."

A jumbo-sized beast-of-a-woman wearing a halter tent top with the phrase "Mama's Little Helpers" emblazoned on top, tried to ease on by behind me on her way to a pork-chum frenzy. I sucked in air and strained hard to get small.

"So everything's handy-dandy now?"

The moment and the woman passed.

"The Gloucesters did their duty and the U.S. Marshalls took all three of them to Never Never Land, which is anywhere but Arizona. I got Wisconsin in the office pool."

"Three?"

"Yeah, Mama Gloucester didn't want to miss out on her boys' lives, so she relocated with them. All in one house. Maternal as a guppy, or somethin' else that eats its young. Said something about grandchildren, if you can believe it."

Occasionally the planets aligned just right, and then loaves and fish started falling. Unfortunately, none of them landed on my plate. I pushed it away after nibbling a stale but 10-40 lubricated sausage, flecks of not-meat crunching with the bite.

"Poor Desmond. I was growing to like the guy in a criminally absurd way. Rodney's a complete moron, but Desmond had a bit of style. One month of them all cooped up together and I'm layin' odds someone gets a steak knife to the disco ball."

"Not my problem anymore," said Juarez, punctuating each word with a shake of an egg-yellowed piece of bacon on the end of his fork. "They can turn cannibal and fricassee themselves for all I care."

"I think this place already beat them to it."

Juarez bulldozered another wad of grub into his mouth, chewing for a four count before swallowing. "You are too particular is what your problem is. Everything's gotta be just right. Right now, it's as right as it's ever going to get in the world. It's righter than it has any right to be. So eat up and try to remember today, because I guarantee you that tomorrow's going to be worse."

"You buying?"

Juarez shook his head.

"Then today's worse."

"I'll throw in the tip though," Tightass graciously offered with what I believed was a first.

"Seriously?"

He nodded.

"Maybe it *is* a good day then."

***

So there I sat in all my IRS-ian regal glory, swivel chair rotating with ease and comfort, lumbar support set to "stun," the master of all my little-but-slightly-bigger-than-my-old-cubicle could survey. Boss, even, which I'd finally gotten used to once the plutonium dust had settled. I headed up my own fiefdom of the bureaucracy within the building. Everyone's got something to hide except for me and your money.

My e-mail ding-a-linged, and I caught the missive from Mr. Aroon: let the decoding begin. "Guinea Pig stink gone, do ronron in a turnstile of infinite glory. I will expect a complete synopsis of everything that occurred by lunchtime...tacos hip-hop my rattlesnake." Rather eloquent for him; no doubt due to the jovial mood he was in from not having to explain my immunity papers to anyone. Or maybe Mr. Aroon simply upped his articulation with my new position. Small favors for small minds.

The workload increased, the miles of piles of files hunkered up in my basket waiting for my perusal and signature. But I'd always been fast, so that glitch in the radar fizzled out once I found a rhythm. Miguel beamed in expectation and wedding plans, texting to Becky at every break and being texted back various china patterns and silverware expectations, which flustered *and* exited him. Wooly Bob discovered a new skin moisturizer that hydrated four times faster than a deep-water calcareous sea sponge and listed no ecologically unsound ingredients. Harry harried me about getting him a raise, or danger pay, or extra vacation days, depending on if it were before or after lunch.

I did my work, until the day came that I knew that Mecca called, and excused myself from the office for "personal" reasons, got into my car and drove. My cell rang. Devon.

"Hey, kiddo," I answered, "What's up?"

A scratchy, frequency-hopping connection mukluked into my ear. "Whatcha doin'?"

I turned left, just branching off the main road and winding across the vista drive. "Errands, not much. How about you?"

"Waldo's got me practicing for a new trick—the Amazing Bisected Woman."

"Bi what?"

"Sected, you nasty man. As in, he puts six metal sheets right through my body, then mixes up the pieces like a numbered slide puzzle. A member of the audience then gets to slide them around some more."

"As long as Waldo puts you back in the right order for me to take apart again later."

I angled into the driveway of the mortuary, the classic Greek architecture on the main building looking staid and afterlife-ish.

"I have to bend in some really interesting ways," Devon continued. "You'll need to rub the kinks out later."

"I'm all about the kinks." I switched off the engine. "Look, Dev, I've gotta get out now, I just got to where I'm going."

"Sure. I gotta go, too. If you need anything..."

She hung up, and I left the car resting comfortably as I parade-marched up the Architectural Digestedly perfect grassy hill toward the eternal rest of Lila. I hadn't noticed the view at the funeral—too busy marinating my anger—but I took both barrels of the full panoramic 3-D spectacle that only a clear day and someone with a lot of money buying the plot could achieve.

It smelled like pine trees and ice cream up there; the sort of scent that meant never changing and almost melted. The plaque, in a marble's marble, told Lila's full name and years from birth to grave, a single gaudy sapphire dotting the "i." I didn't bring flowers. Lila didn't really like flowers, even if she collected more than her share. Too needy for her, she'd once explained.

"So," I began. "Here we are. Together again." At the last, I didn't know what to say. "Nice spot you picked. Very impressive in a eulogy-meets-money way. Nothing but dead people as far as the eye can see, but a person could get used to it."

An onyx-eyed crow mortared down, landing a headstone away. It gave me the thousand-yard stare, then began sharpening its beak on the stone, sounding like a carpenter sanding a rocking chair. Another fluttered down to join it, both sharpening and staring.

"Got the people who killed you. Some of your friends helped, and of course the *guys* helped. Even Mr. Aroon helped. Devon helped, too. Don't know why the minute you're gone she hit-and-ran into my life, but as I'd said before, you'd like her. In fact, if you were around, my life'd be a living hell. But in a good way, I think."

The crows both crapped on the headstone in unison, then took to the skies, Maypoling around each other until they vanished into flecks of black on a blue, blue background.

"I'll come visit when I can. Maybe bring a bottle of something. Mostly for me, but if you want some, I'm willing to share." I didn't know why I dialogued; Lila six feet under couldn't answer, but I knew that if any spirit'd get VIP treatment in the hereafter, it'd be Lila, so maybe she copped backstage passes to Earth to visit here. You never knew with Lila.

I didn't even hear her walk up behind me. First, there was nothing, then the warmth of her hand in mine.

"I thought you were working on a trick," I reminded her.

"Abracadabra, here I am." And there Devon was, radiant and alive and exactly where she should be, oddly enough. "If you get to fib, I get to fib."

"Just saying goodbye, I guess."

Suddenly, it seemed silly and uncomfortable, talking to a headstone with no one at home.

"But you haven't even introduced us, Mark. I've met the rest of your so-called friends." She let go of my hand and knelt down before Lila's marker. "Hello, Lila, I'm Devon. And if you were as close to Mark as I think, you're probably shaking your head in pity right now at my involvement with him. I know, I know, he's a handful, but I like him, and that should count for a lot."

"Gee, thanks."

Bad enough a girlfriend chatting with an old friend, but a *dead* old friend? I was in serious trouble *à la mode*.

"Hush, the girls are discussing," she replied with complete stolen-heart authority, then back to Lila's marker. "I'd appreciate any tips or advice you give me, as I'm in this for the long haul, and I'll need as much help as I can get." She smiled up at me. "I figure great minds can think alike, even in regards to you."

They talked for a while, shootin' the shit, Devon asking questions that scurried from intimate details to obvious banalities. Don't know if Lila answered, but the questions loosened a tightness in me that I didn't know I had, and when it all wrapped up with Devon brushing her hand across Lila's marker, I felt more comfortable in my skin than I had in a long time.

I helped Devon to her feet without a word, and we made our way down that perfect hill of dead to our cars, hers parked right next to mine.

"You know, I still have those kinks to unkink," she said, grinning as she slid into her driver's seat.

I tailed her back to my apartment, the whisper of a friendly breeze sighing in my thoughts, fond memories of fond friends.

***

Sounding like a herd of wind-sucking wildebeest with IRS credentials, we'd humped up fourteen frickin' flights of mucus-gray concrete stairs after a squint-eyed eight-year-old pressed all the buttons in the elevator as a joke. His mother claimed, "Kids will be kids." I only hoped in twenty years' time I'd get to audit him as payback. "Hey kid, remember when you hit all the elevator buttons? Well now, it's my turn. IRS agents will be IRS agents."

Harry graciously let Miguel bust through the rooftop door because Harry'd never put himself in harm's way when a newbie rook could do it for him. First bash almost dislocated Miguel's shoulder. I turned the knob—unlocked—and pushed the door open, matadoring Miguel to try again, "youth before boss."

Miguel grit his teeth, crouched in a television-inspired cop stance, and crab-dashed across the threshold, only to trip on an air-conditioning duct and sprawl, legs spread, right onto an empty paint drum someone had thought they'd discarded in the most unlikely of places, banking his *nards* like a clapper in a bell. He nosedived into chin-tucked, legs tight position, clutching his groin and screaming out prayers to whichever fertility god or goddess would listen to save his parenting abilities from future harm.

Harry shook his head. "That boy just has a way about him."

Gary Blaine Murdock owed the United States government sixteen thousand one hundred and forty-eight dollars from two years' worth of back taxes incurred while working as one of those call-at-dinner-hour telephone pollsters. We'd hustled over to collect after numerous letters of demand and all the legality that entailed. Gary Blaine Murdock claimed penury, but on closer examination of his day-to-day buying records—we at the IRS love credit cards, PayPal, and eBay's digital-paper trails—it seemed that Mr. Murdock invested liberally in collectibles of a Japanese nature.

Wooly Bob edged right, Harry left, ducking behind the same air-conditioning duct Miguel'd prostrated himself across. I moved carefully over the roof, approaching Gary Blaine Murdock, who held in his hand a briefcase full of rare, one-of-a-kind Pokémon trading cards. I knew that because Gary told me under no-uncertain-terms through the downstairs intercom that neither myself, the IRS, or Beelzebub could have them, and that he'd rather throw them over the side of the building and into the Sacramento River below, destroying them forever, than let any of the "mint-condition expressions of his soul" fall into the hands of Philistines. I took umbrage to my artistic sensibilities being called into question, as well as the fact that he owed the cash, so by right, he needed to fork them over, pronto.

Some people took things too far sometimes. And dressed funny.

Gary Blaine Murdock stood a shade less than five feet four, costumed in an eye-stingingly, bright-yellow Pikachu outfit.

"Y-y-you n-n-no c-c-can't have th-them!" he stuttered.

Hearing him out looked to be a long-term process at best. The fact that he feigned a high-pitched Japanese accent didn't help things in the communication department either. Fourteen flights of stairs third-striked him.

"If you throw that bag over the side, Mr. Murdock," I explained, using my Big IRS Agent's voice, "you might as well throw yourself over after, because those cards are the only thing keeping you from going to jail. And little guys who dress in Pikachu outfits tend to have very difficult times in the Big House. Trust me on that."

Harry raised up, holding his pistol nonchalantly, though Gary Blaine Murdock couldn't have known that. "Can't we just shoot the anime bastard right in his cosplay ass and have done with it? Be simpler that way."

Gary held his hands out. "In k-k-keeping with Pik-k-k-kachu's awesome electrical p-powers, I've s-s-s-superglued Tasers to my ha-ha-ha-hands. You c-c-c-come near me, and I'll z-z-z-zap you g-good!" He pulled the costume back from his head to reveal a third Taser. "I ha-ha-have one st-st-stuck to my head, t-t-t-too."

Some people took things too far sometimes.

Harry commented again. "Like I said, let's just shoot him and get it over with."

Gary Blaine Murdock's eyes grew bigger than a little Hentai girl's. "I...I j-j-just c-c-c-c-can't give you th-them."

Wooly Bob'd eased himself around to the side in a clear fifty-meter dash from Murdock. Miguel still squirmed on the ground, just catching his breath, probably feeling the weight of the world on his crotch. Harry knew I'd make a move soon, so he kept talking about blasting Gary Blaine Murdock as I put one foot in front of the other, slowly, carefully, innocuously nearing the poor befuddled owe-ee. Closer examination begged the question: If he superglued the Tasers to his hands, how could he be holding the briefcase? Seemed worth a shot.

"Mr. Murdock..." I kept moving. "I have a question."

"Ok-k-kay."

"Did you accidentally superglue your briefcase to your hand as well as the Tasers?"

Gary Blaine Murdock panicked, tried to fling the briefcase full of cards over the side of the building, not realizing that, being stuck, he'd go along with them.

"N-n-n-n-n-n-no-o-o-o-o-o-o-o!"

Bob, faster than a speeding hairless guy, caught him from the side, half over the edge, Murdock's yellow-costumed legs kicking like a swimming student's. I grabbed Pikachu ears and hauled backwards. Gary Blaine Murdock flailed, accidentally triggering one of his Tasers, which shot out and hit Miguel bull's-eye. I knocked the Taser off, but Miguel, weakened by his previous ball busting, went out like a spastic narcoleptic.

Harry laughed hard, tears rolling from his eyes. "This is better than watching the circus."

Bob and I wrestled Murdock to the rooftop, where he sobbed, pleading with us not to take his precious trading cards. "Th-th-they're all I ha-ha-have!"

I flicked open the briefcase; yup, full of Pokémon goodness.

"Sorry, Mr. Murdoch, but if it's between you and the government, the IRS chooses the government. It's just a matter of who pays our bills."

I managed to pull the briefcase free from Murdock, not without a certain amount of skin coming along, and gathered up Miguel with Harry and Bob's help.

"Come on, Miggy. Just imagine the tender lovin' nursing Becky'll do for you," offered an unrepentant Harry.

We headed for the stairs, leaving behind a crying little man in a bright-yellow Pikachu suit, heartbroken but safe from backdoor jaildom. A win-win in my book.

My name's Mark Douglas, and I work for the IRS. Welcome to my world.

You betchum.

.

Acknowledgements

Whelp, first-off, I should thank Mark L, the wily ex-IRS agent who accidentally gave me the kernel for this book by telling a few stories of his life on the job. Ha! Bet he's sorry now. Much appreciation to justanothermambafan, who read and commented on the first draft when it was done. Hey, she liked it! Always a good sign. A nod to Ken P for noticing a redundancy in my redundancy. A tip-o-the-cap to my agent, Alison P, for even taking this project on and trying to run with it. Many *gratitudes* for my publisher and all-around good egg Ruth W, and her cats. Despite him no doubt denying it, loads of thanks to Art V for getting me to rethink how I write, which galvanized me to get back to doing prose. And, lastly, but hardly leastly, always thankful for my Dad, the original inspiration for being creative, and all the times as a kid he'd yell at me: "Get off your ass and go clean up the dog crap!" which turned out to be the greatest lesson ever about how to be a professional writer.

About the Author

Mark Zaslove – writer/director/producer – Mark is an entertainment industry veteran in both live-action and animation, movies and television, creating content for all the major studios, including Disney, Universal, Paramount and Warner Bros. A two-time Emmy Award winner for writing/producing and recipient of the Humanitas Prize (for writing uplifting human values in television and movies), he also writes short fiction and has served as senior editor on various magazines. *Death and Taxes* is the first in a series of mystery/crime novels following the escapades of IRS agent Mark Douglas and his band of merry revenuers as they bring justice to those in great need of same, while collecting your Federal dollars along the way. Remember: April 15th is the tax deadline unless you get an extension. Also remember to tip your accountant when you leave.